Patty,
Thanks for all
of your support throughout
the years - you are awesome
Love,
Jen

Jennifer Jamelli

Checked

Jennifer Jamelli

a 48fourteen Publishing Trade Paperback

This is a work of fiction. All of the characters, organizations, and events portrayed in this novel are either products of the author's imagination or are used fictitiously. Any similarity to actual events or people, living or dead, is entirely coincidental.

Edited by Kate Wright. Cover by www.ravven.com.

Library of Congress Control Number: 2013957587

ISBN-13: 978-1-937546-24-3
ISBN-10: 1-937546-24-1

Without these people, I never would have been able to write this book . . .

1.) *Max and Derek*
2.) *My family*
3.) *The creators of Zoloft*

Chapter 1
the appointment

{IN MY HEAD RADIO, THE Pretenders start the second verse of "I'll Stand by You."}

"Have a seat, please, Miss Royce," says the red-headed receptionist as she extends a manicured hand to indicate the seating area. Red. Bright red nails. And a small scratch on the pad of her pointer finger. A scratch or perhaps some wayward nail polish? *Please let it be nail polish. Please don't let it be blo—*

She stares at me, waiting. I flush.

"Like I said, I'm fine here, really, if I'm not in your way or anything. I don't mind standing. Really." *Stop talking, freakshow. She gets it—you don't want to sit.* I move slightly away from her desk so I am standing in the seating area. We are both quickly distracted by the jingle of bells at the door. A short, plump man with a trench coat and a briefcase comes flying in the room. *{Frank Sinatra takes over, crooning* "Fly Me to the Moon."*}*

I step back further into the waiting room just in time to prevent the side of his briefcase from touching my black pea coat. Clutching my silky black and white purse, I watch him fling the briefcase on the counter as he talks at the receptionist.

"Cancel my appointments for today, tomorrow, and Friday. I have to get to the airport by three to be in New York by evening visiting hours." He pauses to breathe and quietly adds, "He's in critical condition."

To avoid imposing further upon this conversation, I take another step into the seating area, careful not to touch any of the clustered blue chairs. I look down at my purse and fiddle with the silver hardware on the handles. *{Sinatra moves right on to the second verse.}*

Mr. Briefcase finally gives the receptionist a chance to speak.

"Yes, sir, Dr. Spencer. I'll cancel your appointments right away. Oh but, um…" I can feel her gazing toward me. I keep my hands and eyes on the silver rings on my purse.

She quietly says, "Your two fifteen is here a little early. A referral from Lennox Counseling." I look up at this man who is apparently going to be my psychiatrist. I remember the card from Dr. Lennox hanging on my fridge. Dr. Keith Spencer. Pierce Mental Health. 2:15 p.m.

"See if Dr. Blake can handle it," he says, picking up his briefcase with one hand while fumbling for his keys with the other. "If he starts the initial consultation, he can just leave the paperwork on my desk." He glances over at me, and I move my eyes abruptly back to my purse. He then continues his conversation with the receptionist. "I'm sure I'll be back here by two fifteen next Wednesday."

When I eventually look back up, Miss Receptionist and Dr. Spencer peer intently at her computer screen. Perhaps Dr. Blake can't "handle" me either.

The receptionist taps a red nail on the computer

screen as she whispers, "But he won't treat—"

"It's just an initial consultation," Dr. Spencer interrupts before turning and flying back through the door without another glance in my direction.

Won't treat what? Women? Graduate students? Catholics?

"I'll be right with you, Miss Royce." The receptionist cuts into my thoughts as she stands up from her chair to go toward the back part of the office.

Back to my purse buckle. *{Time for the refrain again. Ready for a big key change.}*

"Ma'am." She is at her desk again. "Dr. Blake, a psychologist in this practice, will be seeing you today. Please just step through this door, and I'll show you to his office."

I look at the brown door to her left, the one those red fingernails point out to me. It isn't one of those swing doors I can just push in with my foot or leg or back. It has a horizontal silver bar handle. *Shit. SHIT. SHIII-TT.*

Since the receptionist appears to be gathering a file (mine?) from the desk, I quickly thrust my coat-covered elbow onto the end of the silver handle and push down and forward at the same time. The door opens. I catch it with my right black pump and try to move my elbow back to a normal spot. But instead, I drop my purse. *Smooth, Callie. So graceful.*

Now holding my file, the receptionist is looking at me. Awesome. I grab the top part of my purse, carefully avoiding any contact with the sections that touched the carpet or door.

"Right this way, please."

Sure, Red. As you wish.

I follow her for what seems like forever. Her slow, calm pace doesn't help matters. We go to the end of one brightly lit hallway only to turn left into another. Uniformly framed pictures line the walls, pictures of meadows and birds.

We make a second left turn and there is yet another large bird staring at me. A robin, I think. I hate birds. They randomly crap on things that would otherwise be clean. Cars. Park benches. Picnic tables. Mmmm…nothing says yummy picnic better than a big white and black pile of—

We are turning again. *{Frankie fades out, and The Beatles slide in with* "The Long and Winding Road."*}*

We're here. The receptionist twists the silver doorknob to open the door and then presses her back against it so I can enter.

"Miss Calista Royce, Dr. Blake."

A quiet, so quiet voice says, "Thank you, Annie."

Annie. Of course your name is Annie.

Annie steps in the room a moment, and soon that quiet, deep voice speaks again.

"Come in, Miss Royce."

The door stays open even after Annie leaves. *Excellent. Not an automatically closing door.* I walk in, and my eyes meet, um, no one. No one sits behind the massive cherry desk that faces me.

"Dr. Lennox referred you to this office?" That hushed voice pulls my gaze around, over to the right corner of the room. Blue dress shirt over muscular arms. Black pin-striped pants. Dark brown hair.

All facing away from me.

"Um…yes." *As you clearly just read in my file. Why bother asking?*

"He wants you to seek further treatment. Medication from Dr. Spencer." This comes as a murmur as he appears to look up and directly out the window in front of him. "Very tense. Obsessions occupying approximately eighty-five percent of the day. Compulsive behaviors linked to the majority of these…difficulty sleeping, working, socializing. Excessive checking habits…"

He turns and gradually begins walking, all the while flipping through my file. Face down…reading…walking. Toward me? To shake my hand? To take my coat?

As he approaches me, I clutch the top part of my purse even tighter in my right hand and bring my left hand down to play with a button on the front of my coat. He stops in front of me but doesn't look up. I hold my breath as he reaches behind me to close the door. Still looking down at the file, he heads back to the window.

I don't resume my breathing until he is again facing away from me.

Silence. *{*"The Long and Winding Road" *ends and then starts right back up again…twice.}* My purse is getting heavy. I let go of my coat button and grasp the top of my purse with both hands.

He clears his throat and speaks. "So you're looking for some quick fix, some medicine from Dr. Spencer."

Quick fix?

I try to explain. "Dr. Lennox suggested that, um, taking some medicine might alleviate some of my issues."

Quiet. Nothing. Just the back of a man—a statue in front of me. His hand moves through his artfully-tousled hair. Silence. I clear my throat.

"He did want me to see Dr. Spencer specifically so I can just wait until next week when—"

"Dr. Spencer wants me to conduct this opening consultation with you." He turns from the window to walk to his desk.

"Just a few standard questions—if you are ready."

I nod my head in agreement. But he can't see me because he is now sitting at his desk and looking down at a clipboard.

"Mmhmm…" I say quietly, pointlessly nodding again. He takes a shiny silver pen out of his left shirt pocket.

Pen poised to write, he speaks again, "First question." He pauses.

He still doesn't look at me. I move my own gaze to the bookshelves behind his desk. Lots of thick books with fancy, complicated titles. A framed degree. Dr. Aiden Blake.

One picture. A young woman holding a maybe two-year-old boy. Both with the same dark hair. It looks like a professional picture gone wrong. The woman has a warm smile directed at the camera. The little boy is sitting on the woman's (his mother's?) lap and his body is facing the camera. His head, though, is turned up toward the woman's face, and his little right hand rests on her cheek. As if the little boy whipped his head around during the photographer's count of three to check to make sure his mother was still there. Sweet. Perhaps Mrs. Quiet and son.

My eyes involuntarily move to his left hand. No ring.

"Why do you spend most of your day seeing problems that do not exist?"

What? That is your "standard" question?

I abruptly move my gaze back to him, but he, of course, is not looking at me. I don't think he is going to speak again until I offer an answer.

"Umm…I don't really…I'm not entirely…I don't know."

"You don't know. I just figured you did know since

you're ready to put a medicinal bandage on this whole problem."

Medicinal bandage? Who says that?

"Um…no. I'm not really…you know, I can just wait until next week. Really. I have to, uh, work at the writing center in just a couple—"

"You're a writer?" he interrupts.

"Well, I want to write, yes. I am taking graduate courses in creative composition at, um, Pierce University, and well, I have to write for, uh, my courses."

Eloquent, Callie. No wonder he thinks you're a writer.

"Well then, Miss—" (He looks back at my chart.) "Royce. These questions can easily be answered in writing."

"Great." *Just tell me what you want me to write about, and I can give my answers to Dr. Spencer next week then. I'll stop ruining your day.*

I start to dig in my coat pocket to find my keys.

"I'd like you to start by writing about some early memories of your issues. Perhaps you can email these to me by, let's say, Friday afternoon."

What? Is this like a homework assignment? As though I don't have enough to—

"Is there a problem, Miss Royce?" Oh—did he see my irritation? I look up.

Of course not. He has now spun his chair around to face the sole picture on his bookshelf.

"Um, well, when I write I prefer to use an old-fashioned pen or pencil." Pause. "By the way, it's Calista."

"That's fine. Try to get it in the mail by Friday then. I see we have your email address on file, so I'll just send you some other topics to think about later in the week."

"Oh. Okay. Thank you." *Again, sorry for disrupting*

your existence.

I turn toward the doorknob on his door.

"Calista." That quiet voice pulls me around yet again.

I freeze. He's looking at me. Sorrowful eyes… heavy…inconsolable. A tragedy in blue.

I can't look away. I begin to feel a dull ache in my left side. *{Damien Rice fills my head with* "The Blower's Daughter."*}*

His eyes hold mine. They are relentless. The sharpening pain in my side weighs me down, cementing my shoes to their place on the floor. My lips part slightly as my body tries to remember to breathe.

In slow motion almost, he releases me, closing his eyes and clenching them shut. The blue eyes that open back up to me are hard, stony.

He swiftly spins his chair to grab the box of tissues on his bookshelf. Without meeting my eyes, he turns back around and holds the box out to me.

"To help you out of here," he says in an almost inaudible voice. *What?*

"Th-thank you," I stammer. I clutch my purse and take six slow steps toward his desk. Three steps at a time. One two three. One two three.

He stares past me, blankly looking at the door. I pull three white tissues from the box he's holding and turn back to his point of focus. When I get to the silver doorknob, I quickly cover it with the three tissues spread out in my left hand.

And I'm out.

The creepy birds on the walls watch me as I walk back through that twisting path in a daze. I use my three tissues to open the next silver-handled door, and I'm back in the waiting room.

The receptionist is on the phone, arguing heatedly with someone about which bar to go to on Friday night. She's mad. She doesn't even look up as I pass.

Later, Annie. Hope your sun shines again tomorrow.

I use Dr. Blake's tissues one last time to push out the main door (no silver handle) to the building, and I hastily throw them into the large trash can right outside the office. Carefully, I hold up my purse with my right hand. I unzip it with my left and remove my wallet, a pen, my phone, deodorant, a package of tissues, a calculator, my checkbook, lip gloss, and three Band-Aids. I shove the items in my coat pockets and drop the purse directly into the trash can.

Too bad. It really was a nice Christmas gift.

I quickly retrieve my keys from my right coat pocket and find my car. After I climb into the driver's seat, I just sit for a moment.

What the hell was that? The longest stare ever, no doubt. Preceded by the most elongated period of time avoiding eye contact. Some kind of game, perhaps? I smile to myself. Maybe this is simply part of the "standard" treatment.

I look at the clock on the dashboard. 2:38 p.m. Better get moving. I have to be at the writing center by 4:00 p.m. I count to three, start my car, count to three again, and turn on the radio.

My little rented house is in front of me eight minutes later. Mandy's car is not in her spot. It's nice to have my sister for a roommate, but she really isn't around much. Busy with all of those stimulating undergraduate courses, maybe. More like all of those parties and sorority events.

2:47 p.m. I open the front door and leave my shoes on the black towel just inside. The kitchen sink is eighteen steps away from the front door. Six counts of three. After rinsing all of the soap off of my hands and lower arms, I dry myself off and hit the "PLAY" button on the answering machine.

"Hey, Callie. Guess you're not back yet. I'm just checking to see how things went. Call me when you can!"

Melanie. I pick up the phone and dial her number. On the first ring, I hear Abby, my six-year-old niece.

"Hey, Abby. Is your mommy home?"

Silence. And then, "Hi, Aunt Callie. I just got a new—"

"Abigail—I'll take the phone now. Hey, Callie." My older sister's authoritative voice interrupts our conversation. I hear some small whines from Abby in the background.

"Hey, Melanie. Couldn't wait for me to call, huh?"

She laughs. "I was just hoping they'd be able to fix you in under fifteen minutes and have you all bouncy and sunshiny before work."

"Not quite. I think it's gonna take at least twenty minutes. Thirty, tops."

Melanie laughs. "Okay. How did it really go?"

"Well, I think I managed to get in and out of the office without contracting any new diseases. Barely, though." I decide not to tell her about my purse. If I try to keep it light, we can talk things out comfortably, normally. Otherwise she worries too much. Besides, she was the one who gave me the purse last Christmas.

I take a new dishrag out of a drawer, drench it with dish soap and water, and begin wiping off the counter.

She's waiting to hear more.

"My doctor couldn't actually see me. Some emergency or something. They passed me off to some other guy." Guy? Super busy man? Terrified, sad boy?

"Oh. What was he like?"

What do you want to know? I can give you a pretty detailed description of the back of his head, his tense shoulders...

"He was pretty busy, really." Busy staring out his window...and at my file...and at his bookcase. "He didn't have a lot to say. I'm just going to fill out some basic information and send it back to the office. My real doctor should be back next week."

"That doesn't sound too bad. Maybe it'll be easier to get yourself into the office the second time."

"Maybe." Although I can't imagine it will be much easier to get out next time. Unless, perhaps, I take six tissues instead of three.

"Okay, I have to make Abby some dinner before I go to yet another meeting. This case is killing my evenings."

"A phone meeting? Or do you have to drive the whole way back to the office?"

"Back to the office. The firm likes us to be all professional and lawery for the big cases. At all times. We'll probably be in Board Room I, the one with the enormous chairs." She pauses. "It is a forty minute drive, though, and that does mean I'll have a total of eighty minutes in the car without hearing any crying or whining. I could use a little peace."

"All right. Please—"

"Be careful. I know. I will be, Calista. Give Mandy a hug for me."

"I will. Thanks for checking on me, Mel. Bye."

2:59 p.m. Not much time before I have to leave again. As I take the dishrag to the hall laundry closet and put it in the washer, I think about this week's to-do list. Work tonight. Groceries tomorrow morning. I pull out the knob to start the washer and grab the Lysol spray on the laundry shelf. Hmm…class tomorrow at 6:00 p.m. Professional Writing Lab I. Our second night of my professor's Publishing Series. Some published writer will be speaking for the entire three hours. Trying to be inspirational. Really just feeding his or her ego.

Going back down the hallway, I disinfect my black pumps. Six seconds of spray per shoe.

Lysol can back on shelf. Hands washed in kitchen sink.

Let's see. TA class on Friday afternoon. College Writing 101. I still haven't done much more than sit and observe. I can hardly be called a teaching assistant. The freshmen yawning through class probably think I'm just a twenty-something-year-old creeper drooling over their teacher. Little do they know it's the other way around.

After Dr. Gabriel officially introduces me to the class in late October, perhaps I'll feel more comfortable about being there. Comfortable, yeah—for about two weeks before I have to teach a couple of the classes in November. With him watching me. *Ugh!*

Quick trip up to my bathroom. Last one until I get back home tonight around 8:00 p.m. As I dry my hands, I look in the mirror to make sure I look together. Make-up—faded, but not running. Hair—a little frizz, but nothing disastrous.

I go back downstairs to the kitchen table to grab my notebook for Monday's Literary Analysis II class. Maybe I'll get some writing done tonight at work.

"You're a writer?" The memory of a deep, quiet voice questions me. Oh. That's right. I have yet another writing assignment to complete this week. In the mail by Friday, he said. Before he sends me more "standard" questions. Fantastic.

Maybe I'll just write my response for him this evening and get it out of the way. I can put it in the mail tomorrow, and we can get this process moving. I'll have all the paperwork done before I see Dr. Spencer next Wednesday.

I smile, thinking of my conversation with Melanie. According to her, I'll need just one short visit in Dr. Spencer's office and my transformation to normal should be complete.

3:05 p.m. Preparations to leave the house.

3:48 p.m. Time to go. I grab my coat and notebook before taking my black leather purse from the closet. I transfer the items from my coat pockets to my new purse, step into my slightly damp heels, and I'm out. Door shut and locked. Handle twist. Handle twist. Handle twist. Locked.

On to work.

Chapter 2
the assignment

THE WRITING CENTER IS PRETTY empty. The usual. No one really comes until after dinner on weeknights. Most of them don't even want help. They just want a quiet place to type.

For now, I'll take advantage of this quiet place to write myself. *Earliest memories*…I begin to brainstorm as I get situated at my corner desk.

Hmm…my parents always tell me that I was a horrible baby. Always screaming.

Not sleeping unless I was on my mother's chest. But maybe that is how babies are for the most part. Maybe Melanie and Mandy were just exceptionally good. Perhaps Jared was only different because he was a boy. Or maybe he seemed really easy because he came right after me. Could this really have started that early though?

"Excuse me." A stick-thin girl with a campus sweatshirt interrupts me. "Can you help me with my paper?" She looks to the left, most likely toward the computer where she is working.

She thinks I am going to go over there? Clearly a freshman. I smile at her as patiently as I can and explain the process of emailing me the paper, attaching questions, and getting a response within a half hour.

"Oh. I just thought..." She drifts off. Thought what? That I would actually take a job where I had to sit and talk with college freshmen? That I would sit close to them and hear them chomp their gum as I worry that they'll accidentally spit while they are talking to me? So close that I can smell their not always clean clothes and the scented sprays they've used to disguise their poor laundry habits? No, thanks. *Sorry, freshman. {Cue Green Day's* "Boulevard of Broken Dreams."*}*

She is still standing in front of me. I manage to give her a smile before she turns to go back to her computer. It's not entirely her fault that I find her disgusting.

This is probably her first college paper, and she really does look worried. I turn on the laptop sitting on my desk so I'm ready for the arrival of her email.

Back to early memories. So why did the baby version of me scream so much? Not bathed enough? Not changed enough? Maybe I was scarred from my experience with swimming in filthy amniotic fluid for months. Maybe a questionable looking doctor gave me my first shots.

Or was the baby me just afraid that if I stopped crying I'd be left alone with my own scary thoughts? Were they already there?

Perhaps my mega-intense doctor man can tell me if this is even possible. Surely this couldn't have been what he meant by earliest experiences though. I really think he meant early as in I could hold my head up and eat solid food but not old enough that I had my driver's license yet.

I don't have the chance to finish this enchanting conversation with myself because my computer dings.

That means I have a paper to check.

My freshman. Brittany at Computer 7, so says her help ticket email. No paper is attached to the email. Just a question about making a cover page. She's only on the cover page? Looks like I will be spending my whole shift with Brittany.

I type her a quick response, attaching some "standard" cover page examples.

Back to my "standard" question. I begin to write my response, and other than four dings from Brittany, I am pretty much left alone...

The Evil Forks and the Dangerous Mouse Droppings

Some of my earliest fears were based on some simple fatherly advice. I don't even know exactly why the advice was given; I'm sure my brother, Jared, and I were doing something questionable to bring it on though.

At dinner, Dad told me that a person could get something called "Lockjaw" from having a fork stabbed into his or her skin. Lockjaw sounded pretty scary.

For the next few years, every fork I saw became a nemesis. Luckily, I found that I could eat many foods without having to use utensils. (Knives and spoons were probably okay, but how could I know for sure? Dad hadn't said one way or another on other eating devices so

I thought it was safest to avoid them all.) But I couldn't avoid them all of the time. Every week (usually during the weekend), there would be four index cards sitting on the kitchen counter, four lists of chores. One for my brother, one for each of my sisters, and one for me. Ah... the dreaded list. Mine always said "EMPTY DISHWASHER" in the small capital letters my dad used for list making. DAMN IT.

Carefully, oh so carefully, I'd pull out each spoon, each knife, and each terrifying fork. If my skin even brushed against one of the menacing prongs, I'd quickly open and shut my mouth a few times to make sure it wasn't glued shut.

Eventually, the scandalous task would be over and, phew, I'd made it through yet another weekend list...almost. After my dad's capital-lettered chores, my mom would often add some of her own in her more feminine, lower-cased writing. And many times it was there, the next worst task: dusting. AHH—people should be forced to read the warnings on some of those cleaning supply bottles before they use them. They are freaking scary. I could go blind. I could have to have my stomach pumped. Hell, I could even die. No way. Not me. If I wasn't going to let the forks get me, there was no way a bottle of toilet bowl cleaner was taking me out. So at the age of seven, I proceeded (very carefully—with gloves) to find out which bottles had the least troublesome warnings. Window cleaner and dish soap won (but this was many years ago—I've found other acceptable products over the years.) From then on, all dusting was done with window cleaner or just water. And when one of those lists said "Clean bathroom sink and tub," my parents could always count on the hall bathroom smelling like dish soap. Who knows how many times I saved my eyes, my stomach, my life...

Okay, so cleaning products and forks were nightmares, but they couldn't even compete with the treacherous mouse droppings.

More words of wisdom from my father. "Wash your hands after you play in the garage. There is probably mouse crap out there." Hmm...sounded pretty bad if this actually merited a warning from my father. (He never really gave random warnings or advice.) What could these mouse droppings do?

It wasn't like there was a bottle I could use to check out warnings for this feces product. This was also obviously before the Internet was really in swing so I had no help there. Instead, I had to leave the potential dangers to my imagination. Smart move, I know—just brilliant.

That mouse crap was almost paranormal—it could paralyze or even blind a person quite easily. All someone would have to do was walk out to the laundry room (in the garage) in bare feet, come inside, and walk on the living room carpet—and the house was suddenly infested.

If I accidentally picked something up from the carpet after an infestation, I would immediately wash my hands, my feet, the thing that I had picked up—all contaminated objects. It was an endless cycle. We are lucky we had no fatalities.

I did my part. I wore shoes if I had to go out to the laundry room, and I refused to use anything that had ever resided in the garage. My other family members didn't do their part though. They still don't. I've seen them countless times doing laundry in bare feet, using tools they've found in the garage, and coming inside without washing their hands. I constantly fear a call from the hospital. One of them is bound to end up there.

I finish my shift pretty pleased with my completed assignment so I grab an envelope and fold it so it fits inside. If I just drop this in the mailbox on the way home, I don't even have to think about it for the next couple of days. I do just that.

I BEGIN MY NIGHT PREPARATIONS shortly after returning home. Thermostat: 70 degrees. Stove: off. Doors: locked. Blinds: closed. Alarm: set. Teeth: brushed. Pictures: straightened. Clothes for tomorrow: out. Mandy's room: cleaned. Nails: painted. Email inbox: empty. Laundry: away. Entire house: dusted. Kitchen: scrubbed. My bathroom: sanitized. Evening shower: taken. Body lotion: applied. Pajamas: on. Hair: dried. Prayers: said. TV: on.

Eventually, I fall asleep while a skinny woman on the television goes through the steps for making ravioli.

Chapter 3
the next day

WHEN MY ALARM RINGS AT 6:00 in the morning, I hear a different female chef preparing some sort of egg soufflé. Sounds wonderful. Like five thousand calories of delicious.

I opt instead for a 175-calorie breakfast of some granola and yogurt before I complete my morning routine and follow it up directly with my leaving-the-house checks.

THE GROCERY STORE IS DESERTED as usual when I get there at 10:00 a.m. Kids aren't screaming. Vested workers aren't stocking shelves. It's nice. I know this tranquil atmosphere will only last until 10:50 a.m. so I pull out my list and get to work right away.

10:42 A.M. SAFE WITHIN MY CAR, I see three disheveled kids get out of a van parked beside me. They are everywhere—beside my car, behind the van, in the aisle of the parking lot. To avoid accidentally harming one of them, I wait to even turn on my car until their mom (or babysitter?) herds all three into the store.

Before I can back out, another car pulls in on the other side of me. *Seriously?* Perhaps I should start coming fifteen minutes earlier.

A scummy looking guy and a short-haired girl step out of the car. They quickly join hands and head toward the store. As I am pulling my foot off the brake, I look again in my rearview mirror and see lover boy drop his girl's hand and head back to the car. *AHH*...brake pedal back down. Guess he forgot something in the car.

While he is searching in the back seat, the girl calls something to him, and he looks up over the car for a moment, smiling. *{Mental picture of Patrick Swayze and Jennifer Grey lip-synching* "Love is Strange" *in Dirty Dancing.}* He has now gone to the other side of the backseat to look. *{Swayze and Grey are now crawling across the floor to each other as the song starts blaring.}* He found it! He found...his...hat? *Seriously?* I've been sitting here for three extra minutes for a baseball cap? Maybe I should've backed out and taken my chances on not hitting—

NO. I didn't mean that. I didn't mean that. I didn't mean that. As I cautiously back out, I make a silent plea to not hit him, or his girl, or anyone else for that matter.

MANDY IS ALREADY GONE FOR the day when I get back home. I see her colorful note on the table as I bring the groceries into the kitchen.

Three classes today. Thirsty Thursday tonight.
Fifty cent drinks. Wanna come?

She asks every Thursday. I guess she maintains hope that somewhere down the line a Thursday will come along when I won't mind the sticky floors and tables, the sweaty dancing people, the appallingly disgusting bathrooms…and so on and so forth in her favorite college bar.

She asks every Thursday, but she really never expects an answer. Nor do I need to give her one. The offer is just always on the table, literally so today.

AFTER SPENDING THE AFTERNOON IN our quiet house, I complete my leaving checks and head to my 6:00 p.m. class. Tonight's published presenter writes movie reviews. I half listen and half jot down ideas for my lit analysis paper on the poetry of Pablo Neruda. I also pick off half of my nail polish. Mr. Speaker talks about the process of watching a movie, engaging with it, and capturing it in writing…or something. He lectures for over two hours. I can't even recall his last name—I'm pretty sure it wasn't anything close to Ebert though…

WHEN I GET HOME, I take a nice long bath with my notes about Pablo Neruda's poetry. 9:30 p.m. Mandy knocks on my bathroom door to tell me that she is heading out.

"Okay. Have fun. Be careful!" I yell over the running water.

"I will. I guess you are working on a paper," she half asks, half states. That is her simple way of acknowledging that I will pass on her offer to go out tonight.

"Yep. Pablo Neruda tonight. Wild and crazy evening ahead."

"Okay. Good luck. Night!"

"Good night. Careful, Mandy."

I get out of the tub when I hear the door click shut. I run in my towel to the thermostat and then to the stove so I can go see if the door is acceptably locked while still maintaining my night preparation schedule. If I get out of order, I have to go back and retrace, and I'll never get to bed.

The bar lock on the door is in the correct vertical position. I twist the door handle three times to make sure it's adequately locked. Then I move on to the blinds.

When it is time to check my email, I flip open my laptop. Sometimes there is a quick note from Mom or Melanie. There are always a few junk emails that somehow made it through the filter. I guess the filter gets confused over whether or not I would be interested in giving my bank account information to a stranger in Nigeria. Terribly puzzling for even the most intelligent of filters, I'm sure.

I quickly respond to a question sent from a fellow student in my nonfiction class and then take a second to review Dr. Gabriel's email about tomorrow's lesson plan. At the end of his email, he says he has to run because he has a date. He writes something like that at the end of every email. I guess he's just letting me know that his schedule is still pretty full even though I refused to go out with him. Letting me know that he's still dating a bunch of other girls. And probably sleeping with them. Little does he know, that's the exact reason I refused to go out with him. Pretty ironic.

Under Dr. Gabriel's email, I see a brand new email address: dablake@throughlink.net. DA Blake, eh? *{The pounding beat of 50 Cent's* "In Da Club" *overtakes my thou—}*

Okay. Enough, Calista.

Why is he writing to me already? Did he really already get my letter? Freakishly fast campus mail must have a late pick-up time.

Maybe I shouldn't have been so anxious to drop it off last night.

All right. Time to rip off this hot strip of wax. Silent, brooding, angry wax. Here goes. One. Two. Three.

Click.

Calista,

This isn't a writing composition assignment. Please try not to make it one. I'm going to send you a few lists of topics over the next few days. Consider each topic briefly, and then quickly type your feelings on the subject. No more letters. No more crafted sentences or sarcastic side notes. Just your feelings and fears. Quick and uncensored. If you need to respond to the prompts in sets of two, or five, or whatever, that is fine.

Respectfully,
Dr. Blake

Respectfully? *You respectfully found the fears I told you about to not be worth your time? You respectfully want to know every uncensored thought that runs through my mind?*

He wouldn't even look at me for most of my appointment, yet he sends me this. *Bastard. Is that uncensored enough for you?*

After a (very) prolonged stare at my computer screen, I finally start putting laundry away at 11:15 p.m.

Much later, as I turn on the television and climb into bed, I try to stop thinking about the email so I can get some sleep. It doesn't work. I am able to move past his interpretation of "respect," but I can't stop thinking about his last sentence. *If you need to respond to the prompts in sets of two, or five, or whatever, that is fine.* A teeny tiny dab of ointment after his monstrous bite of an email.

First the tissues, now the counting. This harshly blunt man somehow seems to have an uncanny knowledge of the way my mind works. Well—almost. He did say sets of two or five. He didn't mention three.

Thoughts run through my mind for quite some time. Almost a full course meal is prepared on television before I finally drift off. The last thing I remember hearing has something to do with preparing a workspace to make pumpkin cheesecake.

Chapter 4
lists

FRIDAY MORNING. AS I WAKE up, I have the odd sensation that I'm about to set off on an unprecedented suicide mission. I know I cannot wait until night preparations to see if he has sent me a list so I decide to check my email now.

As I open my laptop and click on the little email icon, I can't really decide whether or not I want a list to be in my inbox. I'll probably waste a lot of time thinking about it either way.

My inbox appears on the screen. DA Blake has written. The subject line says, "First List." I wonder how many more lists he will send.

Guess I better attack the first list before I worry about future ones. I spend a few minutes picking at my nail polish and then take the plunge. One. Two. Three.

CLICK.

Calista,

Here is your first list of topics. Remember, give me your initial reactions and feelings. Do not overthink this.

1.) Dirty
2.) Family
3.) Television
4.) Church
5.) Dating

The email is signed the same way as the last one. "Respectfully." Yuck.

Okay. The list is not terrible. Especially since I've been granted permission to only answer three items for now. Don't have to touch number five just yet.

It's funny. Now that I've opened the email, I realize that I can't NOT respond to it right away. It has somehow become a to-do list in itself, and to-do lists must be completed swiftly and efficiently (as Mandy says when she is making fun of me). I warily recognize that I will just have to move promptly to my morning preparation routine AFTER the list is completed.

One. Two. Three. I type.

1.) Dirty
- Public bathrooms
- Needles
- Syrup
- Public transportation
- Hotels

- People
- Gas pumps
- Hospitals/Doctors' offices
- Movie theatres
- Bars
- Doorknobs
- Spit, blood (all solids/ liquids coming from a human, animal, or bug)

I consider mentioning mouse droppings specifically, but I don't want to get too writery on him.

2.) Family
- Mom and Dad
- Two sisters (Amanda and Melanie)
- One brother (Jared)

Enough? I guess so. I wouldn't want to overthink this…

3.) Television
- I don't watch much television. I guess I mainly watch shows on the food station before I go to bed.

Okay. I scrutinize my email for grammatical errors or typos. None. Do I sign it? Hmm…

I smile as I sign the email.

```
Respectfully,
Calista
```

Might as well give him a little competition for douchebag of the year.

One. Two. Three. Send.

Laptop closed. Morning procedures commence. Leaving-the-house procedures follow immediately.

NOON. COLLEGE WRITING 101 BEGINS. Dr. Gabriel is discussing the use of foreshadowing and figurative language in narrative writing. Pretty basic stuff, but I don't think the three muscular freshmen in the back row are really getting it. Or perhaps they don't care.

Yes, that's it, I decide as I see that they are actually texting during Dr. Gabriel's lecture. It looks like they are even texting each other. I'm sure their lack of attention will be really awesome for me when I'm the one up front talking.

Class drags on a bit. I take a few notes on Dr. Gabriel's teaching style. Each time he makes what he must feel is an interesting point, he looks at me out of the corner of his eye to see if I'm paying attention or perhaps realizing what a literary genius I turned down. Gross. *When I see you I don't see a genius, Dr. Gabriel. I see a living, walking STD.*

I try to keep my head down as much as possible. I spend some time wondering what I should do differently to hold the students' interest. I pick at my nail polish. I think about my email. Did I do my "assignment" correctly this time or is there already a mean email in my inbox? Maybe he won't even respond until Monday. It is Friday afternoon, after all.

I wonder if I can quickly check my email on my cell phone. The students are working silently on their narratives, and Dr. Gabriel is sitting and writing at the table in the front of the room. Really, I have nothing to do right now.

My purse is hanging on the back of my chair. I begin to reach for it, but that is as far as I get into my devious plan. At that moment, Dr. Gabriel's little timer goes off, signaling the end of the writing portion of the class. *{And now a quick appearance from Ke$ha with* "Tik Tok."*}*

"Time to share our narratives," Dr. Gabriel says. I listen to the first few writing samples and make comments when Dr. Gabriel asks me for them. Yes, he asks me for comments even though he hasn't ever told the students who I am.

I get rather stuck when one student uses a sentence beginning with, "I seen a girl." SAW SAW SAW! Or "have seen" perhaps? That drives me freaking crazy.

I, of course, don't mention that when Dr. Gabriel

asks me for my commentary. Instead, I praise the young girl for her foreshadowing techniques. I don't want to humiliate her in front of the whole class. She would probably go home and cry and then maybe start cutting this class, which might lead to her dropping out of school… and then what? She would end up a self-conscious woman struggling to make ends meet in this poor economy all because a creeper in the class (me) couldn't keep her (my) mouth shut. No, thank you.

Who knows? Maybe she'll come to the writing center sometime where I can privately help her with her irritating verb usage.

Eight more students read their narratives before it is 3:00 p.m. and class ends. I guess the rest will go next Friday.

I hurry out of the room so I don't end up walking out with Dr. Gabriel. I head home. After spraying my shoes and washing my hands quickly, I go up to my room. My hands are not even one hundred percent dry when I open my laptop. DA Blake has written me two emails. The man who wouldn't even look at me two days ago has now sent me two emails within an hour.

Count and click. First email open.

Calista,

Nice work—very succinct. I have just a couple of follow-up questions for you.

2.) Family
- How often do you see your family?
- Do they know about your OCD?

```
3.) Television
  • I enjoy watching food
    shows myself. You don't
    cook though, do you?
               -Dr. Blake
```

How does he know I don't cook? I can't even convince my mother that I'm not watching cooking shows in the hopes of being some big sort of chef. I swear she buys me a new cookbook every Christmas.

I hit reply.

```
Dr. Blake,
  2.) I see my parents and my
      brother a couple of times
      a month. I live with my
      sister, Amanda, and I see
      my other sister, Melanie,
      every Friday night for
      Girls' Night. Yes, they
      all know.
  3.) No, I don't cook at all.
                  -Calista
```

I force myself not to ask how he knows about my cooking. It would probably inspire a whole new list of questions.

One. Two. Three. Send.

One. Two. Three. Click. Second email.

Calista,

Here is your second list.

1.) Church
2.) Dating
3.) Weight and food

-Dr. Blake

Geez. So many personal questions. Like he mixed up his OCD "standard" topics with a questionnaire for speed dating.

I hit reply quickly. This will have to be fast. Girls' Night starts at 8:00 this evening, and I need to get everything ready. Here goes.

Dr. Blake,

1.) Church
   - Every Sunday
   - Catholic
   - Confession on Saturdays
2.) Dating
   - No one currently.
3.) Weight and food
   - I step on my bathroom scale every morning.
   - I eat 1,400 calories a day.

I sign my name. Short and to the point, just like he asked. If he needs more personal specifics to work his doctor magic, he'll have to tell me.

Laptop closed. I head to the kitchen to get things in order for tonight, and the answering machine light is blinking. I'm momentarily shocked that I missed seeing the flashing light when I rushed to my room to check my email.

I press the "PLAY" button.

"Hello. This is Annie from Pierce Mental Health. This message is for Miss Calista Royce. Unfortunately, Dr. Spencer will not be back from New York for your appointment at two fifteen next Wednesday. Dr. Spencer has spoken to Dr. Lennox, and they've both decided that you should spend one more session under the care of Dr. Blake. Dr. Blake has confirmed that he will be here for your appointment on Wednesday. See you then!"

Thanks, Annie. Good to know in advance, I guess. Now I can get a whole five and a half days of worrying in. *Awesome.*

It is just one more week, though, and he is being nice now…even respectful. I smile at the thought.

As I prepare to mop the kitchen floor, I wonder whether he'll actually look in my general direction during our next appointment. *{A solo spotlight shines on Phil Collins as he begins his* "Against All Odds (Take a Look at Me Now)."*}* Kitchen floor: mopped. Pictures: straightened. Living room: swept. *{The refrain repeats again and again.}* Mirrors: cleaned. Blinds: dusted. Shower: in progress. *{And again.}* Legs: shaved. Hair: shampooed and conditioned. *{And again and again and again…}* Thoughts: running rampant.

The counting in "sets of two, or five, or whatever,"

the tissues for the door—anyone who has read one article about OCD could have guessed.

I thought that the cooking channel was my own unique piece of crazy though…

Chapter 5
girls' night

OUT OF THE SHOWER. MANDY'S home. I hear her moving around in the kitchen, probably preparing tonight's margaritas. Melanie will want one when she arrives.

I get dressed in shorts and a big Kelly Kapowski-style off-the-shoulder t-shirt. When I get out to the living room, Melanie is already sitting on the couch in button-down flannel pajamas. She says hello as she hurriedly moves her margarita from the bare glass table to a coaster.

"I saw that," I say with a smile.

"Just practicing for when you are all fixed."

"I'll bet those drink rings will still piss me off even when I'm 'fixed.'" I smile again and join her on the cushiony couch.

"Who is getting fixed?" Mandy comes into the living room and heads right to the DVD player. "Callie? Does this mean she'll be having more than one margarita tonight?"

"Not fixed yet, Mandy," I say as I join her by a bag of DVDs. "What are our choices for tonight?"

Mandy grabs the bag of DVDs before I can even see

the title of one.

This week's choices are…" She pauses for dramatic effect. *"Friends* Season 5, *Friends* Season 8, or *Friends* Season 9." She holds up three DVDs, fanning them out in her right hand.

Before Melanie or I can begin to voice an opinion, she continues.

"I know I don't get a vote here since it is my week to select our three options, but…" She plucks out Season 9 with her left hand and holds it up by her face, pouting her lips.

"Cheater," Melanie scolds while nodding her head and agreeing to the choice. I quickly offer my own agreement. It's sometimes such a relief when one of us has some sort of watching preference; otherwise, we sometimes waste up to an hour trying to decide which DVD we are probably going to talk the entire way through anyway.

Mandy smiles and randomly puts Disc 2 in the player as Melanie and I spread out a blanket to share on the couch. We start talking before the characters even jump in the fountain during the opening credits.

Melanie tells us about Abby's dance lessons and Doug's attempts to make dinner on the nights she's been working late. As she finishes a story about a burned batch of macaroni and cheese, I think about how nice it is to see her so relaxed. I bet she won't be able to keep her eyes open very long tonight.

When we decide to stop and switch to Disc 3 of *Friends*, Mandy goes to the kitchen to refill Melanie's drink. She comes back with a margarita for me too—my one drink for the evening. She also brings out some pretzels and Doritos.

I sip my drink as Mandy whines about a science

project she is expected to do.

"I actually have to study windmills. Where am I even going to find some?" She bites into a pretzel as she groans. "What is a future art teacher supposed to do with all this stupid windmill information anyway? It's taking up room in my brain that should be devoted to something else."

"Like what—all the fruit you spend hours drawing?" I tease. She knows I love her artwork, but she also knows that I find still life paintings of food incredibly boring…and also somewhat tempting when I've already had my calories for the day. We currently have four paintings of food up in our house—one in the kitchen, two in Mandy's room, and one in the hallway.

At least they're not pictures of birds. *{A nice big welcome back to The Beatles with* "The Long and Winding Road."*}* Perhaps I should check my email again.

"So when is your next shrink appointment, Callie?" Melanie asks, somehow following my train of thought.

"Next Wednesday. Two fifteen."

"When do they give you the magic pills?" Mandy chimes in from the loveseat.

"I don't know. They want to know pretty much everything about me before they'll give me any medication."

"They?" Mandy asks.

"She has a real doctor and a busy surrogate doctor right now," Melanie answers before I can even start to explain the situation. Much simpler the way she puts it, I'm sure.

Before either of them have a chance to ask more questions, Monica starts singing "Delta Dawn" on the television.

We all know our conversation is going to have to be

put on hold for now.

Initially, we begin singing in unison, taking care to stay in pace with Monica. That only lasts for a few seconds though. I continue to sing the melody while Mandy quickly creates a descant and Melanie hums harmonic notes. Poor Monica can't even be heard anymore. That's probably for the best, though, because I don't think we are even singing the same version as she is.

We all stand. Mandy takes the straw out of her margarita and uses it as the world's smallest microphone. Melanie grabs a fake flower from the arrangement on the end table and pushes it behind my ear, without missing a note.

By the time we get to our big finish, Monica has been done singing for at least a minute and a half. Melanie and I plop back down on the couch, but Mandy announces that it's time for her to call Josh. She grabs her cell phone and heads upstairs to her room.

"How long will this call last?" Melanie asks in a nauseated voice.

"At least forty-five minutes. Be nice," I tease. "She could be sleeping around with all the other college sophomores on campus." And then I'd have to move out. I have a hard enough time when she has friends over who may or may not be sleeping with multiple guys. Just the thought of her sorority sisters makes me want to stop everything and disinfect the living room. *Thank God I have my own bathroom...*

"I'm not saying anything. They've been pulling off this long distance thing much longer than I would've bet on." *Yeah—much better than I did.* Is she thinking that too? She reaches over to me and takes the fake white rose out of my hair.

"If I have forty-five minutes, I'm going to take my

shower now." She stands up and puts the rose back in its vase before walking to the hall bathroom.

As I straighten up the living room, rearranging the throw pillows and taking my empty margarita glass to the kitchen, I decide that now is probably a good time to check my email. So, after washing my glass, drying it, and putting it back in the cupboard, I head upstairs. I can hear Mandy giggling across the hall as I step into my room and gently shut the door.

Laptop open. One email from DA Blake.

The subject line reads, "Follow-up Question." Count. Click.

```
Calista,
    3.) 1,400. Every single day?
                            -Dr. Blake
```

Count. Reply.

```
Dr. Blake,
    3.) Always 1,400. Yes.
                            -Calista
```

One. Two. Three. Send. Empty inbox. Shut laptop.

When I get back to the living room, Melanie is on the couch playing some word game on her phone. We decide to begin Disc 4.

Mandy comes back in after we finish about half of an episode. She carries a pitcher of margaritas and fills up Melanie's glass and then her own.

"How's Josh?" Melanie asks, sounding genuinely interested. Impressive. I try to catch her eye to silently thank her for her efforts, but she is still looking at Mandy.

Mandy plops down on the loveseat. She tells us how much she and Josh miss each other. As she divulges her plans to see him next weekend, I try to catch Melanie's reaction. She, however, is already looking at me with a concerned glance.

Oh. Right. The being left alone thing. She knows I can spend entire nights when I am alone searching for hidden murderers around the house. I used to stay with her when Mandy went away, but recently I've been trying to suck it up on my own. No murderers have shown up as of yet so I must be doing something right.

I try to ignore Melanie's anxious look and instead focus on Mandy's babble of plans. Melanie eventually turns to Mandy as well. It appears that she is softening a bit to this whole relationship between Mandy and Josh. I know she thinks they are young to be so committed, but maybe she finally recognizes that she and Doug were also young when they got together.

Besides, it's probably better to be nineteen and committed instead of twenty-four and alone. Somehow, Melanie seems to be following my thoughts yet again.

"So, Callie, how is class with Dr. Gabriel?" She sounds all sing-songy as she says his name. She knows I hate talking about him.

"He's somehow managing to balance having me as an assistant and trying to impress me while simultaneously pretending that I don't exist. I think he's still pretty pissed about last year."

I had Dr. Gabriel for my Journalistic Writing I class last fall. We ran into each other on campus in the spring, and he asked me out. After I said no, I, of course, was assigned his class for my TA position. That's just the miserable way the world spins for me.

"You should have just said yes," Mandy chimes in.

"Now there is a piece of journalism," I reply with a smile. "Sex-crazed professor captures virgin extraordinaire."

Melanie laughs. "You are probably the only one who has ever said no to him. All those literary grad students can't resist living out the handsome, poetic professor falls for young, naïve student storyline."

I smile, thinking of the girls I've seen walking with him on campus.

"You're right. I'm pretty strong to settle for the Emily Dickinson-style 'just me and my writing' character."

I do hope things get less awkward with Dr. Gabriel. I guess I should be glad that he actually asked for my commentary today in class, even though he seemed rather disinterested when I gave it. Eventually, he will have to give in and introduce me to the class, especially before I start teaching in November. He'll probably wait until the last second. My discomfort in class seems to be my punishment for turning him down.

Oh well. At least the TA job is paying for my tuition. The awkwardness must be worth that. I think.

We watch another *Friends* episode and discuss Mom's upcoming birthday. I'll pick out the gift and wrap it, we'll split the cost among the three of us and Jared, and we'll all have dinner with Mom and Dad to celebrate. Pretty standard.

11:30 p.m. Mandy and Melanie both seem to be

dozing off. I pull Melanie's blanket over her and take Mandy's glasses off of her face, setting them on the end table. I power off the television and DVD player and turn off the living room light.

Time for night preparations. But first, I head to my laptop.

One email, sent shortly after my last reply. Count. Click.

Calista,

3.) For how many years?

Aren't you supposed to be at Girls' Night?

-Dr. Blake

Count. Reply.

Dr. Blake,

3.) For as long as I can remember.

Yes, it is Girls' Night. There was a break in the action.

-Calista

Count. Send.

Laptop closed. Night preparations—GO!

IT'S AROUND 12:45 A.M. WHEN I finish cleaning Mandy's room and begin painting my nails. As I wait for my nails to dry, I wonder if there will be any more questions tonight.

After three minutes of drying, it is time to open my laptop again.

He wrote.

```
Calista,
    3.) What would you eat if you
        had a day when calories
        didn't count?
                    -Dr. Blake
```

That is his question? At almost 1:00 in the morning? Fast count. Onetwothreeclick.

```
Dr. Blake,
    3.) Nachos covered in melted
        cheese.
    Why do you keep replying to-
night? I'm sure you are well
aware that I can't go to sleep
until my inbox is empty.
                    -Calista
```

Onetwothreesend.

What the hell? It's Friday night. Doesn't he have something else he could be doing? Sleeping, perhaps?

I remember that little dark-haired boy in the picture on his bookshelf. He'll probably be up and ready to watch cartoons or something in just a few short hours.

DING. Another email.

Count. Click.

```
Calista,
   Yes. I am aware. Just testing
to see how long it takes you to
offer some unsolicited informa-
tion about your condition.
                  Good Night,
                  Dr. Blake
```

This was a test? *Damn it.*

I can't shake my irritation as I continue my routine, folding, dusting, and scrubbing. Did he even need answers to those follow-up questions or were they just stupid pawns in his little game? *{And here is Avril Lavigne with* "Complicated."*}* Shower. Cleaned. Shaved. Dried. Lotioned. *{Avril begins her thirty-third rendition of the song. This one goes out to Dr. Aiden Blake.}*

Finally, I get to the point where I can turn the television on. Spicy meatloaf tonight—doesn't sound very appetizing. Doesn't matter. Sleep.

Chapter 6
saturday

APPARENTLY, DR. BLAKE CLOCKS IN on Saturdays too. There is an email waiting for me when I wake up. He sent it at 7:00 a.m. Maybe that dark-haired little boy did get him up to watch some cartoons. I briefly wonder if his wife or girlfriend, or whoever the mother of that boy is, gets irritated that he works on the weekends.

All right. List number three coming up, no doubt.

Count. Click.

```
Calista,
    Here is your third list.
    1.) Drugs/Alcohol
    2.) Money
    3.) Flowers
    What time is confession to-
day?
                    -Dr. Blake
```

Why? Does he want to come? I can't see how knowing the time will lead to any help in my treatment. *Ugh!*

Reply.

```
Dr. Blake,
    1.) Drugs/Alcohol
      -  I have never touched
         any drugs (nor will I).
      -  It astounds me that
         people using drugs have
         such a blind eye when
         it comes to germs. Of
         course, I'm terribly
         appalled that anyone
         would voluntarily stick
         a needle into his or
         her skin and repulsed
         by the fact that that
         very needle might have
         just been lodged under-
         neath someone else's
         skin. However, I also
         find it disgusting that
         people merely pass a
         joint around in a cir-
         cle without reflecting
         on the germ-infested—
```

I stop and sit, picking at my nail polish. I'm probably giving him too much information.

I quickly delete everything but my first sentence.

```
1.) Drugs/Alcohol
  -  I have never touched any
     drugs.
  -  I have one margarita every
     Friday night.
2.) Money
```

What does he want to know? My current checking account balance? Maybe he is asking for my bank account number like that stranger in Nigeria.

I smile at the thought. I won't be giving that information to either of them, although I am giving this man all kinds of other information about myself that I don't really tell anyone else…

Okay, money.

```
2.) Money
  -  Some money saved to buy a
     house after grad school.
  -  Trying to pay down under-
     graduate school loans.
```

Hmm…good enough.

```
3.)  Flowers
```

Seriously? Flowers? *I don't know, Dr. Blake, what kind of flowers do you like to buy for that woman in the picture with your son? Does she like it when you ask your patients such date-like questions?*

Calm down, Callie. One. Two. Three.

```
3.) Flowers
  -  Yellow roses
Confession is at 4:00 p.m.
                    -Calista
```

Count. Send.

8:00 a.m. Time to get my morning routine moving. Melanie has already gone home to spend the morning with Abby. Mandy will be asleep in her room until around noon. That will give me plenty of time.

Thermostat: 70 degrees. Stove: off. Door: locked. (*Thank you, Melanie*. She hasn't forgotten once since I gave her a spare key.) Blinds: opened. Alarm: off. (It was set for 8:30 this morning—just in case.) Teeth: brushed. Pictures: straightened. Living Room: cleaned. Floor: swept. Refrigerator: sorted. Dishes: washed. Kitchen Floor: scrubbed. Doorknobs: wiped. Laundry: started. Prayers: said. Bathroom: sanitized. Bathroom Floor: steam-mopped. Shower: taken. Body: cleaned, shaved, lotioned, and weighed. Hair: dried and styled. Clothes:

on.

11:05 a.m. Mandy's up early. She knocks on my bedroom door.

"Hey, Callie. I'm heading out. I have to work on a group science project thing."

"All right, Mandy. Careful."

"See you later."

Minutes later, I hear the front door close. I run out to check the lock and then return to my room.

Maybe I should just quickly check my email before I continue to work on my paper. If I keep up this pace, I will soon have checked my email more times in one week than I did in my entire career as an undergraduate student.

Laptop: open. Inbox: empty.

After scraping off the last bit of clear nail polish from my left pinkie finger, I press the "check email" icon.

Still nothing. *{The refrain of Whitney Houston's* "I Have Nothing" *plays broken record-style.}*

Focus, Callie. Paper time.

THREE HOURS LATER. THREE PAGES, hand-written. Many more to go.

3:03 p.m. Email inbox is still empty.

3:05 p.m. Almost time for confession. Leaving-the-house routine.

3:45 p.m. On my way. I drive and consider the mean things I've thought since last Saturday. I remember the grocery store parking lot. Those loud kids and lover boy with his girl. Unnecessarily mean thoughts just because

I had to sit in a parking space for a few extra minutes. Irritation toward Dr. Gabriel. Just like every week.

Perhaps you ought to tell Father Patrick about your incessant desire to check to see if a potentially married man wrote you an email. And about the fact that you are disappointed he hasn't written more today even though he is probably off spending quality time with his wife and son. I'm pretty sure the big J.C. really doesn't like it when you think about messing with family units.

I tell my conscience to shut it as I pull into St. Anne's parking lot. I want him to email me because I want him to help me so that maybe in the future I won't be pulling into this parking lot for confession every Saturday until I die.

4:02 p.m. Confession.

4:04 p.m. Out with a penance. Father Patrick wants me to say the Hail Mary three times. I say three sets of three. Just to be sure.

4:35 p.m. Home. Mandy's already out for the night. Dinner and a movie with some sorority sisters. I see her standard note sitting on the table as I'm drying my hands. I know what it will say before I even make my way across the kitchen.

Title of the movie she'll be seeing. Time it starts. Theatre number. General area in the theatre where she'll be sitting. The fact that she'll save a seat for me "just in case."

Just in case I miraculously forget the story I heard somewhere about people with AIDS sticking themselves with needles and then placing the needles in movie theatre seats so you can get a side of disease with your movie experience.

Still haven't forgotten, Mandy. Check back next week.

As I walk back to my room, I have to admit to myself that it's nice that she still asks.

More Pablo Neruda tonight. I force myself not to open my laptop until I'm scheduled to during night preparations.

11:30 P.M. THREE MORE PAGES WRITTEN tonight. Night preparations complete.

He didn't write.

I fall asleep as the chef on television is pulling a specially seasoned prime rib out of the oven.

Chapter 7
sunday

EMAIL INBOX: EMPTY. MORNING PREPARATIONS. Leaving the house routine. Church. Home. Email inbox: empty. Pablo Neruda paper: completely typed. Night preparations. Email inbox: empty.

{U2 performs one song over and over all day: "Sunday Bloody Sunday."*}*

Chapter 8
more lists

6:00 A.M. MONDAY MORNING. DA BLAKE is back in the house. Three emails sent about fifteen minutes ago.

I force my hands to shut my laptop so I can't open any of them. He didn't write all day yesterday—he can wait. Besides, I'll never make it to my class on time if I start replying to his emails now.

Morning and leaving routines. One. Two. Three. Start.

9:40 a.m. I grab a 225-calorie cereal bar and head to school. At the beginning of class, I turn in my Pablo Neruda paper and then sit and listen as Dr. Sumpter discusses poetry analysis in depth.

She has now been discussing the poetry of Tennyson for over forty-five minutes. I stopped listening when she hit the thirty minute mark.

What will be on his list today? Why didn't I just open the emails before class? Then I could have had something to think about during this Tennyson sermon.

How many more lists will there be? *{Bob Dylan steps up to the microphone with his guitar for a little* "Blowin' in the Wind."*}* Will he be finished with the lists by the time I have my appointment on Wednesday? *{Actually, it's a lot of* "Blowin' in the Wind," *enough to get me through most of class anyway.}*

When class finally starts to wrap up, I realize that my nail polish is gone. I am going to have to paint my nails again before work this afternoon.

Dr. Sumpter gives us our next assignment. An analysis of any work by Fyodor Dostoyevsky. *Step aside, Mr. Neruda; I'll be taking a new man to the bathtub with me this week.*

1:25 p.m. Home. Shoes: sprayed with sanitizer. Hands: scrubbed. To the laptop.

First email. One. Two. Three. Click.

```
Calista,
    One clarification.
    2.) Money—How do you feel
        about money itself? The
        actual green stuff?
                      -Dr. Blake
```

Oh. He doesn't want my bank account information. This makes much more sense.

```
Dr. Blake,
    2.) Money is one of the filth-
        iest things on the plan-
        et. I buy everything with
        credit cards.
                      -Calista
```

Count. Send. Not too bad.
Second email. Count. Open.

Calista,
Another clarification.
3.) Flowers—How do you do with flowers themselves? Planting them, watering them, working with soil, etc.?
-Dr. Blake

Now I feel like an idiot. Of course that is what he meant by flowers, but why didn't he just write that?

Count. Reply.

Dr. Blake,
3.) I like to look at flowers and smell them. I don't plant them or have a garden or anything. You never know what gross stuff is waiting for you as you dig up soil.
-Calista

Count. Send. Okay. Last email. Count. Open.

Calista,

Here is your fourth list.

1.) Music

2.) Spare time

3.) Sex

-Dr. Blake

What? I'd really like to see an official copy of this list of "standard" questions.

Deep breath. Count. Reply.

Dr. Blake,

1.) Music
- I listen to most types of music.
- Not a big fan of country music.

2.) Spare time
- I don't really have much spare time.
- Spare time can be a bad thing—too much time for thinking.

3.) Sex

As I try to scrape off some nail polish, I'm harshly reminded that it's already gone. What the hell am I supposed to write about here? My rather short history of somewhat intimate encounters? People I'd like to hook up with? Positions? How I cringe when I think of the sexual promiscuity of others?

Okay, let's go with that. Sexual promiscuity of others.

```
3.) Sex
  -   Irresponsible people with
      different partners/no pro-
      tection.
  -   Diseases/babies/emotional
      baggage.
  -   Not getting tests for dis-
      eases/spreading more dis-
      eases.
```

Enough? It'll have to be. As I count and click, I pray that he won't have follow-up questions on this one.

I repeat the prayer two more times. Just to be safe.

Laptop: closed. Nails: repainted. Salad (three hundred calories): eaten. Dostoyevsky's *Crime and Punishment:* downloaded and twenty-five pages read.

3:00 p.m. Time to get ready to leave.

3:45 p.m. Off to the writing center.

Pretty quiet evening, once again. Brittany is sitting at Computer 7, but she follows procedures perfectly tonight. In three hours, she has me answer two questions and proofread a rough draft. In between answering her questions, reading Dostoyevsky, and picking at my nail polish, I observe as a new student gets up from Computer 9 and starts toward my desk.

Brittany stops him and points to the list of procedures hanging on the wall. *Well done, Brittany.* I'd like to hire her to do that for all of the scummy freshmen since they can't freaking figure out something so simple by themselves.

Soon after, Luke at Computer 9 submits a ticket. Excellent. I proofread his draft and go back to my book.

It's 7:00 p.m. before I know it. Time to go home.

After six hundred calories worth of dinner, I catch up with Mandy and then begin preparing for bed.

10:00 p.m. I congratulate myself on not checking my email before schedule.

Two pieces of junk email. One email from Mom about a family dinner on Sunday. I send a quick response, telling her that I'll be there and that I'll make dessert. She knows that means I'll buy some pies at a local bakery.

Mom's email ends with "Hope all is well." That is her way of checking to see if I want to talk about my doctor's appointment. I don't. Melanie will fill her in on what she knows anyway.

I send my response and delete my junk mail. Inbox: empty. No DA Blake.

Look on the shiny side of it, Callie. No follow-up questions either.

11:30 p.m. In bed, lulled to sleep by the sound of a knife chopping onions and celery for some sort of crepe-wrapped meal.

TUESDAY MORNING. TWO CLASSES TODAY. One email.

```
Calista,
   Here is your final list.
   1.) Parties
   2.) Grammar
   3.) Clean
                      -Dr. Blake
```

Last list? Does that mean last email?
Count. Reply.

```
Dr. Blake,
   1.) Parties
     -  Uncomfortable
     -  Spills
     -  Loud
     -  Sweaty
     -  No personal space
   2.) Grammar
     -  Very important
     -  People don't spend
        enough time proofread-
        ing.
   3.) Clean
     -  My bathroom
```

- My sisters and mother
- Shower/bath
- Kitchen sink
- Antibacterial soap (not the waterless kind)
- Organization
- Sanitation
- My bedroom

-Calista

One. Two. Three. Send.

Morning routine. Leaving routine.

11:00 a.m. Poetic Writing II class. Today's subject—a bowl of fruit. Around five hundred calories sitting in front of me. *UGH.* I sneak a picture of my subject and text it to Mandy; at least she'll get some amusement from my three hours of misery.

I write as many poems as I can about two apples, a bunch of grapes, and a banana. I manage to scrape five poems together.

They all suck. *{A big welcome to Gwen Stefani with* "Hollaback Girl."*}* A few classmates eagerly volunteer to share their poems during the last part of class. They've obviously tried to make their poems all symbolic and inspirational. Really, though, their poems suck too. Their poems might even be worse than mine.

Dr. Emery is delighted by the sucky poems. She claps and gives glowing feedback each time a new volunteer "shares" a poem. *{And Gwen Stefani sings her refrain over and over and over again...}*

2:00 p.m. Suckfest over. *Thank God.*

Home. A 450-calorie lunch. Seven chapters of *Crime and Punishment.* No new emails.

Leaving routine. Another stupid professional writer presentation tonight. Okay. We get it. It's important to research other published writers and articles prior to trying to get a piece published. Message received. I don't need to hear seven more professionals tell me this.

Seven more published writers. That means twenty-one more hours of presentations before I will be allowed to pick up my own pencil and write in this class. *Brutal.*

Chapter 9
publishing series

I GET TO CLASS TEN minutes early and go right to my usual seat. Three rows back, first seat in. Close to the door for leaving, but back far enough that every person who walks through the door in the next ten minutes won't walk right past me. No awkward smiles or forced conversation. No latecomers accidentally brushing against me as they rush to a seat. Safe.

To kill some time, I decide to keep reading *Crime and Punishment.* Before I can even pull my Kindle out of my purse, though, my gaze is drawn to the center of the classroom. I briefly register the sight of my professor's mouth moving as he gives some quick information to, presumably, tonight's speaker.

Tonight's speaker. He has his back to me.

As usual.

Fitted black pants. Long-sleeved white shirt. Strong, toned arms underneath. Tousled dark, dark hair.

Him.

{Cue Damien Rice with "The Blower's Daughter."*}*

His body remains rigid, statuesque, as Dr. Harper flails his arms around, explaining something about the class.

Why him? Why this class, my class?

And can he really talk for three hours? He had me standing in silence for most of my appointment. Now he's going to do some Bruce Wayne/Batman morph into a presenter with a three hour song and dance presentation? Impossible.

I reluctantly peel my eyes away as I watch Dr. Harper move to a seat in the front row of the classroom. The song and dance is about to begin.

He begins talking in that deep, soft voice before he even turns around. To the other students, this probably comes off as a dramatic technique. For me, well, it makes me start to wonder if he really is as socially awkward as he appeared at our first meeting.

I listen.

"My writing begins when I encounter a burning question about a patient—a question I can't simply answer by thumbing through textbooks or recounting hours of lectures from graduate school."

He is turning around. Slowly. My eyes immediately leap to see if his blue eyes are sad or angry—the only two emotions I've seen them express.

They are both and neither at the same time. He's looking straight ahead, at the back of the room. The sadness is there, in the center of his blue eyes, but the edges are tense, angry…hardened against the sadness. It feels like he is trying to use this deadly combination to look contemplative and poised.

He's good at it. My classmates are probably buying it, as I'm sure many others have in his past.

I don't buy it.

"A question like this: How do I uncover and mend a debilitating fear that lurks inside the mind of a patient who feels compelled to dispose of an expensive luxury item such as this upon leaving my office?"

What? I push my eyes down to his arms.

Oh. My. GOD. He has my purse! My beautiful, black and white silky purse from Melanie. What the hell? He's come to my class to talk about me?

And the douchebag of the year award goes to Dr. Aiden Blake. Hands down. No drum roll necessary.

I move my body quickly in my seat, preparing to bolt out the door. Unfortunately, my elbow hits my notebook. The notebook bangs as it hits the floor. Of course. *Shit.* Some of my classmates glance over at me. *Shit.* I have to pick it up. Up from the probably disease-covered floor. *Shit.*

One. Two. Three. Cringing, I bend over. I position my fingers so they only grab the top cover of the notebook.

Before I can lift it from the ground, I have to stop. He stops me.

He's looking at me. My head is down, my eyes are lowered, but I know. I feel. My heart begins to throb as I helplessly lift the top cover of the notebook. The pages and back cover flail open and fly through the air as I bring it back up to my desk. I keep my head and eyes down as I sit back in my seat, but I can still feel his scorching gaze.

I know he's still watching me.

And I can't help myself. I slowly raise my head, my eyes. One. Two. Three. Click. Our eyes come together. Fuse together. *{The volume on Damien Rice rises to an almost deafening level.}*

The genuine shock in his eyes forces me to tone down the hurt loathing in my own. He didn't know. He's not here to mortify me.

He did though. *{I use all of my mental strength to*

turn down the volume so I can think.}

One…Two…Three. I disentangle my eyes from his.

I will my eyes to remain focused on my notebook, the cause of all of this, for the next few hours. My ears strain to hear how he will transition back to his presentation.

He clears his throat. "Questions like these consume me. They drive me to work. And research. And write. Until I have an answer. Some solution. Some way to help."

I hear a tiny thump, and I can only assume that he has placed my purse on the desk in front of him. He continues.

"I don't search frantically for a quick fix, a temporary solution. I strive to find something lasting, something that works for the individual who inspired my question, my thinking, my obsession."

Obsession? My eyes try to force my head up, but I lock my head in place just in time.

"I write about my findings. For me. For other doctors. For other patients who might have similar problems. Every patient is unique. Every set of problems has new variations. But every bit of information gathered and explored means one step closer to finding a solution. It is always my hope to find solutions that help the individual first and then maybe others eventually.

"This is what drives me to write—the slight possibility that my research might mean breakthroughs for other patients makes me spend the time getting my work published.

"I'll be honest—publishing your work is a tedious, frustrating process. Drafting. Proofreading. Citing sources. Changing citation formats for different journals. Selling your ideas, your words, yourself. It's exhausting. But if you have a purpose, you can ignore all of the irritating parts.

"That is my advice to you: Have a purpose. Don't publish just to put something on your resumé. Or for money. Find a reason. A reason why other people will benefit by reading your writing. If you do this, your work will be better. Then the publishing experience will also be better."

He pauses. I hear the sound of a zipper being opened briefly, another thump on the table, and then the zipper being closed.

"I don't want to bore you by lecturing for hours about writing. I've made you each a copy of a paper I had published back when I was in graduate school. This was my first publication. I've included a copy of my first draft and also a copy of that draft with all of the comments and corrections my teacher added to it. Some of those comments were hard to swallow. I'm glad I got over that, though, because those corrections made the paper more professional. After two more rounds of corrections, the paper was publishable.

"I've included copies of all of those drafts and all of those suggested corrections in your packet. You have everything I did from the first draft to the final publication. The full process. Seeing that process will help you more than listening to me ramble on about it will."

I hear his hand sweep across the table and his feet as they begin to move toward us. The class is still rather silent, as though afraid to miss any extra sentences uttered by that quiet, quiet voice.

The silence is a blessing for once. I hear his feet on the right side of the room and can follow their soft taps as he moves to the middle of the room. I hold my breath as the taps get a little louder, coming my way.

I keep my head down and try not to exist. I don't

move. I don't even pick at my nail polish to relieve some of the tension. That has to be a first.

His feet stop in front of my row. What is he doing?

"Calista—here." A female voice. The blonde in front of me. Oh. She is handing me some of his packets. One for me and two to pass back to the classmates behind me. I mumble a thank you, grab the packets, and extend my arm backwards to pass on two of the copies. I don't look up or back. Just down.

His feet are walking away. My body again enjoys the luxury of breathing.

"Take your time and look at these drafts. We'll have an official question and answer session after about forty-five minutes. I'll take individual questions as you have them while you are reading."

I plead silently with the classmates around me. *Do NOT feel inspired to ask him an individual question. Save it for the Q&A. Or send him an email. Better yet, just don't think up anything to ask him.*

Touching only the bottom corner of the front page, the part untouched by the blonde in front of me, I pretend to look through the packet. Pages and pages of handwriting and typing and red ink. I have to admit, giving us these packets is not a bad technique for a writing presentation. Better than talking for three hours.

Too bad I can't focus on any of the words—all I see is a blur of red, white, and black.

Silence in the classroom. I have no idea where he has positioned himself while we are reading. Well, while my classmates are reading. I fold over the packet and pretend to examine page three as I pick at my nails under my desk. *{Fade into Destiny's Child singing* "Survivor."*}* Page four. There is no more nail polish on my left hand. Gotta slow down if I want to make it through class.

Page five. Page six. Page seven.

"Um, Dr. Blake, I have a question." The girl behind me. *Are you kidding me?*

"Over here, Dr. Blake." She isn't kidding. *Bitch.*

Body: frozen. Head: looking down as far as possible. We're talking chin in neck. Breathing: halted.

His shoes are clicking over this way. They come into my view as he reaches the front of our row. Black. Leathery. Clean. Closer and closer.

The heat from his body paralyzes me further as he walks past me. If my chair was two inches closer to the door, his arm would be grazing mine…right…now.

Now he's standing behind me. Directly behind me. I clench my eyes shut, trying to think of something, anything else. I allow myself a cleansing breath but breathe in his cologne. There is no escape. His smell. His heat. His voice. *{Damien Rice's voice overtakes Destiny's Child in a swift motion.}*

My lifeless limbs are becoming too heavy to hold up. I keep my eyes shut and try to focus on not falling out of my chair. *Hold on, Callie. Hold on. Hold on.*

He's moving. Back down my row. Two inches of air between our arms as he passes.

The clicking of his shoes is quieting. He is somewhere up by the center desk once more. I begin to feel my limbs again so I straighten my body in my chair.

Great survival techniques there, Callie. If you handle a bear attack this well, I'm sure you might last for two whole seconds.

"We are going to start the official Q&A session now. I'll answer any questions you have, and then we'll probably wrap up early. I've already received Dr. Harper's blessing."

Thank you, Dr. Harper, my mind sings slowly in

Gregorian chant. Almost done.

"If you think of more questions later, please don't hesitate to email me at the address on the front of your packet." I hear pages rustling and assume some classmates are checking out how to contact DA Blake.

I don't listen to the questions or answers spoken over the next twenty minutes. I plan my escape. *{I turn up the volume on Gloria Gaynor singing* "I Will Survive" *for inspiration.}* Hmm…if he dismisses class and turns around to gather his papers in his briefcase, I can bolt out the door. Just like a genuine coward would.

I'm not trying to be a hero here. I wait for the questions and answers to stop. My heart is bouncing all around and my ears are ringing. *{My survival anthem is now blaring.}*

It's quiet. A lull between questions. I wish I could look up to see if any classmates appear ready to ask anything else. I decide not to risk it.

Judging from the last taps I heard from his shoes, I surmise that he is front and center in the classroom. His eyes could be looking anywhere.

It's still quiet.

"Okay. If you think of more questions, you know how to contact me. Have a good night."

Papers start shuffling on the desks surrounding me. Pens are being capped. Cell phones are switching on.

Then, a miracle. The girl behind me, the bitch with the individual question before, walks quickly past me, calling out to him.

"Oh, Dr. Blake. I have one other thing I'd like to know." *Thank you! Sorry I called you a bitch.*

I can't hear what they are talking about, but I hear the low hum of his voice as he is responding to her. They are right in front of the room. By the desk. The one with my purse on it.

No time to think about that now. *Time to go, Callie.*

Once again grabbing only the top cover, I shove my notebook under my arm and then yank my purse strap off the back of the chair, leaving the copy of his study on my desk. Standing up quickly, I keep my eyes down and start moving straight to the door at my left. I should be out the door in one slow count of three.

Slow doesn't seem right in this situation though. I opt for three quick counts. Onetwothree. Onetwothree. Onetw—SLAM. I run into the guy in front of me. And my notebook falls out from under my arm and bangs on the floor. Of course. *Stupid freaking notebook.*

I quickly apologize to the guy in front of me, and he continues on his way after telling me not to worry about it.

Sure, like that will happen.

As I turn and bend to retrieve my notebook yet again, his eyes somehow manage to find mine once more. My cheeks heat up, and I freeze, crouched down, left hand about to secure the top cover of my notebook. His eyes are as disconsolate as they were the first time he looked at me in his office. A blue tragedy.

{Back to Damien Ri—} No, Callie. He humiliates me and then expects me to lose myself in his sorrow? Unreal.

I find the strength to close my eyes and lower my head. I scrape my notebook off the floor, turn around, and leave.

Onetwothree. OUT. Out the classroom door. Six more fast counts of three and I'm out the main door of the building. Out into a downpour of rain. Of course. Because my world is just that awesome.

I don't take the time to worry about my hair, my

shoes, or my purse. I can't afford to. I bolt to the parking lot, not stopping to breathe until I'm safely in my car.

In the driver's seat, I breathe. I let my head fall back onto the headrest. And breathe.

Quiet. Car on. Time to go home. *I survived.*

I think.

Chapter 10
cancellation

HOME. QUIET. AFTER TEARING OUT my notes, I throw my notebook in the trash can and thoroughly wash my hands. I start night preparations right away, already planning to skip the "check email" part. I convince myself that Dr. Gabriel probably wouldn't have sent me an email about Friday's class this early in the week. And if Mom or Melanie emailed, it's probably nothing urgent. They'd call or text if it was.

I do take the time to write myself a reminder on a sticky note.

Call Annie. Cancel 2:15 p.m. appointment.

I'll reschedule once Dr. Spencer returns from New York. Or maybe I'll find a new doctor, a new practice. Or maybe I'll just be done with this therapy thing altogether.

{Damien Rice is back.} Teeth: brushed. Pictures:

straightened. Clothes for tomorrow: out. Mandy's room: clean. Nails: painted. *{I can't fight his song out of my head.}* Laundry: away. House: dusted. Kitchen: scrubbed. Bathroom: sanitized.

As I'm about to get in the shower, my phone makes a vibrating beeping sound. The text message alert. Probably Mandy. She is still not home.

Yep.

Grabbing some ice cream with my class project group. Home in an hour.

Reply.

I'll probably be in bed by then. Have fun. Careful driving! Night.

To the shower. I let the hot water run over my hair and down my sore neck. I don't think I have ever held my head down for that long—not even back in second grade at Catholic school while the teacher was showing us how to kneel in our pews, fold our hands, bow our heads, and pray in correct form. It seemed like forever back then, but I bet we were only positioned like that for about fifteen minutes.

I move my dripping head first to one side and then to the other, stretching out my neck. I feel better. Not great, but better.

I wash and shave and lotion myself. Air dry. Put on pajamas. Turn on the TV. Some sort of cake baking competition is going on tonight. An oven timer goes off on the television just as my phone starts vibrating again.

I don't recognize the number. My phone doesn't either as it's labeled "Unknown Number." One. Two. Three. Open.

```
Calista, please check your email
tonight. I'm sure you are still
awake. -Aiden Blake.
```

Did he memorize my patient contact form? Does he carry it with him at all times? *Unbelievable.*

One. Two. Three. Delete.

Bed. I try to concentrate on the sounds of the cake competition, but the noise isn't turning into a calm, peaceful blur like usual. Instead, it sounds like a few loud bakers trying to make the most elaborate cakes. Unreal. I spend the next hour trying to force their voices to blend into a dull, unimportant melody.

Nope. Not working. I reluctantly throw back my comforter and get out of my soft, immaculate bed. And I start my night preparations again.

Thermostat: still at 70 degrees. Stove: still off. Doors: still locked. Blinds: still closed. Alarm: still set to go off at the right time.

As I'm brushing my teeth again, I hear my phone buzz once more. I walk out of the bathroom into my adjoined bedroom, mouth full of toothpaste.

Unknown Number. *Ugh.*

One. Two. Three. Open.

```
Calista—come to your appointment
tomorrow. I need to talk to you.
Please don't cancel.
```

Of course he knows I'm going to cancel. He probably knew before I did.

{Roberta Flack begins a soft, soulful rendition of "Killing Me Softly with His Song."*}* Damn it. He knows freaking everything. He probably even knows what grade I'll get on my next paper, how many children I'll have, what I'll be wearing tomorrow…

I go back to the bathroom to rinse out my mouth before making sure that the pictures in my room are still straight and checking to see that my clothes are still set out properly on my chair.

Quick decision. I hastily rip the black knee-length skirt and red boat neck top off the chair and rush to my closet where I grab a short, simple black dress and a pair of black stiletto pumps. Then I hang up my old outfit and return to the chair with my new one. I smooth out the black dress so it sits neatly over the chair's back and then switch the black Mary Janes on the floor with my black stilettos. There. *Get out of my head.*

After I put the Mary Janes back in place in my

closet, I head to Mandy's room. Not as clean as I left it. Mandy's sprawled out in bed, sound asleep. The clothes she must have worn to class are on the floor beside her bed and her third dresser drawer is open.

It only takes me a minute to put her clothes in the hamper, shut the dresser drawer, and pull her pink blanket up over her. I then leave her room, wondering when she got home. I'm surprised I didn't hear the door open.

Perhaps I shouldn't keep the TV volume so loud when I go to bed. Maybe I'm just making it easier for the murderers to swoop right in while I'm sleeping.

Back to my room to repaint my nails. I ceremoniously walk right past my laptop as I again skip the email step in my routine and go right on to look at my already folded laundry. I then dust, scrub, and sanitize before hopping back in the shower.

It's almost 3:00 in the morning when I am finally back in my pajamas. Just as I am climbing into bed, my phone buzzes. Does he actually know that I'm still up?

One. Two. Three. Open text.

`Please, Calista.`

{Roberta Flack keeps singing her refrain. Repeating and repeating.} I put the phone back down on my dresser, and I put myself back in bed.

At some point, hours later I'm sure, the voices on the television finally morph into my soft, soothing lullaby, and I fall asleep.

MY ALARM RINGS ALL TOO soon. Wednesday morning. *{Roberta Flack transforms completely into Lauryn Hill. Same song but in hip-hop now.}*

My cell phone is ringing. Now he's calling me? It's only 7:30 in the morning! Give me a second to breathe.

It's not him. I answer.

"Hey, Melanie."

"Morning, Callie. Quick story for you."

I smile. "An Abby story?"

"What other stories do I have time to observe these days? Yep, Abby."

I listen. I love Abby stories. Her views on life are pretty hilarious. Her more recent funny comments have involved school mishaps. Some stories we call OCD moments because Abby does have some obsessive-compulsive tendencies. When she does something that reminds Melanie of me, Melanie calls. My favorite call came a few years ago when Mel heard Abby screaming in the bathtub. Melanie ran to the bathroom and found Abby lining up all of her toy ducks on the bath ledge. Melanie asked her what was wrong, and Abby said that she needed to go to the potty. Melanie told her to get out and go. But Abby resumed her screaming, saying she couldn't go until all the ducks were lined up. Melanie told her that the ducks could wait and that she should stop and go to the potty. To this Abby exclaimed, "Mommy, you just don't understand."

Priceless. The girl literally had to get her ducks in a row before she could go to the potty.

Today's story isn't duck or OCD-related however.

"I picked Abby up from daycare yesterday, and her face was streaked with blue paint. I asked her if she had fun, but she must've seen me examining her blue face. She hurried to reassure me, saying, 'It just happened while I was painting, Mommy. I'm not turning into a Smurf.'"

I laugh. Hilarious.

"I love it, Mel. That is adorable."

"Just thought I'd try to start your day with a smile before your big appointment."

I ignore the appointment reference.

"You definitely did. Thanks, Mel. Give Abby a kiss for me. She's coming with you on Friday, right?"

"Oh, yes. She's already packed her bag."

"Awesome. I'll see you both then."

We say our goodbyes and hang up. I'm so glad Melanie brings Abby to Girls' Night every other week. I wish I could spend even more time with her.

Phone back on dresser. Time to start the day. And almost time for my cancellation phone call.

The office probably won't be open until at least 9:00 a.m. so I grab a 200-calorie breakfast bar and start plugging away at my morning routine.

10:30 a.m. I'm getting my supplies (dish soap and window cleaner) ready to clean my bathroom, and my phone buzzes.

Unknown Number…again.

Count. Open.

Five minutes? Can you give me that? After that, I can send your paperwork directly over to

```
Spencer's office. Really. Please.
```

UGHHH. I know I'm going to give in. He doesn't need to beat himself up this much over the purse. He didn't do it on purpose. I know.

Besides, he seems to already have plenty of things to make him sad. *{There go those Soggy Bottom Boys with* "Man of Constant Sorrow."*}* He pissed me off, but I don't need to add to his troubles—whatever they are. With my luck, something bad will happen to him, and I'll read about it in the paper. A car crash. A fall. A house fire. Something. I don't want to feel responsible for that. None of that.

I hit reply.

```
Fine.
```

Count. Send.

Another beep from my phone. A new message appears on the screen.

```
Would you like to add this num-
ber to your contact list?
```

No. Click. Phone down.

FINISHING MORNING PREPARATIONS. FOR ONCE, I'm glad I have to do such a long, structured routine. Keeps my mind almost busy enough to not obsess about 2:15 p.m.

Almost.

12:45 p.m. Done. I stare at the text of *Crime and Punishment* for a half hour. I read none of it.

1:15 p.m. Preparations to leave the house. Thirty-three checks. Bathroom shower: water off. Bathroom sink: water off. Hair dryer: unplugged. Hair straightener: unplugged. Bathroom counter: empty. Mirror: clean. Toilet: not running. Air vent: uncovered. Light: off. Bedroom floor: clean. Air vents: uncovered. Bed: made. TV: off. Light: off. Mandy's room: clean…ish. Air vents: uncovered (at least). Light: off. Hallway light: off. Thermostat: 70 degrees. Laundry closet light: off. Laundry closet: closed. Hallway bathroom sink: water off. Toilet: not running. Air vent: uncovered. Light: off. Kitchen sink: water off. Stove: off. Refrigerator door: shut. Air vents: uncovered. Light: off. Living room floor: clean. Air vents: uncovered. Light: off.

Repeat.

Repeat again.

Out the door. Door locked. Handle twist. Handle twist. Handle twist. Locked. And I'm off. Just like that.

2:14 p.m. I discreetly (I think) use my own clump of tissues to open the main door to his office building, catching the door with my foot and hastily discarding the tissues in the outside trash can. I begin to move past the blue waiting room chairs to check in with Annie. Before either of us can say anything to the other, however, the brown door to her left opens. We both freeze as we hear a deep, quiet voice.

"Miss Royce."

Annie looks shocked. *{Cue Michael Jackson singing out her name in* "Smooth Criminal."*}* I'm sure my face looks much the same.

One. Two. Three. I allow my eyes to move from Annie's face to his. Our eyes are all knotted together before I even have the chance to inhale.

Annie interrupts. "Oh, Dr. Blake. Is there something you need me to do? Miss Royce just arrived, and I was just about to lead her—"

She rambles on. It seems that Dr. Blake doesn't make a habit out of escorting patients to his office. He looks at Annie briefly, saying, "I don't need you for anything right now, Annie." He pauses. Even quieter voice now. "I might need you to transfer some records later.

"Miss Royce, if you'll follow me back…"

He has put his back against the door so I can walk right by. Annie is staring at me. Gotta move. I hug my purse close to the side of my body and instruct my black heels to start moving. I don't look up as I pass him; I'm too busy mentally scrunching up all of my limbs and praying that I don't accidentally brush against him.

Made it. I stop in the hallway, wait for him to shut the door and then lead the way down his ridiculously long hallway. *{Michael Jackson's song begins to morph into a reprise from The Beatles with—}*

NO! Concentrate, Callie.

Grey pants today. Dark purple dress shirt. He walks slowly but with large strides. I match his pace. Two small steps for every large masculine stride.

One. Two. Three. Turn. One. Two. Three. One. Two. Three. Twist. One. Two— We are here. He twists the silver bar handle and again leans back on the door to let me through.

One. Two. Three. Body scrunch. In. Standing in the same place as before—just far enough inside that the door won't graze my body as it closes. If someone closes it.

He does. Then he walks around me to his gigantic desk.

Silence. Again. Didn't we do this already? I can't believe I'm standing here again. Looking down at my purse. Again.

"Thanks for coming."

I nod. I don't even know if he can see it. Recalling his history of time actually spent looking at me, I decide he probably can't.

I don't say anything. I wait.

Still waiting.

"I haven't had a patient like you in a very long time, Calista."

Okay. Not really sure where this is going. Silence. Again. Since I've gotten pretty good at determining the placement and direction of his voice, I risk a glance up.

He is sitting in his desk chair facing his bookcase. Perhaps I should look into getting a freaking degree in voice location.

I keep my head up. He seems to be staring at the picture of his son and wife or whatever she is.

He still isn't talking. Am I supposed to have some sort of intelligent response for him? I don't. So I keep standing. When he asked me for five minutes, I don't think he remembered to add in all of his moments of silence. It feels like each one is at least five minutes.

He sighs a long sigh. I lower my head again, just in case he decides to turn around. *{A power ballad is brewing; Bonnie Tyler steps up to begin* "Total Eclipse of the Heart."*}* Nothing. Quiet. *{Verse one. Verse two. Verse thr—}*

He speaks.

"I have to keep you as my patient."

Huh? He has brought me here to tell me that Dr. Spencer won't be returning for a while? Annie could have told me on the phone.

"Calista?"

He wants a response. I try quickly, too quickly, to give him one that will free us both from this awkwardness. I even look up as I talk.

"No. Oh. No. You don't have to worry about that," I stammer to the back of his dark head. "Annie didn't say that Dr. Spencer would be gone so long, but really, it's fine. And I am just going to call Dr. Lennox and be referred elsewhere and then everything—"

"Dr. Spencer will be back tomorrow." He cuts off my super-sized sentence.

Oh.

"Let me rephrase this." He continues our face-to-back conversation. "I need you to let me treat you. I need to help you."

He feels guilty. I'm sort of glad he feels guilty, but letting him dwell on it won't get me out of here any faster. And it won't change what happened. I cut in before he can say any more words.

"Really, it's fine. You don't need to worry about the purse thing. I get it. You didn't know I'd be there. You didn't do it on purpose. You don't owe me anything." I look back down at my purse. If I could just make myself move, now would probably be a good time to go. Before he even turns around. *{Refrain.}*

I'm too late. He starts to speak, and his voice is a fraction louder than it was before. I know he has turned around.

"This doesn't have anything to do with the purse, Calista."

Sure. I keep my head down. Quiet. He is looking at me now. I feel him.

"I have come up with a unique twelve day program of immersion treatment for you. If you commit to this, we'll take a major step in helping you. After twelve days, you won't be suddenly cured, but I think you will experience some marked improvements."

Ah. There it is. His motive. Some experimental research—grounds for a brand new fancy article.

"I know Dr. Lennox sent you to this office to seek medication," he continues, "but if you begin taking medicine it won't start to take effect for quite some time. Perhaps this treatment will give you earlier and more natural relief." *Yeah, and perhaps it will get you a sizable paycheck. Or another presenter spot in one of my classes. No, thank you.*

"Our research doesn't have to be put into an article. Or a textbook." Of course he knows what I am thinking even now.

"If you don't want me to, I won't tell anyone about this. You won't have to sign any information release forms, and we'll follow only your personal doctor-patient confidentiality agreement. Your terms." His voice is intense but sincere. I know his eyes haven't left the top of my head.

I realize I've started to pick at my nail polish. I consider stopping, but really, what is the point? He already knows about my crazy. And about every thought that flickers through my brain.

"Calista. Please trust me on this. No one has to know." Quieter now. "I won't embarrass you."

Again. Shouldn't he have said "again" at the end of that sentence?

"I spend most of my time here in this office. The other doctors and Annie won't even ask about your treatment. They know all about confidentiality agreements." He pauses. "And I live completely alone. My closest relative, Uncle Dan, lives over two hours away. So I'm not going to go home and spill your secrets to anyone." Another pause.

"I know I embarrassed you before. I won't do it again. Your information will go nowhere if that is what you want."

"And where would it go otherwise?" My own voice stuns me. My curiosity must have unfrozen my lips. Luckily, it didn't also raise my head…or ask the real questions I can't stop thinking. *How do you know I just watch cooking shows for background noise? Why are you so sad? Why did you keep my purse? If you live alone, who are the people in that picture?*

He replies rather quickly (for him), seemingly grateful for my first bit of participation in this discussion.

"I would only ever share our program, our findings, if you wanted me to do so. And then, I would only do it if I felt the information would lend help to other OCD patients like you or to other doctors willing to try experimental treatments."

Oh. He has every possible base covered. Of course. That was probably easy for him though, what with his crazy super mind-reading powers.

"Calista." So quiet. "Look at me." Almost a whisper.

He knows. He knows I'll say yes if I look at him. If I see whatever expression he's chosen to manipulate me.

"I don't want to look at you," I mutter bluntly, verging on angrily.

"Why not? Because you want to say yes?"

DAMN IT.

I thrust up my head and meet his gaze with all of the frustration I can express without exploding my eyes.

"How do you keep doing that?"

"I don't understand." His blue eyes look surprised, confused.

"You don't understand?" I push on without giving myself time to question or regret the words. "Right. That would be a first. You know everything. You see everything. It's like you've read some all-inclusive tell-all journal that I've never even written."

He stares at me, mouth slightly open.

I can't stop.

"Or maybe you foresee that I'll eventually take the time to write all of this down, and you just haven't told me yet. Please, Dr. Blake, tell me what I'll do next. Amaze me with—"

Oh my God.

His eyes are miserable, devastated. Just like the first time I was in this office. But it's worse. Much worse. I did this.

"I-I'm sorry." As I say the words, I feel a transformation in my eyes, my face. From harsh anger to sorrowful regret in an instant.

It doesn't change the look on his face. I'm too late. He's staring past me now. His seated posture is perfect, professional. His large hands sit on the desk in front of him. Still. Rigid. Shoulders tensed. I watch the movement in his throat as he swallows at an excruciatingly slow pace.

I have to fix this. Now. And then I have to get out of here.

"Look, I'll do your study or experiment thing. You can do whatever you want with my information. Just email me or have Annie call me to set it up."

He is still staring past me. Can he even hear what I am saying? *I can't just leave him like this.* But what else can I say? He hasn't moved a gazillionth of an inch. His troubled eyes are in some sort of trance. Wide open. Seeing nothing. Nothing here in this room anyway.

BEEEEEP. The phone on his desk breaks through our silence. His eyes blink quickly, and he turns his head to listen to his message.

"Dr. Blake, your three fifteen has arrived." Annie. *Thank you, Annie.*

He verbalizes my thoughts yet again as he pushes a button. "Thank you, Annie."

I've got to go. While he's lucid. I mumble, "I… um…I'll just wait for your call or, um, email or…whenever you are ready to begin…" Good enough, I think. But he's still looking at the phone. *Damn it. Look at me. Acknowledge that you hear me. Blink. Or cough. Or nod. Do something so I can leave and not feel worse than I do already.*

He doesn't look up but instead begins to spin around in his chair. Seriously? He turns back rather quickly. He has the tissues again. Oh. I've spent years trying not to use tissues on doorknobs in front of people. Now I'll be doing it for the third time in one week.

As I step forward, he keeps his eyes lowered. Just like the last time we did this little dance. I gently pull out each tissue. One at a time. One. Two. Three.

"Thank you, Dr. Blake," I mumble, standing right in front of him. And he doesn't move. Or talk. So I turn and go out his door, down the bird-infested hall, out the brown door, past Annie and presumably his "three fifteen" patient, out the main entrance, by the trash can where I deposit my tissues (his tissues), and into my car.

And I breathe for a little.

Chapter 11
the aftermath

I DRIVE STRAIGHT TO THE writing center. If I drive home, I would have to prepare to leave again before driving to work and would probably be late so instead I use the extra time to catch up with Raskolnikov in *Crime and Punishment.*

Quiet night at the writing center. Brittany's not even here. I get through most of my book during my shift.

When I get home, I mix a salad and microwave some instant soup for dinner. Around four hundred calories total. I begin my night preparations, knowing that I won't skip the "check email" step tonight.

10:30 p.m. When I finally sit down at my laptop, five new messages show up.

He wrote. One. Two. Three. Open.

```
Calista,
    Please come to your appoint-
ment tomorrow. I'm sorry.
                    -Dr. Blake
```

Oh. He hasn't written. That is from last night. Now it's twenty-four hours later, and I'm the one who should be sending an apology message. But I don't. I apologized. He ignored me. I delete his message. If only it was so easy to get his tortured look out of my mind.

I press on. Two pieces of junk mail. One about erectile dysfunction. The other about penis enlargement. Awesome job, once again, email filter.

The next email is from my dad.

```
Hey Cal,
    You know your mother's birth-
day is coming up. Do you have any
time to shop with me next week?
See you at dinner on Sunday.
                  Love,
                  Dad
```

I smile to myself as I reply. These emails come from him like clockwork when a holiday or anniversary approaches. I write him back to check his plans for next Thursday and then get to my email from Dr. Gabriel.

Ugh. Just a copy of the university's grading policy. "In case you need it when you start teaching in November," he says.

As though I don't already know the university's grading policy. As though I wasn't just a student in his class last fall. *Please stop emailing me.* The email ends with his signature comment about having a date with a new girl tonight. *I get it, creepshow. You are spreading diseases all over campus. Stop reminding me, please.*

No count necessary. DELETE.

I hit "check email" once more. Just in case. Nothing. *{Schoolgirl-style Britney Spears begins "...Baby One More Time."}* I close my laptop and head to the laundry closet. Maybe he'll write tomorrow. Or perhaps Annie will call with an appointment time.

Or maybe nothing will happen. Maybe he changed his mind.

Time for dusting. I grab my duster from the shelf above the washer. *{On to the desperate refrain. And repeat. And rep—}* My cell phone is ringing. It's almost 11:00 p.m. He didn't give up.

I pick up the phone. It's not him.

"Hey, Melanie."

"Callie—I know it's late. I had a really busy night, but I'm out of the office now, and I couldn't wait until tomorrow. How did it go today?"

She wants to know how the appointment went. *Get behind me in line.*

"Well, I don't really know, Mel," I start out. "It's still early yet. I think I'm going to be starting some intense immersion treatment."

"Wow. Is that like touching dirty things and then not washing your hands?" I feel my body convulse a bit at her words.

I decide not to tell her that I only agreed to the therapy as an apology. Might sound ridiculous. "Well, uh, I think there's more to it than that. I don't really want to think about it just yet."

"I understand," Melanie blurts out before smoothly changing the subject. Her new subject is Mandy. "What is Mandy up to tonight?"

"I think she is on the phone with Josh. Making plans for next weekend." I pick up my duster and get to work on my dresser as we talk. It is already pretty late, after all.

Melanie has that motherly, worried ring in her voice. "Are you sure you don't want to stay with us, Callie? We could do a whole sleepover weekend thing. Abby would love it if we did makeovers and junk food and all that girl stuff."

"We'll see how things go, Mel. I really do need to be able to stay here on my own. I can't still be bringing a sleeping bag to your house when I'm fifty." I finish dusting my room and take the duster out to the living room.

"Well, we'll just see how you feel at the end of next week, okay?"

"Sounds like a plan. Thanks, Mel."

"All right—I've got to get to bed. That alarm will be going off in a blink."

"I know what you mean. Okay—see you Friday night."

"Good night, Callie."

"Night, Mel."

I finish dusting, scrubbing, and sanitizing. Time to get clean. Shower. Apply body lotion. Dress for bed. Check email...one last time. Nothing. Television on. Filled pasta dishes tonight. Heavy food to be thinking about so late at night. Luckily, I don't have to listen for long. Last night's lack of sleep has rewarded me tonight...I'm exhausted. I drift off just as the manicotti is being put in the oven.

I DREAM ABOUT HIM. WE are jousting in some inflatable game type thing, like the ones rented for freshman orientation activities every year. We are standing on four-foot blow up round stands, both wearing ridiculous, gigantic masks as if we might be severely injured by our inflatable swords. The mask covers his face so I can only see those miserable eyes. When a whistle blows, we try to knock each other off the stands. I'm terrible at the activity. I almost knock myself off of my own stand a few times. He seems pretty steady on his stand, but he isn't getting anywhere in our match either.

After a few minutes of a very lame battle, I lose my balance yet again and start to fall. As I go down, I reach out and grab his arm. He loses his balance and we both plummet to the cushy game surface below.

That's it. The dream ends and then starts all over again.

And then again after that. I even dream in threes.

When my alarm finally rings, I don't feel very rested. But I know I have to get moving if I want to beat the grocery-getting crowd.

Before I can start my routine, I know I have to check my email. No new messages. I briefly consider writing to him, but then realize that I have nothing to say. *Hey...I just dreamt about you all night—thought you might like to know. Oh, and P.S.—are you still mad at me?* Yeah. *Awesome idea, Callie.* I close my laptop and get moving.

9:45 a.m. Grocery shopping. No major drama beyond my normal blueberry fat-free yogurt being completely out of stock. I decide to try another brand even though each cup is ten calories more than usual.

I leave the parking lot with no trouble. 9:45 a.m. it is from now on...

Home. As I'm soaping up my hands, I hear my phone buzz. A text message. I get through the hand-washing process as fast as I can. My hands are almost dry when I reach into my purse for the phone.

Not him. Still.

It's from Mandy. The Thirsty Thursday invite. I quickly type my reply.

```
Thanks but not tonight. Have a
good time. Careful!
```

Send. No other texts. *{Damien Rice comes rushing back in with* "The Blower's Daughter."*}* I spend my afternoon finishing *Crime and Punishment* and taking notes for my paper. *{It plays over and over and over and over and over and over.}*

5:00 p.m. Leaving routine.

5:43 p.m. Check email. Nothing. *{The song begins again.}*

5:58 p.m. In my seat, ready for another presentation. I pull out my fresh notebook to jot down more ideas for my paper, but I cannot concentrate. He stood only a few feet in front of me in this very room. Only forty-eight hours ago. *{And again and again and again.}*

Class begins. Tonight's speaker is a young woman. Late twenties. Early thirties at most. Long, pin straight hair. Acrylic French manicure. Fitted black suit. Probably a size two. She writes for a celebrity magazine. In a sugary voice, she tells us how she researches her stories (pretty much by stalking people, it seems) while I manage to remove all of the polish from my nails.

She moves around the front of the room as she talks, heel clicks accompanying her presentation. We are given some time to examine a few of her latest articles. Pregnancy. Affairs. Shopping splurges. Arrests. As I skim the pages and half listen to the Q&A session, I can't help but wonder how many of these articles are actually true. Probably not a good question to bring up.

Finally, it sounds like she is wrapping up her presentation. Wishing us luck. Giving us contact information. Yep, sounds like an ending.

8:35 p.m. Class is over. Only twenty-five minutes early. Still better than ending at the scheduled time, I guess. I gather my stuff and head out. No mishaps this time.

It is one of those fall nights outside. Slightly chilly sweatshirt weather. Leaves blowing around. I take a slow walk to my car, breathing in the new season and letting my step match the beat in my head radio. *{The owner of the beat is Lady Gaga with* "Paparazzi."*}*

I hear a rustle of leaves behind me. A classmate in a hurry to get to the parking lot, I'm sure. I slow my step and move to the grass on the side of the walkway.

Hasn't passed me yet. I can't slow down much more without completely stopping.

"Calista." Quiet. Low.

Him.

Chapter 12
immersion eve

I STOP. *{LADIES AND GENTLEMEN, Mr. Damien Rice.}*

"Calista."

I can hear him breathing behind me now. I try to look back out of the corner of my eye, but I can only see my own dark ponytail. Gotta turn around. This is awkward—even more awkward than it usually is when we are in the same space. If that is even possible.

Inhale. One. Two. Three. Exhale. Turn. He is two steps away from me. Lit by a dim walkway light. Dark pants. Hands in his front pockets. Light dress shirt with the collar open and no tie. Mouth—serious. Eyes—haven't made it there yet.

"Are you ready to begin?"

What? My eyes accidentally meet his as my head snaps up. "Um, what?"

"Your twelve days?" His eyes aren't sad. They are almost calm. Almost.

Maybe the lighting is just bad.

I clear my throat. "Um, now?" *So articulate, Callie. I'm sure this university won't regret giving you a degree for a mastery of the English language.*

"Why not now?" He slides his eyes away from me momentarily. "Unless you have plans." Well, I do have a hot date with my stove, my laundry, and my alarm clock, but they'll all be waiting for me when I get home.

He hasn't looked back at me yet. He's looking past me, and some of the calmness in his eyes has seemed to disappear. I decide to go along with his plan before his eyes get any worse.

"No. I don't have plans."

He blinks back over to me. His eyes have a new expression. Relief? Anticipation? I'm not sure. "So you'll come with me?"

Sure. What the hell? I'll go with this mega-intense, super sad stalker guy who waits for me for God knows how long outside of my class. At 9:00 at night. *Good plan there, Callie.* I try to reassure myself that there aren't too many doctors slash ax murderers out there. I really don't think he is a Hannibal Lecter-type exception to that. I take my chances.

"Sure," I say pseudo-confidently. I wait for further information. Where is it that we are going? What is he going to try to fix at this hour of the night?

"Great. I'll drive." He takes his right hand out of his pocket and motions for me to keep heading toward the parking lot. As I start to move, he catches up to walk beside me. Beside me, leaving enough room for each of us to have a comfortable bubble of personal space.

We don't talk. Leaves crunch. Twigs snap. Trees rustle. Crunch. Snap. Rustle. Crunch Snap Rustle. Crunchsnaprustle. We reach the parking lot, and he leads me to a car right next to my small grey Hyundai. Unbelievable. Parked right beside me. Was he already there when I parked?

He opens the passenger door for me. A black Lexus. Clean black leather seats. Immaculate floor. I can do this. This part anyway. I slide into the car, and he gently shuts the door behind me. As he climbs into the driver's seat, he breaks our silence.

"I'll drive you back to your car when we're done."

"Okay." *Okay. Okay.*

No music. Breathing. Soft clicky turn signal sound now and then. More breathing. Two sets of eyes staring straight ahead. *{The track finally changes, and Simon & Garfunkel come in with* "The Sound of Silence."*}* Eventually, we arrive at his office building. The parking lot is empty. Two dull lights shine from the front of the building. He parks. I don't wait for him to get around the car to open my door. This isn't a date.

He meets me as I step out, and we walk together to the front door. Right by the trash can where I threw away my purse…

I allow him to open the front door for me. As a doctor protecting me from doorknob germs—not as a suitor following the rules of chivalry.

Everything is dark in the waiting room. I step to the side of the door to let him pass so he can lead the way. *{The song begins again.}* I hear only his soft footsteps as he crosses the room. I stand. Wait. Listen. A door is opening. Probably that brown one beside Annie's desk. A dim light flickers on beyond the door.

There he is. Standing at that brown door, waiting for me to pass him. Just like last time. Yet totally different from last time. No other patients. No Annie. Us. Nothing else.

I squeeze past him and then pause, waiting for him to lead me down the hallway. He steps in front of me, and I begin to follow. The birds hanging on the walls, looking creepier yet in the dim lighting, by the way, stare at me as I, well, stare at him. At the back of him. As usual.

We get to his door. He lets me in, turns on the light, and closes the door behind us. As if it matters. As if anyone else is in the building.

I stand in the same spot as usual, right inside the door. My spot. He heads right to the left corner of the room. I've been in this office twice before and never even glanced at that side of the room. Until now. There is a large brown microfiber couch against the left wall. Looks comfortable. Until you consider how many other crazy people have sat there…

In the far corner of the room, a few feet away from the couch, is a door. A locked door, apparently, because he now sorts through his keys as he stands in front of it.

He finds the key and opens the door. It appears to be a decently-sized closet, but I can't really see much with him standing right there. I can see his back, but of course, I already have that memorized.

He leans down a little and starts pulling something out of the closet. Something pretty big. He keeps pulling and backing up until he is in the middle of the room, at the corner of his cherry desk.

Finally, he turns to me, mumbling, "First things first." I am only caught in his hopeful eyes for a moment because he abruptly moves aside so I can see.

Wow. This is pretty big. Sitting at the corner of his desk is a tall-backed office chair. Or maybe a conference room chair, like the ones Melanie sits in during important meetings in Board Room I. If it was larger, maybe. Or if it didn't have wheels.

At the top right corner of the chair, a white square is hanging. A tag.

Holy shit.

"This is for you. Just you." My eyes rise again to his. "When you aren't here, it will be locked up in that closet."

A clean, new, untouched place for me to sit. All bases covered yet again.

He nods his head toward the chair and points to the tag.

"Go ahead—it's yours."

I reach out and remove the tag and the little piece of plastic that secured it to the chair. When I look back at him, he holds his hand out toward me.

Oh. I hold my hand over his and drop the tag and the plastic piece into his palm. Careful not to drop anything. More careful not to graze his hand.

He moves his hand slightly to drop the items into the trash can to the left of his desk. I simultaneously pull my hand back and let it rest by my side.

Now he's looking at me again. Waiting.

"Thank you," I murmur, hoping that is what he is waiting for.

It's not.

"Aren't you going to have a seat?"

Oh. The first time he's ever said those words to me.

"Sure." I sit down in the dark, soft chair. My chair. I really have nowhere to put my purse so I hold it in my lap. *Okay? Time to begin now?*

No. Not yet, it seems. He leans on the left corner of his desk so we really aren't all that far apart. A couple of feet maybe.

"Before we start our therapy, Calista," he begins, "I have to know that you are in the necessary physical condition for this to be safe."

What physical exertion is part of psychological therapy? Rock climbing? Bungee jumping? My face must reveal my confusion.

He goes on. "I need to know that you can physically handle the emotional strains we will be putting on your body."

I still must look confused. He continues. "If you have high blood pressure, an irregular heart rate, or a similar condition, this won't work."

Makes sense. Guess he doesn't want me to have a heart attack in his office. Probably a good plan. No doctor has ever told me that my blood pressure is abnormal or that I am at risk for any kind of heart issues. Is that what he wants to know?

"How long has it been since you've actually entered a doctor's office? Are we talking months…or years?"

I can tell from his tone of voice that he knows it's been years. Of course he knows. I twist my mouth slightly and bite my lower lip.

"I'll take that as years," he says quietly.

I nod my head slowly. I think he even sees my head nod for once. He has looked in my general direction more tonight than he ever has before. He stands up from the corner of the desk before pacing a little in front of me and running his right hand through his dark head of hair.

"This leaves you with a choice then, Calista. You can schedule an appointment with a local doctor or…"

Or what? I can refuse the treatment? I can't believe he is going to give up so easily.

He stops pacing and his blazing eyes meet mine head on. "Or you can let me perform a quick preliminary examination. Just so we can get started." He pauses. Waits. But he doesn't look away. I don't know how much longer I can endure the intensity of his stare. Squeezing my purse, I silently wish I still had some nail polish on my nails.

I open my mouth and try to make my lips form a response, but I can't produce any words. My effort causes a small gasp to escape instead.

"It's too much. I know it is." He looks away. "Like diving right into one of your major fears before we even really get started." He's pacing again. "If there was a way for me to verify your physical health without medical instruments or um...touching, believe me, I'd jump at the option."

I still don't talk. *Touching?* I swallow the colossal boulder in my throat.

He presses on, pacing now in the direction of his closet. "I know the traditional OCD fears in this area: the 'dirty' doctor's office, the sick patients, the germs, the used and reused instruments, the invasion of personal space, etcetera. I've tried to find a way to eliminate most of these issues."

He pauses as he leans into his closet again and reappears with a brown shipping box in his hand. As he walks to his desk with the mystery box, he begins talking again.

"Right now, there are no other patients. You are already here, in my office, safe in a chair that no one else has ever touched." He pauses and opens the brown box. He pulls out a heavy-duty plastic bag and another smaller box. In silence, he begins to break open the securely sealed plastic bag. He unrolls some protective bubble wrap and reveals a stethoscope.

A brand new shiny stethoscope.

Before I can say a word, he moves on to the next step in his little magic show. To open the smaller box, he rips off several layers of packing tape. When the box is open, he pulls out more protective bubble wrap. He removes some more plastic and uncovers a blood pressure cuff. Immaculate. Straight from the medical supplier, no doubt.

All. Bases. Covered.

Almost. There's still the part about the touching. I've spent years of my life perfecting the art of avoiding human contact. Steering clear of popular places. Sitting on the edge of classrooms. Paying with a credit card at a grocery store (so I can just swipe the strip of the card by myself) and then having the cashier put the receipt in the bag even though I'm scared to death of losing a receipt, not recording it, and having an inaccurate checking balance. Pretending to sneeze or cough or be otherwise indisposed when we get to the handshaking part at church. Oh, and pretty much entirely neglecting my medical, dental, and visual health.

I have finally gotten to the point that I can hug my mother. And Mel and Mandy. Abby too. They can actually get away with a lot of physical contact with me as long as they haven't been messing with heavy-duty cleaning supplies or using a public bathroom or something.

I'm also doing pretty well, I think, with Jared and Dad. It would be easier if they weren't always sweating and working in the garage or outside. Or scratching themselves. Or itching their belly buttons. Sometimes I think Jared only does some of those things to help me see a lighter side of my situation. He's always teasing me about my bathroom. My personal bathroom connected to my room. For me…just me. Forever clean. Everything always just as I leave it. A safe place to wash off my day. Jared knows all of that, but he's always texting me or calling to tell me that he stopped by my house while I was at class to use my bathroom. "I hope you don't mind, Callie." It makes me smile every time. I know he would never actually do it, and I also know he is simply trying to make me laugh.

I remind myself to hug him the next time he is around and not dirty.

That thought jolts me back to the problem at hand. *The touching.*

I look up at him. He is still waiting for my response. His eyes have everything in them. Concern. Sadness. Confusion. Hope.

Hope. He really wants to do this treatment. And I've already gotten this far. I'm here, I've given him pages of personal information, and he already somehow knows intimate information I've held back. I know I'm not going to be able to get myself to another doctor. Not a physician for this little medical check, not another therapist. If I'm going to try anything, this is the time.

"Okay." It slips out of my mouth in a whisper.

His eyes widen as his eyebrows lift in surprise. *Wow.* He did all of this, planned it all perfectly, but he never actually believed I would say yes.

"Okay," he finally murmurs back.

I watch him push his desk chair toward me. He wheels it to a spot next to my chair. Close. Not touching. Going back behind his desk, he starts to pick up the stethoscope to put it around his neck. He pauses, though, and places it back on the desk. He glances at me briefly and then walks away.

What?

He starts toward the right side of the room. Great. Is he going to take an hour or two to stare out the window? We don't have time for that. I'll definitely lose my nerve.

He doesn't walk to the window though. Instead, he goes to a door in the center of his right office wall—another door I hadn't noticed before. He opens the door and pushes it out as far as it will go before he turns on the inside light to unveil a bathroom.

He rolls up his shirtsleeves, goes in to the sink, and begins washing his hands. Scrubbing them with soap and water. Making sure I can watch. And I do watch. Intently.

After he finishes rinsing off all of the soap, he lifts his hands and pauses, deep in thought. He throws a quick contemplative look my way before grabbing a few paper towels from the dispenser and drying his hands. When they are dry, he awkwardly balls up the paper towels and places them over the left faucet knob. Twist. Water off.

Just like I would have done it.

I know my mouth is hanging open a little bit, but I don't get the chance to clamp it shut because he's not done yet. He tosses the paper towel into a trash can by the sink and then turns off the light with his covered elbow. Just. Like. Me. *Seriously?* I crash my lips together so I don't accidentally blurt out the question I know I'll regret asking…asking again.

It must be carved in my face though. He stops just outside the bathroom door and stares at me. He closes his eyes and squeezes them. For five seconds? Ten seconds? Feels like three years.

When he opens them again, every bit of the misery from before is back. After a beat, he looks away, down. And then he answers my unspoken question. He exhales, and the words breathe out of him.

"It's because of my mom."

I don't speak. I wait for more.

He must sense that I don't understand from his one simple sentence. Another deep breath and he continues. "She was diagnosed with this condition, your condition, when I was really young. Probably shortly after that picture was taken of us." He nods toward the picture on his bookshelf.

Even though I can imagine the photograph clearly

in my mind, I follow his nod. His mom. Of course. Her dark hair matching his. And…him. Tiny him. A little man checking on his mother just as the photographer snapped the picture.

I don't have the time to process this because he has started to speak again.

"I watched her day in and day out when I was little. The hand washing. The checking. The routines. All of it. It was my childhood." He stops and lifts his anguished eyes to mine before continuing. "So yes. I know. I understand." Another deep breath. "And that is why I can help you."

Just like that, he has moved back to me. He is done talking about his mother, I know that. But I have so many questions…

"So…," he lingers on the word, waiting for me to allow him to press on with our arrangement. With his little medical examination. I close my eyes and let my head nod slowly. Up and down. Up and down. Up and down.

"Okay, Calista, I'm going to start with your blood pressure." Back at his desk, he puts the stethoscope around his neck and grabs the blood pressure cuff. "Why don't you lean back in your chair. Rest your head."

I do as he says, though I can't really say my body is "resting."

"All right. Hold out your right arm, palm up, and rest it on the arm of your chair."

Okay. Done.

"Good." He's right beside me now. He sits down on the edge of his chair. "Now, I'm going to place this cuff around the top of your arm. I think your shirt is thin enough that I won't need you to roll up your sleeve."

I give myself an imaginary high five for my wardrobe selection tonight. *Good work not wearing a sweat-*

shirt in sweatshirt weather, Callie.

Okay, enough accolades for now. I have to get through a lot more tonight before buying myself a trophy.

I look over at him. The stethoscope buds are in his ears. The blood pressure cuff is unrolled, waiting for my arm.

One. Breathe. Two. Breathe. Three.

I lift my arm and slide it over to rest in the open cuff. Meticulously, he wraps the cuff around my arm. His quick fingers touch only the cuff. I hear the connection of Velcro as he secures it in place.

I hold my right arm up stiffly, trying to take all of the weight out of his hands. Struggling to keep my body balanced, I hug my purse with my left arm.

He notices. "Calista, do you want me to stop?" Gentle. Soothing.

No. I shake my head.

"Okay. You can place your arm back on the arm rest."

As I lower my arm, I notice that it is shaking a little. It knows what is coming next just as well as I do.

He takes the little bell of his stethoscope and slides it under the cuff, in the middle of my upturned arm. It's cold. It's smooth. It's...the only thing that is touching me. Somehow he has arranged his fingers so that they firmly grasp the bell but don't touch me at all. Did he practice this?

He looks up, right to my eyes, as he begins squeezing the bulb that in turn starts the squeezing of my arm. His eyes are questioning, concerned, and reassuring all at the same time. *{Chantal Kreviazuk's voice begins a slow, sweet rendition of* "Feels Like Home."*}* Still squeezing the bulb. Still holding onto my eyes with his.

The look in his eyes takes me back to nights in my

parents' house. Every time I had a nightmare, I would get out of bed and head directly for my parents' bedroom where I would stand right beside Mom, crying as she slept peacefully. She'd open her eyes, see me, and give me that same look. Now his look. Dad gave me the same look the day he first took the training wheels off of my bike, the day he first let me try to keep myself up. That look. Endless patience. Unconditional concern.

"One-twenty over eighty. Perfectly normal." He sounds relieved.

He gingerly removes the bell of the stethoscope and then the blood pressure cuff from my arm. As carefully as he put them on. After moving to his desk to put down the blood pressure monitor, he pushes his chair to face mine. Our knees are facing each other. Close, very close, but not touching.

"Okay, Calista. Now I'd like to listen to your heart."

It's been years since I've been to a doctor, but I remember well what this entails. I count and slowly nod my head.

Warily, he lifts his right arm and places the bell of his stethoscope on the left side of my chest. Again, his middle and index fingers hold the top of the bell securely while the other fingers are strategically placed away from my body.

Once he has the bell positioned, he slides his eyes up to mine. He exerts a tiny bit of pressure on the little bell and listens, not once removing his eyes from mine. *{And now, finally, the refrain of* "Feels Like Home."*}*

It feels like more than that. But I'm not ready to think about that just yet.

I try to ignore the scorching heat tiptoeing throughout my body. I feel a power ballad starting up in my head. I try to ignore that too. His penetrating eyes aren't really helping.

I really hope he isn't using his special mind-reading powers right now. I also hope that my heart isn't really beating as fast as I think it is.

It must not be. He pulls the bell away, simply saying, "Sounds good." Before I can relax and rejoice a little over the end of my fake doctor's appointment, he continues.

"Now, one last thing." *What?* There are no other instruments left to use.

I wait. He pushes back his chair and spins it around to place the stethoscope on his desk. He doesn't pick up anything else. His hands are empty as he turns back to face me.

With a guarded look in his eyes, he reluctantly speaks. "The last thing I need to do is check your pulse."

I know my eyes widen. There was no mention of this before I agreed to our non-appointment.

He starts spitting out words. "Calista, this really is the last check we need to do. Then we can get started and put this behind us." He takes a breath and then continues. "Would you like me to wash my hands again? Or find some gloves?"

No. His hands are already clean. Gloves aren't really necessary. They'd be nice if they would somehow prevent or dilute the response I fear my body will have. But I don't think that really has anything to do with my OCD.

He looks at me. All concerned and waiting for my response.

Shaking my head, I say, "No. It's fine, I think."

"All right," he murmurs. Not very confident. He just stares at me nervously. I nod again to reassure him. To reassure me.

"I am going to use these two fingers," he says as he holds up his right middle and pointer fingers, "and I'm going to place them right on the underside of your wrist."

I nod again, hoping that he'll stop staring at me. He does but only for a moment to place his fingers on my wrist. As his fingers connect with my skin, the heat that has been slowly spreading through me floods my entire body. The pieces of songs streaming through my head are moving so quickly that I cannot place even one of them.

I feel my body sway a little, and my head falls back on the chair. And then he breaks me out of the moment. He jerks his fingers from my wrist.

"Calista, I'm sorry. It was too much."

He doesn't get it. He thinks he's hurting me. I can't speak yet.

In his desperation to make it better, he grabs my wrist and clutches it, calling my name again and again. Before the tsunami can reclaim much speed throughout me, he lets go, shocked. His eyes give away tremendous remorse. He thinks he has made two major mistakes. In quick succession. The premeditated pulse check and then the spontaneous wrist grab. Such transgressions. I imagine him telling a priest about them in confession, and I feel a smile creep onto my face.

But I stop. I can't smile now, not when he looks like this.

Or maybe...maybe a smile will be just the thing he needs. Something new for us.

Keeping my eyes on his, I allow a soft smile to break out on my face. He looks surprised but not better. I need to do more...to fumble for the right combination of words.

Through my smile, some words do spill out. "We

did it. Am I cleared now for treatment, Doctor?"

My words snap him out of his guilt. He blinks and moves right back into business mode. "Um, yes. I was able to get your pulse, and everything seems fine. You are ready to begin the treatment plan. It is, ah, getting late, though, so perhaps we can meet to tackle the next step tomorrow afternoon."

He gets up from his chair while he awaits my answer. As he pushes his chair back to its spot behind his desk, I formulate a response.

"Sure. Tomorrow's fine. What is my next step?"

I don't really want to know, but I want to keep him talking. I guess I ask it as part of my silent apology for getting all weird during the pulse reading. Very similar to the fact that I'm doing this whole therapy thing primarily as a penance for upsetting him with my curiosity.

"Yoga-type relaxation," he answers, interrupting my own conscience examination. I must look confused because he continues. "We need to familiarize you with some meditative concepts of yoga so that you are prepared to encounter some scary situations."

"So I am going to what?" I blurt out. "Break into Downward Facing Dog when I think I touched something dirty? Wouldn't I look a little less ridiculous just washing my hands for an hour?"

He doesn't answer immediately, but wait, is he smiling?

Well, that is new. *And rather adorable*, some loud corner of my mind informs me. Shut it.

The smile hasn't completely left his face as he says, "No, you'll learn some yoga relaxation techniques, not positions. You'll see. Tomorrow."

I simply nod my head for the three-millionth time.

"Let's lock up your chair."

"Oh. Okay, great."

I stand up, still holding my purse, and he grabs the back of the chair so he can push it to his closet. As he puts the chair away, I briefly wonder if he is serious about it being my chair. How would I know if he is lying? Perhaps I should break into his office during one of his sessions with another patient. I could distract Annie and run down the hallway without anyone noticing.

Just as the *Mission: Impossible* theme song gets started in my head, he interrupts.

"This chair really will be just for you, Calista."

So his mind reading isn't limited to OCD tendencies; he can predict criminal intentions as well.

He goes on as he moves back to his desk. "The same goes for these medical instruments. I'll box them up and keep them locked in my closet. Just in case we need to use them again." He places the box of instruments in his closet and then locks the closet door. Just like he said he would.

"You are going to have to trust me a little, Calista. Or else this won't work." I know he's right. Whether or not it'll ever happen, I can't say, but I know it would be best. I give him my signature nod.

"Ready to go?" He is standing by the office door.

"Mmmhmmm," I murmur before walking past him as he holds the door open yet again. No touching. He gets me through the other two office doors in the same fashion and goes back to turn out the lights after I am already safely outside.

It's darker outside now and much chillier. It would be nice to have a sweatshirt. That would have complicated my "appointment," though. It's difficult to imagine having to take off a layer of clothing while holding on to my purse and then having nowhere to put the sweatshirt and having to hold it too. I decide to be grateful I didn't bring a sweatshirt. As for the cold? I can just suck it up.

He locks the main office door, and we walk to his car. As he is opening the passenger door for me, my cell phone rings. I grab it from my purse after I slide into my seat. It's Melanie.

"Hey, Mel. What's going on?"

As Melanie starts questioning me about birthday presents for Mom, he gets into the driver's seat and starts the car. He looks over at me and gives me a face that seems to be asking if it's okay to start moving. I nod and give him a little smile. Which he returns. And it really is adorable.

Shit. Melanie must've just asked me a question. She seems to be waiting for my response.

"Um, Mel, I missed that. I must have bad reception right now."

"Oh, well, I just wanted to see if Dad called you about getting his present for—wait, you have bad reception? Where are you?"

Shit. Shit. Shit. I glance over, and he appears to be trying to ignore my conversation. Perhaps that would be a bit easier if the car wasn't so deathly silent.

"Um, I am on my way back to campus to pick up my car. I'll be home soon."

"Wait—don't tell me Mandy finally got you out for a Thirsty Thursday. I never thought that day would come."

"Well, it hasn't. I was doing this, ah, therapy thing."

"At 10:30 at night? That sounds more like a date."

"No…um…just some prep work for that immersion thing I was telling you about."

I glance over at him. His face shows no reaction to my words even though he obviously hears them. This guy's gotta get an iPod or some CDs or something.

Melanie isn't done with her inquiry. "So you are going to go through with this immersion therapy. Do you think you can handle it?"

"Well, I'm going to try," I answer honestly. Before she can think up any more questions, I come up with one for her. "What are you up to tonight?" Okay, so I came up with a pathetic question. It still works. Melanie begins lamenting about her latest case and about the fact that she keeps losing evenings with Abby.

"So you are driving home now?" She knows I hate it when she calls when she is driving. If she crashes, it would essentially be my fault.

"I am. I just thought I'd catch you quickly about Mom's gifts."

"Well, okay, I will take care of picking those up. Maybe we'll get to talk about some ideas tomorrow night."

"That sounds like a good idea."

"All right, you just drive now. And be careful."

"I will. Good night, Callie."

"Night."

He glances over at me as I put my phone back in my purse. "Your sister?" he asks and then looks back at the road.

"Yep—that was Melanie."

"Not the one that you live with?"

"Right, that's Mandy. She's out tonight. Thirsty Thursday every week."

"And you don't go with her."

He didn't even put that in question format. Do I have to answer?

I don't get the chance. He goes on. "Why not?"

Where do I begin? "Drunk idiots. Sweaty bodies.

Accidental brushing and touching. Disgusting bathrooms. Sticky floors and tables."

He nods. And then changes the subject. "You'll see both of your sisters tomorrow night, right?"

"Yep, every Friday."

"What time do you want to meet tomorrow then?"

As I tell him about my schedule for tomorrow, we pull into the campus parking lot, right next to my car. It feels like forever since we were last here.

Still sitting in the car, we decide to meet at 4:00 p.m. so I'll have some time after my TA class to grab some lunch before I drive to his office. With our plans settled, he comes around to my side of the car to open my door. When I stand up out of the car, we are face to face, only inches apart.

Our eyes find each other. Everything's quiet.

Eventually, he speaks. "Thank you, Calista."

He has no reason to thank me. He is giving up his time to fix me.

"No. I am the one who should be thanking you, Dr. Blake."

He shakes his head as soon as the word "doctor" comes out of me.

"Aiden," he says softly.

"Aiden," I repeat.

"Until tomorrow?" he asks.

I nod. Of course. He steps aside, and I get into my car. He stands and watches as I back out of my spot. I give him an awkward little wave and then go home.

10:50 p.m. Night preparations.

1:52 a.m. Bed.

Chapter 13
breathing

I WAKE UP NOT RESTED at all. Some people would say that they tossed and turned all night, but that would not be accurate for me. I am a side sleeper, and I remained on my left side for hours. Most of my body didn't move even a centimeter throughout the night. The only exception was my eyes—they opened and closed all night long. Every time they closed, I saw him. His blue, serious eyes. Watching me.

I couldn't sleep with him watching me. So I'd open my eyes and stare at my alarm clock on the nightstand. And think about him watching me.

Unfortunately, I couldn't fall asleep thinking about him watching me. Or with my eyes open. So I'd shut them again, and see him again, and force them back open again. And so on…

So no, I don't feel rested this morning. But I drag myself out of bed anyway. Can't be late for class or it will give Dr. Gabriel an excuse to talk to me. No, thank you.

When I get to the end of my morning routine, I wonder what I should wear for my afternoon therapy session. Yoga relaxation—does that require special exercise clothing? Mandy would probably know, but asking her means opening myself up to a wide assortment of uncomfortable questions. I decide to pack a bag with sweatpants, a t-shirt, and sneakers just in case the short blue dress I'm wearing to class won't work.

I leave my bag in the car when I get to campus. As I walk into class, Dr. Gabriel corners me right away. *Fantastic.* He runs down his game plan for the morning's class, as if it makes much of a difference for what I'll be doing. No matter how he arranges it, I'll be sitting and avoiding eye contact with him. Regardless of this, I humor him and listen to his plans, nodding to show my (fake) appreciation for his lesson scheduling abilities while simultaneously praying that he doesn't touch me as he makes erratic hand gestures to illustrate his ideas.

I get out of our little pre-class conference unscathed. Untouched. *Thank God.* I take my seat and class begins. *{And now Jeff Buckley, a guitar, and* "Hallelujah."*}* Dr. Gabriel is talking to the students, now explaining to them the same game plan he mentioned in our little chat. I'm sure the students are finding it as brilliant as I did.

The students who didn't get to read their narratives last week start presenting. More attempts at using foreshadowing and figurative language. Dr. Gabriel doesn't ask me for my thoughts as he gives his commentary for each presenter. He seems to be trying to move things along quickly so he can start teaching the lesson. Fine with me. The less interaction I have with him, the more comfortable I am.

His lecture begins. Persuasive writing tips today. The students don't care. The same ones from last week are texting again. The blonde in the front row is sleeping. In the front row! She's not even trying to pretend that she is awake. Dr. Gabriel doesn't really look at the students as he lectures anyway. He does this strange thing where he focuses his eyes toward the pictures on the back wall of the room. Just like we were taught to do in my ninth grade public speaking class to help with nerves. Is he nervous? Or is he just trying to avoid having to acknowledge the disinterested looks on his students' faces? Either way, I'm sure the kids do great impersonations of him outside of the classroom.

Dr. Gabriel starts his timer for the individual work portion of class. I use the time to work on my *Crime and Punishment* paper. Last night's surprise therapy session put me behind.

I can't believe I'll be back in another therapy session in just over two hours. Back with him. *{Quick record change—Buckley right back to Damien Rice.}*

Callie, focus. Paper. Due. Monday.

I do focus on my paper over the next hour. Sort of. As the clock gets closer and closer to the end of class, closer and closer to my appointment, my stomach gets more and more nervous. I try to shift in my chair to relax, but every time I move, Dr. Gabriel glances over at me like he thinks I'm trying to get his attention. I try to keep still so he stops. Luckily, my stomach's skips and tumbles don't make noises that he can hear.

Once his timer rings, Dr. Gabriel walks around to check the students' progress. He decides to give them until the end of class to write. I use the time to work on my paper, to look at the clock, to pick off my nail polish, and to worry about 4:00 p.m.

At 3:00 p.m. sharp, I duck out of the classroom as a student corners Dr. Gabriel with questions about his paper. *Thank you, pimply freshman boy.*

I don't have time to go home so I drive right to his

office. After eating a 110-calorie granola bar, I pretend to continue writing my paper. Really, I just watch the clock and try not to notice the other patients going in and out of the office. My attempts don't work. I notice each and every one. The Pierce football fan (so says his t-shirt) who screeches into the parking lot at 3:31 p.m. and runs to the main entrance doors. The crying brunette who uses the tissues in her left hand to wipe her eyes as she opens the office door with her bare right hand. The petite blonde who exits moments later talking on her cell phone. I watch them all. 3:55 p.m. As I prepare to get out of my car, the main office door opens again.

It's him.

White dress shirt with a royal blue tie today. Eyes searching the lot. Looking around…for me?

Yes. He catches my eye as I get out of the car and then waits patiently while I lock the car and pull on the door handle to ensure that it's locked. One. Two. Three. I walk toward him, toward the main door that he is now holding open for me, thanking him as I walk past him and into the waiting room. He immediately moves ahead of me to open the next door, the brown door next to Annie's desk. He completely ignores the surprised look Annie gives him. I give her a tiny smile as she turns her stunned eyes to me.

And we are off. Down the endless, twisting hall, past the birds, and into his office yet again. He goes right to the closet where he unlocks the door and pulls out my chair. After moving it to the same place as last night, I sit, again clutching my purse on my lap. Without saying a word, he points to a hook on the wall to the left of his desk. A new hook. For me. For my purse. He doesn't even have to tell me.

Mumbling "thank you," I hang the purse on the

hook, my hook, and return to my chair. Another "my" in this office, I think, as I watch him go over to the bathroom and wash his hands. My way. Well, his mom's way too, I guess. *{Let's pause to welcome back Mr. Frank Sinatra, now with* "My Way."*}*

He sits behind his desk, clean and ready to go. "All right, Calista. Breathing. The relaxation techniques I'm going to teach you today will be the foundation for our entire immersion procedure. You will be exposed to situations that you don't like, ones that will make you uncomfortable at a variety of different levels."

I must flinch at the thought because he pauses for a moment and starts again in a gentler, less clinical voice.

"You will be uncomfortable at times, Calista, but I'm going to show you some ways to lessen that discomfort." He stops and catches my nervously wandering eyes. "Trust me, Calista."

There is that word again. Trust. I'm supposed to trust him entirely for this to work. I tell myself that I can do this. I am pretty convinced that he is genuinely trying to help me. I trust that he's not going to just leave me in an unsafe location or seriously dangerous situation. I do. What I don't trust is the idea that I'm going to be able to use relaxation techniques to make me calm. I don't trust that I'm going to have the patience or endurance to not run away. I don't think that I'll be able to just breathe when I'm in one of these tough spots. With him around, I'm having a hard enough time breathing as it is…

He looks at me, concerned now. *Gotta fix that.*

"So…what are these techniques?" I sidestep the trust conversation. Hopefully.

"Okay, if you are ready, I will teach you." He leans back in his chair as he begins his explanation. "I referred to this as yoga-type relaxation only because I thought that might be a familiar point of reference for you. Since it's not, I will refer to it as what it really is—Progressive Muscle Relaxation." Never heard of it.

He continues. "It's rather simple, really. When feeling overwhelmed or highly uncomfortable during our sessions, you may have difficulty with controlling your anxiety. Your first instinct will be to run from the place, from the circumstances, from me." *From him? Doubtful.* "I am teaching you some relaxation skills today so I can perhaps help you prevent yourself from running. Essentially, I want to show you how to relax before I cause you any anxiety."

I nod slightly.

"All right, to get started, I am going to go through some steps with you." He stands up and wheels his chair around the desk. He sits down, and we face each other. Again. Knees not quite touching.

He looks right into my eyes, searching for approval to continue. So gentle. So concerned. So, so sad…still. *That's pity, Callie. He feels sorry for you, just like he does for his mom.*

Pity or not, I hate seeing that sadness so I nod. Nod number 6,003, I think.

He nods slowly in return, somewhat convinced that it's okay to move on. As he starts to explain, he catches my eyes every twenty seconds or so–to check if everything is okay, I guess. Kind of like when I check my alarm clock at night. Maybe he understands this disease even more than he knows…

Pay attention, Callie.

"And the first thing we'll need to do involves recreating some of the tension you experience when uncomfortable or scared. To do that, we'll concentrate on specific areas of your body, ones that you personally feel are most affected when you are stressed."

And these areas are? How the hell could he know when I don't have a clue?

"Calista?"

Oh. He wants an answer. I have no idea. I don't really concentrate on specific muscle groups that I can't even name while I'm trying to avoid catching Hepatitis or the Swine Flu. *I kind of have a lot of other things to worry about in those situations, Doc.*

I, of course, say none of that and just shrug my shoulders instead.

"That's okay, Calista." Understanding, as always. "I understand that you probably haven't really thought about any of this before. We are going to practice with some commonly tensed muscle groups for now. If later in the week you find that some areas become more strained than others, we'll focus on those at that time." Pause. "Okay?" Quiet. Concerned.

Yes, I think so. I nod.

"Okay then."

He says "okay" a lot. "All right" too. He probably remembers to spell it as two words instead of—

"Let's start with your stomach. Many people talk of nervous stomachs when discussing anxiety."

I wonder if he knows how spastic my stomach gets when he looks at me. Probably does.

"I want you to lean back in your chair like this." He rests his back and head against his chair. As he moves, his knee brushes mine ever so slightly.

Yep, there goes my stomach. Tense and fluttery at the same time.

"Sorry," he says quickly, and his face reddens a bit. Guess that wasn't the way he intended to create tension.

I do as he says, leaning back in my chair. Careful

not to move my legs.

"Okay, now…"

Okay. Okay. All right. All right. Okay. All right.

Focus, Callie.

"—should inhale and tightly squeeze the muscles in your stomach for about ten seconds. As you do this, really concentrate on that tension. Feel it. Become familiar with it. After that, you will exhale and relax that muscle group and again concentrate on the experience. The feeling of it. And the power you have over your body." *{Enter Debarge with* "Rhythm of the Night."*}*

"Ready, Calista?"

Nod. Nod. Nod.

"Close your eyes and begin."

I close my eyes and suck in my stomach as hard as I can. Think stomach. Stomach. *{The DJ turns up the volume.}*

"Now, release the tension."

Release. Exhale. Concentrate. Stomach. Stomach. *{BIG refrain.}* Stomach. Stomach. *{And repeat.}* Stomach. Relaxed…ish.

"Okay. Open your eyes. Let's move on. We will use the same process, but this time you will focus on creating and relaxing tension in your hands. Ready?" Nod. Eyes closed again. "Begin."

We continue this process over and over. Neck, face, legs, etc. It's not too bad. Not going to make me calm about catching MRSA or anything, but not too bad. A little relaxing.

After tensing and untensing my feet, he tells me that he would like for me to practice these exercises at home a few times a day. He even tells me about a website that gives tips for the techniques. I should probably write the website down, but I don't have a pen or any paper. Well,

I do, but they are in my purse. Which is on my hook.

Behind his desk again, he paces a little. *What now?*

"Calista, there is one other relaxation technique I'd like us to practice." Still pacing.

"Okay...?" I borrow a piece of his sophisticated vernacular. *What is the problem?*

Still pacing.

"Well?" I push for an answer, raising my eyebrows for emphasis. Wasted emphasis. I'm sure he doesn't see it.

Nothing. Just stupid pacing.

"Dr. Blake?"

He stops.

"Aiden," he almost whispers, looking straight into my eyes. He is sad again.

I am suddenly very aware of the tension building in various parts of my body. Acutely aware.

"Aiden," I repeat softly. "What do we do next?"

Silence. Eyes. Locked. Together. *{Damien Rice cuts ba—}*

Focus, Callie.

"Please tell me."

He squeezes his eyes shut for a moment. When he opens them, they are still sad but also a tiny bit hopeful, I think.

"Calista, I'm afraid that your anxiety level might sometimes reach a stage that you won't be able to breathe your way out of yourself." He pauses, breathes, and continues very slowly. Each word seems to take an entire minute for him to say. "When that happens, I want to be able to help bring you out of it. I want to try one last technique that might stop you from running away."

Okay...

"I promise we'll only try this in extreme circumstances, and only if you want to do it. If you want to drop this part right now, we can." He breaks our eye contact and starts pacing again. *UGH.* Gotta pull more information from him. Who is the therapist here?

"Tell me." Pause. Nothing. "Now, Aiden."

That stops his pacing. His eyes fly right back to mine. I nod gently.

He opens his mouth to talk. *Good counseling, Callie.*

"It's a massage technique," he mumbles while lowering his eyes, "for your shoulders. Something I can do to take away some of your tension when you don't have the strength to do it on your own." He keeps his eyes and head down, almost as though he is waiting for me to throw my chair at him or something.

Oh. More touching. That explains the sad eyes. He thinks he's going to get me all freaked out.

He's wrong. I'm starting to realize that he doesn't actually know *everything* about me. He doesn't know that I do allow some people to touch me. Mandy, Melanie, Mom, Abby. Jared and Dad on occasion. And it's okay. Not something that really takes any special effort on my part.

He doesn't know that some people are clean to me. Okay to touch. And he can't possibly know what I am just now realizing. *He* is clean to me. Somehow.

Well, I know how. He's earned it. The tissues, the chair, the special instruments, the hand washing, his mom…I do trust him.

Now to explain that without being gushy or creepy. It would be easier to refuse the massage. Besides that, he may be clean to me, but the thought of him massaging my shoulders still gets me all nervous.

He is still looking down, but I know his eyes are upset, concerned, distraught. I can't be responsible for that.

One. Two. Three. Here goes… "Let's do it."

His head snaps up. Eyes on eyes. "Really?" More hope than sad in his eyes now. Some relief too. Good.

"Yes."

He starts to explain the massage technique he'll use, but all I hear is, "I'm going to touch you, I'm going to touch you, I'm going to…"

Well, at least I won't have to fake tension in my body for our little practice session. *{Another quick change. Rice to Finger Eleven with* "Paralyzer."*}*

"Are you ready?"

Why not? Deep breath. Nod number 9,306.

He slowly walks away from his desk and around me to the back of my chair. I resist the urge to turn and watch him as he passes, instead keeping my tense body rigid and facing straight ahead.

"Move slightly forward on your chair, Calista. Just a little so I can, uh, get my hands behind you." I adjust myself. "Now, try to recreate some of the tension from our earlier exercise."

Already tense, Dr. Blake.

I close my eyes and go through some of the motions from earlier, pretending to make some new tension.

"Good, Calista." Glad he appreciates my efforts. "Are you ready?"

At least when I nod this time, he gets to see a new view of the move.

No more nodding. I feel the heat of his hands as they crawl to my shoulders. Closer. Closer. Contact. A warm, slow ache begins in my shoulders.

His hands. Strong. Searing. Moving now.

Oh my God.

The slow ache begins to spread throughout my entire body, scorching and paralyzing as it moves. As he moves. Fingers making circles. Pressing into my skin slowly and cautiously. Infusing heat throughout me.

As I sink further into my chair, my eyes close and my mouth falls slightly open. I feel my neck lose all strength and start to drop back…back…back…

I snap forward just in time, managing not to crush his hands with my dead weight. My movement startles him, and he tears his hands from my shoulders.

"Is it too much?" he asks quickly. Quietly.

Too much? Too much heat? Too much aching?

"No, it isn't," I say softly, without turning around. I don't know how to explain the whole neck jerk thing without embarrassing myself so I try to ignore it instead.

"So you think it might work? If you're in a tough spot, it might help you with relaxation?"

Relaxation. I don't think that is the right word for it. Definitely not relaxing. Definitely not helping me breathe. A distraction, though, for sure. I didn't think about Tuberculosis or Meningitis or even Chicken Pox once during his massage.

So I'm speaking honestly when I say, "Yes. I think it could help me change my course of thinking in a rough situation." *Or at any time whatsoever.*

"Really?" There is relief in his voice. I can hear it.

"Really."

He starts to move around me. "All right then. Okay."

All right, okay, all right, okay, okay, all right…

"Let's go over our general procedure then." He sits on the corner of his desk as he begins to explain. I listen, trying to move my eyes slightly every ten seconds or so, working hard not to get trapped by his eyes. I nod here and there to show I'm listening. Hoping it all seems natural.

Doubtful, Callie.

"When we initially get you into an uncomfortable position, I want you to let yourself feel your fear. Don't try to ignore it. Face it. Allow your stomach to get tense, your body to get nervous. As soon as that nervousness begins, which I assume will be rather immediately, you and I will engage in conversation."

Seriously? He's going to make me all nervous and then expect me to be able to carry on a normal discussion? About what? The rainy weather? Upcoming sporting events?

I wait for him to say more, trying to appear ambivalent about this conversation idea, but he must see confusion or disbelief on my face.

"Calista, we are only going to have this conversation once you feel you can talk. If you are absolutely too worked up to talk, I will ask you to begin your relaxation exercises. Hopefully, you will succeed in relaxing yourself enough to talk…"

And if I don't, he'll try to relax me.

"When we have our conversation, we will make a game plan—a worst case scenario game plan. You won't be just worrying about your fear anymore or doing little rituals or routines to avoid it. Instead, you will be dropped right into a situation where your fear is your reality.

"What will you do? How will you handle it when it really happens? What concrete actions will your gut tell you to take to try to make it better?" He pauses. "You cannot really answer these questions honestly until you are actually in the feared situation."

This doesn't sound too awful, I guess. As long as he is helping me through it. I'm still not convinced that I'll be able to keep myself from running though.

"That is the first thing we'll discuss." There's more?

Great. "We will also discuss what specific events would have to fall into place for the feared outcome to occur in your undesirable situation."

What the hell? Gonna have to break that sentence down for me, Doc. A lot. Once again, my face must express that sentiment. Mental note: Sign up for acting classes.

"Okay, Calista. Let me explain that better."

Good plan.

"You are only scared of going to certain places—public restrooms, crowded restaurants, bars, etcetera, because you think they hold some danger for you. Right?" I nod slowly.

"The danger is what you are really afraid of, not the places themselves." I nod again. "And the danger is what this condition, this disease, has created in your mind. Within your mind, you have determined certain horrible consequences for going to each of these places. You've determined that you'll contract unavoidable, specific diseases or that you'll cause definite harm to others or yourself. You associate these places with these diseases or harmful events, convincing yourself that going to these places will automatically result in you acquiring diseases or provoking harm."

I nod slowly again. While this all makes sense, I still don't quite get his point. I also don't get why he had to say "these places" so many times.

"While perhaps there have been times in the past where people have truly experienced these feared outcomes, the likelihood of this is very rare."

Still confused.

"For example, somewhere in the world, on some date, yes, a person might have picked up some rare disease in a public restroom or at a bar. However, ninety-nine times out of one hundred, this doesn't actually happen. You and other people with this condition are worried about that one percent of the time. Many times, you are even worried about something that has never happened before."

That's true. I do know that.

"So we will discuss what conditions would have to fall perfectly into place for your worst fear, your frightening outcome, to really happen. Oftentimes, five to ten specific events would have to occur before that outcome could ever be a true possibility.

"Thinking about how many things would have to fall into place may help you to see your fears in a new light, to understand how unlikely it is that your feared outcomes will ever occur."

I nod again. This sounds reasonable.

He goes on. "One of the most unbelievable aspects of this condition is the fact that most people with OCD realize that their fears are ridiculous. I can tell from your emails and our few meetings that you feel this way."

Of course you can.

"We will simply use that feeling, that knowledge, to help you get through some of these situations. Perhaps we'll even be able to make you see some fears in an even more ridiculous light."

Not a bad plan. Definitely worth trying anyway.

He stands up and begins to push his chair back to its spot behind his desk. I guess we are done for today. I probably should be getting home to get ready for Girls' Night anyway.

Standing behind his desk now, he begins to speak again. Cautiously, but sincerely. "This isn't going to be easy for you, Calista. I do want you to push yourself to work as hard as you can during our sessions, but I also want you to relax when we aren't in session.

"It's crucial for you to practice your relaxation at home and during your down time. This will help you to prepare for our sessions, but it will also help you with relaxation in general. It's essential that we take care of you so you don't become overly anxious or even more stressed out than you already are."

We are going to take care of me? How does that work exactly?

As my heart starts climbing mountains considering the possibilities, he goes on. "We will have sessions Monday through Friday for two weeks and then on Monday and Tuesday of the third week. While we won't formally work on the weekends, I will give you some tasks to work on by yourself. This weekend, for example, I have one area of concentration for you."

I'm sure I'll do a bang up job on that. If I could do these things on my own, I wouldn't be here.

He comes around to the corner of his desk yet again to sit. "I'd like for you to write down all of the, um, sins you'd like to report at confession this week. Then, I'd like for you to wait until next week to go to confession. Keep the list so that you have it next week, adding anything else you'd like during the week. Do you think you can do that?"

Skip confession this week? I don't know. He's looking at me, waiting for an answer.

I shrug, quietly saying, "I'll try." An honest answer. I will try. But I'm not making any promises or anything.

"That's all I am asking of you, Calista."

His eyes are so serious. Determined. He really wants this to work, needs it to work. For a paper? To help his mother? I don't know.

I don't want to disappoint him. "I will try," I whisper. Sincerely.

"Thank you," he whispers back. And he keeps his eyes on mine for an endless moment before blinking away and moving back behind his desk.

Back to a business, doctor-like tone. "I will be in contact with you later this weekend to schedule a time for Monday. I'd rather not set up anything until later." He pauses. "Gives you less time to worry about it." Probably a good idea.

As we work together to lock my chair back in the closet, he asks me to email him my weekly class and work schedule. He then nods to my purse, and I move to take it off its hook, my hook, while he goes to open the door.

I follow him down the hall, through the door next to Annie, and out the main office door. As I get in my car and begin to drive off, I see him raise his hand in a slight wave. Quite a send-off from such a busy, important doctor.

Seconds later, I hear a ding from my phone. I wait until a red light to dig the phone out of my purse. Unknown Number.

`Have fun at Girls' Night, Calista. Relax. -Aiden`

{Cue Damien Rice.}

Chapter 14
the weekend before

IT'S ALMOST 5:30 P.M. WHEN I get back home. Not a lot of time to prepare for tonight. After scrubbing my hands and before starting to clean the kitchen, I unpack my sweats and sneakers. Didn't need them after all. My dress was just fine.

More than fine. His face appears in my head, flushed right after he brushed against my bare leg.

Why the blush? And why the text only minutes after our appointment?

I guess I should respond to that. I grab my phone and hit reply.

`Thanks.`

That's all I have. What else can I say? Have a nice weekend? See you Monday? Doesn't seem natural. I decide to just sign my name under the "Thanks," and I push send quickly so I don't have to think about it anymore.

Just as the little message asking if I want to add him as a contact appears, another text comes through.

`You're welcome, Callie.`

Callie? *What?* Why would—

Shit.

I click back to my sent messages to see what I wrote to him.

Yep. Callie. I wrote "Callie." Only my family members call me Callie.

Until now, I guess. *{Here comes Carly Rae Jepsen with* "Call Me Maybe."*}*

Stop, Callie. Time for cleaning.

7:45 P.M. CLEANING DONE: KITCHEN, LIVING room, me.

Pajamas on.

Since I have fifteen minutes, I decide to start my little weekend assignment. Get it over with now. I write "Confession" at the top of a new sheet of paper. Number one on my list is Dr. Gabriel. I have to seek forgiveness about him every single week. I try to remember how many times I have wished he would just go into a coma or something over the last week.

For number two, I list the patients going in and out of Dr. Blake's office building. I judged each one. As if I should be judging anyone when it comes to psychological issues.

Lastly (for now), I add a number three. Him. I keep hurting him. Keep causing that painful look on his face... Somehow I need to—

"Aunt Callie?"

Abby's here, outside my bedroom door. I put down my pen and go with her to the living room. It's time for Girls' Night.

Melanie and Mandy already have their first margaritas in their hands. Abby and I join Melanie on the couch while Mandy gets the DVD ready.

"What are we watching tonight?" I ask Abby as I pull a blanket over both of us.

"Enchanted," she exclaims. I smile and hug her closer to me. She gets so excited about her movie choices. I get excited too. Since Abby gets to pick what we watch every other week, I only have to pick once a month at the most. That means I only have to worry about disappointing others one time every six weeks.

Well, once every six weeks when it comes to movie choices. Somehow I seem to cause a lot of other disappointment during the course of a month.

I think of Mandy's texts and phone calls, invitations to go out, each one met with a negative response from me. I think of Dr. Gabriel. For only a second. I have a hard time even worrying about that—he's so creepy.

And I think of *him*. Those miserable eyes. *{Damien Rice again!}* What is he doing tonight? All alone in his house. Still working?

I remember that I need to email him my schedule for the week when Abby asks if we can make popcorn.

I'll have to email him later. Melanie and Mandy would ask all kinds of questions if I left to do it now anyway.

I take Abby to the kitchen and put a bag of popcorn in the microwave. While we wait for it to finish popping, Abby tells me about her first grade class. She sounds pretty happy about school. I hope it stays that way.

As we head back out to the living room and start the movie, I begin to remember my own life as a six-year-old.

Catholic school. Long brown curls. Plaid uniform. Already nervous all of the time.

I remember picking at the skin around my fingernails during religion class. Going to bed every night only after Mom put lotion and then socks on my dry, cracked, already over-washed hands. Not sleeping much. Thinking about the sins my teacher warned about in class. Contemplating hell and eternity. Crawling into bed with Mom. Eventually creating a makeshift bed on the living room floor right beside the television.

No cooking shows back then. Old sitcoms worked almost as well, providing my six-year-old body with about a quarter of the sleep it actually needed.

Abby snuggles closer to me on the couch, and I run my hand over her soft blonde curls. I know that we laugh at her OCD moments, but I really hope they remain just that. Little moments every once in awhile.

Not taking over her entire existence.

She nudges me as Amy Adams wanders through New York in a puffy wedding dress.

"Isn't her dress beautiful, Aunt Callie?" I smile and nod. It is beautiful. Well, it was before she started to walk through the filthy New York streets.

Abby isn't finished adoring the dress. She turns a bit on the couch so she can see Mandy. "Do you want to wear a dress like that when you marry Josh, Aunt Amanda?"

Melanie catches my eye, and neither of us attempts to hold back our laughter.

Mandy's stunned expression doesn't help matters. As she spits out partial sentences about being young, about the long distance, about not knowing if Josh is "the one," all items of little importance to Abby, Melanie starts the song.

Mandy's song. Barry Manilow's "Mandy." We've been singing it to her for years any time she does something clumsy or asks a ridiculous question or is left speechless—like tonight.

Abby and I join in for the refrain, and Mandy throws a pillow at us, hitting Melanie on the head. Abby and I raise our hands in the air melodramatically, and Melanie jumps off the couch to prepare for the big finish.

We are interrupted by Mandy's cell phone. I'm sure it's Josh. Unbelievable timing.

Mandy answers her phone and stands to go to her room, rolling her eyes and flashing us a smile before leaving. Melanie decides it's probably a good time to give Abby a bath so I head up to my room to send my email.

It doesn't take me long to type out my schedule. I attach it to the email and type "schedule" as the subject. Then I sign the email. Calista. Not Callie.

One. Two. Three. Send.

As I reply to another email from Dad about next week's shopping trip, a new message appears in my inbox.

DA Blake.

One. Two. Three. Open.

`Thanks, Callie.`

Callie. Guess all further attempts at formality will be futile.

I wonder once again what he is doing tonight. No little boy running around his house because he is that little boy. Was that little boy. With his OCD mom.

No wife. No girlfriend. Presumably.

Unfortunately, there is no more time for me to think about him right now. I can hear Amy Adams singing again in the living room.

I go back out, have my one margarita, and talk a little with my sisters (not too much though—Abby gets annoyed when we talk through the "good" parts). Mandy talks about her plans for next weekend. She'll be driving into Pittsburgh to stay with Josh at his dorm room in Oakland. Since she'll only be about twenty minutes away from Mom and Dad's house, she and Josh will meet us there for Mom's birthday dinner next Sunday.

We talk about Mom's birthday and also about this Sunday's family dinner. Two Sundays in a row—doesn't happen often. I'm glad I'll get to see so much of my parents, but the thought of all of us making that hour drive two weekends in a row makes me a little nervous. Like we are just tempting fate to put one of us in a car accident.

After Mandy reviews the plans she and Josh have made, Melanie looks at me warily as she begins to speak.

"I didn't tell you guys yet," she begins slowly. "Doug has a work assignment in Ohio at the end of next week. The meeting place is only about half an hour away from his parents' house." She pauses. "We decided last night that we'll go up together on Thursday afternoon and make a long weekend out of it. His parents will love the time with Abby, and I'm sure I can get some work done in the car."

She's looking at me, quite obviously gauging my reaction.

Mandy will be gone. Now she'll be gone too. I won't be able to make the twenty minute drive to her house if I can't take it here by myself or if I have to run from the murderers.

I hurriedly tell Melanie not to worry. I was already planning on staying here by myself. She still looks concerned, but we are all distracted by Abby, who begins babbling about all the things she wants to bring to see "Gram" and "Pap."

Melanie looks at me, clearly wanting to say more. I already know what she is worried about. Sunday. The trip. Mom's birthday dinner. She knows I hate driving long distances by myself. I've only driven from here to my parents' house once by myself. And I hated it.

But it only makes sense for her to leave from Ohio and drive straight to the birthday dinner, and Melanie doesn't need to spend her time worrying. I will figure something out.

After piecing together a small, reassuring (I hope) smile for Melanie, I tell Abby how lucky she is that she gets to see both sets of her grandparents in one weekend. Abby continues talking about even more stuff that she wants to bring. I am glad she is here tonight. An adorable little tornado of distractions dancing around the living room, practicing ballet moves to show Gram and Grandma, discussing what she'll eat, what she'll wear…

{Kelly Clarkson begins "Beautiful Disaster."*}* Now she's asking Melanie what she'll do about missing school on Friday. Mel's trying to convince her that missing one day of first grade won't mess up her educational future. *{And now her slow, soulful refrain.}*

Sorrowful, grief-stricken eyes on a mesmerizing, rugged face spring into my mind. *This song is about him. {Repeat ref—}*

Melanie attempts to change the subject, but she doesn't take the heat off of me. "So, how was your late night therapy date, Callie?"

Rolling my eyes and shaking my head, I remind her, "Not a date, Mel."

"Sure. Doctors always keep those hours open for therapy sessions."

Mandy chimes in, "Wait? What? When was this?"

Melanie explains what she knows—she called late in the evening, and I was still with him.

Mandy teases, "Oh, I see, you turn me down for Thirsty Thursday every week, but he asks you out once and you jump right in his car."

I roll my eyes at her. No point in actually explaining. Besides, what would I even say?

Fortunately, sweet little Abby saves me once again, shushing their giggles so she can hear "the best part." That quiets them, but it doesn't stop them from shooting each other suggestive looks.

The movie ends soon after that, thankfully, and everyone looks pretty tired. Mandy wishes everyone a good night and then heads to her room so Abby can have the loveseat. I give Abby a hug, say my own good nights, and head up to my room.

11:15 p.m. Night preparations.

2:25 a.m. TV on. Foie Gras tonight. I don't even

know what that is. Doesn't matter—I'm exhausted. Bed.

I DREAM ABOUT HIM AGAIN. Same dream. For most of the night, we are jousting. Jousting and falling. Jousting and falling. Jousting and falling. Together. Over and over.

I'm kind of surprised my limbs aren't sore when I wake up—how could all of that physical dream activity not take any toll on my body?

I wonder if I should ask for forgiveness for all of that fighting when I go to confession. And then I remember that I'm not going to confession today. Well, I'm not supposed to go today. We'll see…

I finish my morning routine around 11:00 a.m. and then spend most of the afternoon working on my *Crime and Punishment* paper. As I write, I remember mean thoughts I've had throughout the week, things I would normally confess. I do as I'm told and write each thought, each sin, neatly on my confession list.

I remember the girl behind me in writing lab. I thought-called her a bitch several times in class. My thoughts were also less than positive about students in the writing center who came too close to my desk.

As the afternoon goes on and my confession list grows, I start to worry more and more about 4:00 p.m. How can I save this entire list for next week? Some of these thoughts happen on a weekly basis. Like irritation with Dr. Gabriel. And with people at the grocery store and freshmen at the writing center. If I wait until next week to confess, will I be forgiven for both weeks of the same sin? Will I need to tell Father Patrick that some of these sins happened two weeks in a row?

I try to write my paper. I try to concentrate on Raskolnikov's struggles throughout the book, but I really can't stop thinking about my own struggles with missing confession.

3:00 p.m. I begin my leaving-the-house routine, just as I do every Saturday. Just in case I have to go.

3:45 p.m. I finish. I sit in the kitchen with my notebook and try to focus on my paper.

4:00 p.m. I'm still sitting at the table with my notebook, but I've written nothing during the last fifteen minutes. Tension begins to build in my stomach. Just like he said it would. Like he knew it would.

4:03 p.m. I decide to try my relaxation exercises. In the heat of the moment, I can't seem to remember anything. When to inhale. How long to keep the area tense. How to even begin to release some of the tension.

I give up and pick off all of my nail polish in under two minutes.

Now what? I have to do something. I pull my confession list out of my pocket and read it aloud. Hoping that maybe it will count somehow. Maybe I'll be forgiven.

I read it aloud again. And again. The tension is still there. So I read it three more times. And say the Hail Mary twelve times.

Still tense. Maybe even worse than before.

This doesn't count. I know it. If I go a week without forgiveness, what will happen? What if I don't make it until next week? What if I die before then? A car crash? A freak earthquake? Dead with an overflowing conscience.

My mind starts to conjure up the same images of hell that kept me awake at night as a six-year-old. Still just as powerful eighteen years later.

No more. I grab my purse and I'm outside in record time. Door shut and locked. Handle twist. Handle twist. Handle twist. Locked.

On my way.

I PULL INTO THE PARKING lot at St. Anne's at 4:46 p.m. Fourteen minutes to go.

Two people are ahead of me in line when I get in the church. 4:52 p.m. Father Patrick welcomes me into the confessional. He looks surprised by my tardiness but says nothing. He's probably not supposed to keep tabs on who goes to confession and when.

I confess everything without glancing at my list. Father Patrick gives me a penance of three recitations of The Lord's Prayer.

After repeating the prayer twelve times in a church pew, I leave.

Just as I open my car door, I hear a buzz in my purse. My phone silently vibrating, telling me I have a new text message. I get into the car and grab the phone.

Unknown Number.

Ugh.

One. Two. Three. Open.

`What time did you go to confession?`

DAMN DAMN DAMN.

Throwing the phone back into my purse, I start to drive home. My phone buzzes again as I drive, but I try to ignore it.

Bastard. He knew I wouldn't be able to do it. He set me up to fail.

I don't check my phone again until I am back in my room at home, all set up to continue writing my paper. I know I'll never get any work done until I check the message so I grab my phone out of my purse.

One. Two. Three. Look.

It's not even a message from him. Or from anyone really. It's that same message from the phone itself.

```
Would you like to add this num-
ber to your contact list?
```

Ugh. Now, when he's just sent me that message? I don't think so. I click "no" before putting down my phone and working on my paper.

7:00 p.m. Mandy comes in to see if I'm up for a party tonight. She already knows I'm not, of course, but she lets me know where she'll be and how to get there.

"You can even call me, and I'll come back to get you if you change your mind."

"Thanks, Mandy. I really do have a lot of work to do with this paper so I probably won't end up going." As if the paper really has anything to do with my decision. Mandy knows that too but lets me get away with it anyway.

"All right, Callie. I'll see you tomorrow then."

"Thanks, Mandy. Have a good time and be careful."

"I will. Night."

She goes and leaves me to my paper. I work. I write and type until it is time for my night preparations.

11:30 p.m. Just as I'm getting out of the shower, my phone buzzes yet again. As I walk to my dresser, still wrapped in a pink towel, I hope that Mandy is not in some sort of trouble.

She's not.

It's him. My Unknown Number.

Count. Open.

It's okay if you went to confession. Really, it is. In fact, I'd be shocked if you didn't go—if you have that kind of control already, you don't even need me!

Before I can even consider responding, another text comes through.

Him again. Count. Click.

I would like to log the time that you went so I have the results for our little assignment. It's important to have that informa-

```
tion for our treatment program.
Please don't be mad, Callie.
```

He has me cornered again. How does he keep making me feel so guilty? Like I'm overreacting? Like I'm wounding him if I don't do as he asks.

Well, however he manages, he's done it again. I count and reply quickly.

```
I went around 4:45 p.m.
```

One. Two. Three. Send.

The phone buzzes again almost immediately. No, phone, I don't want to add him as a contact. I'm still irritated. I do somehow feel less guilt though. *{Kelly Clarkson begins* "Beautiful Disaster" *once again.}* Just as I'm connecting my phone to the charger for the night, it buzzes again. What now?

Him. Of course.

```
I'm impressed you were able to
wait that long. Nice work! Good
night, Callie.
```

I don't write back to say good night or to tell him that I was impressed too. I was though. I waited an entire, painful forty minutes before going to confess. Pretty amazing for my first try, I think.

After applying my lotion, I turn on the TV and get into bed. A rather young chef is making a cod salad. It seems pretty simple. Not that I would (or could) make it.

I give no more thought to the chef, or the salad, or my lack of cooking skills.

Sleep.

SUNDAY. MORNING ROUTINE. CHURCH. PAPER all afternoon. Final copy printed at 4:00 p.m.

Leaving-the-house routine. Mandy and I leave for dinner at 5:00 p.m.

Mandy drives, and we stop at a local bakery so I can "bake" a couple of pies before we get to my parents' house. 6:15 p.m. We arrive at the house. Melanie's car and Jared's truck are both in the driveway.

We enter the living room. It's noisy. Crowded. The perfect setting for a family Sunday dinner.

The night goes rather well with only a few small glitches. Before dinner, Dad pulls me aside to talk about potential gifts for Mom, and Mom herself walks in during our conversation. Not really a big deal. We didn't come up with anything good, and it's not like she doesn't know that I help Dad with his shopping.

During dinner, Abby gets excited while telling a story about a classmate and she accidentally bumps over her milk cup. She cries. The pure irony of her literally sobbing over spilled milk seems to be lost on everyone but me. Mom hurriedly tries to comfort Abby while Melanie and Doug rush around to clean up the milk. Jared has brought a new girlfriend to dinner and doesn't focus on this or much else all night. This has worked out well for me. Jared hasn't tried to do anything to disgust me all evening. No jokes about using my bathroom. No trying to stick his finger in my face after itching his belly button. Pretty nice.

After dinner, I serve "my" pies, and Mom once again asks me if I've found a local cooking class yet. She saw me put on a food show one time while I was napping at her house.

Maybe I'll try to nap to a porn channel next time she's around. Just for fun.

Mom and Dad dance around the therapy subject, asking how I'm feeling and how things are going. I don't give in, not once mentioning my therapy. What would I even say? I don't know what I'll be doing for this treatment thing. Or when to report to his office tomorrow. He did say he'd let me know over the weekend…

I check my phone for a text as Mandy and I head home around 8:30 p.m. Nothing.

9:30 p.m. Home.

11:00 p.m. His text arrives as I am in the middle of night preparations.

Count. Open.

```
I'll pick you up at the writing
center at 7:00 tomorrow evening.
Good night, Callie.
```

Not a lot of information. But he doesn't want me to worry too much. Or to chicken out, I guess.

When my phone asks me AGAIN if I'd like to add him as a contact, I give in.

First name: Unknown. Last Name: Number. This way my phone doesn't completely win. Neither does he.

I decide to finish some of my night preparations before replying. Don't want him to think I was waiting by the phone.

11:30 p.m. When I open my laptop, I find the same message from him in an email. He must really want to make sure I get the information. 11:45 p.m. I email my response.

```
Thanks. See you at 7:00 p.m.
Night,
```

I pause. Hmm…why fight it?

```
Callie
```

Chapter 15
day one

I TURN IN MY *CRIME and Punishment* paper at the beginning of class. Dr. Sumpter gives the class a new assignment about five minutes later.

The Scarlet Letter. After giving us a little background on Nathaniel Hawthorne as well as some period history, Dr. Sumpter asks us to free write for a while. She wants us to consider the thoughts and feelings we'd experience if we were forced to wear a symbol of an embarrassing indiscretion, a notable weakness, etcetera.

As I write, I cannot help but think of my own defining scarlet letters…

O – C – D

How would I feel if everyone knew? *Don't they already?*

After a while, Dr. Sumpter asks for volunteers to "share." I hate the way she uses that word. Teachers shouldn't use it in classes that are higher than the first grade level.

As I begin to wonder if it's even annoying for first graders like Abby, classmates begin the "sharing." A teeny little brunette in the first row confesses that she'd be mortified if her weight was posted on her shirt…especially after the holidays when she gains a few pounds. Like when she weighs twenty-three pounds instead of twenty, I guess. *Shut up.*

{Fade in Katy Perry and "California Gurls."*}* A blond guy is now talking about an embarrassing moment involving a dare and some fraternity brothers. Sounds like he is just bragging, not "sharing." {Even louder now.} Now a quiet girl is talking about causing a serious car crash. I feel really bad for her—she is pretty worked up.

This "sharing" goes on for another half hour or so. I pick at my nails, trying to be invisible. I don't raise my hand, and Dr. Sumpter doesn't call on me. Thank the Lord.

Class eventually ends. When I get home, I repaint my nails right away. For tonight.

As they dry, I try to decide what to wear for my top secret therapy session. I have no idea. Perhaps I should text him to find out his opinion. He would love that, I'm sure.

As I consider how he'd react, the house phone rings.

It's Annie. Apparently, Dr. Spencer still plans to have an appointment with me, to make sure I am aware of my medication options.

That makes me think of Dr. Blake sounding like a total toolbag when he used the phrase "medicinal bandage."

Still, I am going to try his therapy first so I begin to tell Annie that I don't need Dr. Spencer's appointment. Before I can do that, she tells me that Dr. Lennox called the office recently, concerned that I haven't yet discussed medication with Dr. Spencer. To shut Annie up, I allow her to schedule an appointment for next Monday, after I have already finished a week of my treatment program.

After Annie says goodbye, I hang up the phone and settle on my bed with *The Scarlet Letter*. The rest of the afternoon passes swiftly as I read and take notes.

3:00 p.m. I put my work down, do my leaving-the-house routine, and head to the writing center wearing a brown and white dress, boots, and a brown pea coat—the same outfit I wore to class this morning. If I need to change, he'll just have to give me time to run home.

MY SHIFT AT THE WRITING center drags on and on and on. The three undergraduate students who are actually here work quietly. No one needs my help.

I try to focus on *The Scarlet Letter*, but I get nowhere. My eyes move from my Kindle to the clock on the wall approximately every three minutes. {Damien Rice. "The Blower's Daughter." Over and over.}

When the small hand on the clock finally hits the seven, I feel as though it must already be Friday. Or May.

After gathering my stuff, I head out, wondering where he will be. I get all the way to the parking lot before I see him leaning casually against his car. Dark grey pants. White, slightly unbuttoned dress shirt. He turns toward me as I approach and gives me a, well, almost a smile. A reassuring turning up of his lips and nervous concern in his eyes. Don't they cancel each other out?

He opens the back door of his Lexus and gestures for me to put my bag in the back seat. After I do, he closes the back door and opens the passenger door for me.

Here goes. Getting into his car. No idea what I'm doing or where I'm going…

The car is again silent as he drives away from campus. I wait for him to speak, to tell me the plan for tonight. But he doesn't say anything. He stares straight ahead. So do I.

Five noiseless minutes later, he turns into the mall parking lot. Shopping? With him? Nope. He drives the entire way around the mall, finally parking by the adjacent movie theatre.

Oh.

Shit.

He wasn't messing around when he said we'd be jumping right in to this immersion thing. At this rate, he'll have me sharing recreational drugs tomorrow and shaking hands with patients in the infectious diseases ward of the hospital by Wednesday.

I cannot do this.

I open my mouth to tell him so and realize that he's staring at me. For how long, I wonder.

"Relax, Calista."

I'm guessing that he has been staring for quite awhile.

"Begin your exercises right away, starting in your most tense area. Your stomach, perhaps?"

Okay. Right. My stomach is pretty tense. I try to focus on that tension, really I do, but he's still watching me. And he wants to take me into a movie theatre.

"Gradually release the tension now. Concentrate on the release."

Yes, the release. The release. Him staring at me. The release. The movie theatre. The seats with the needles in them. The diseases. The hospital. The crying. The coffin. The—

"Calista." He quietly breaks into my thoughts. I look at him, unsure of what to say.

"What happened there? How did I lose you?"

What? How did he lose me? I hope I'm not blushing.

He rephrases. "How did you get lost during the exercise? What were you thinking about?"

Deep breath. "Um, just the movie theatre."

"What about the movie theatre?"

I can't say it aloud—I know some of my fears sound ludicrous after they pass my lips. I settle for a quick answer, a non-answer. "Silly stuff."

His eyes go from genuine concern to intense anger and sadness all at once. *Way to go, Callie.*

"Your fears aren't silly or insignificant, Calista. They drive our therapy sessions, create the course for these immersion treatments. If we ignore them, what are we even doing here? What is the point?"

Jeez. Well, there's an explanation for some of the anger in his voice. But why the sadness right now?

I keep my eyes on his, still not quite ready with an answer. The specifics of my fears, I know, will sound ridiculous. They're so personal, too personal to just blurt out.

As he watches me process his words, his anger, his eyes begin to soften to just sadness. He gradually looks away from me and stares out the front window.

"I understand, Calista." So quiet. Even when only rivaled by the silence of the car.

"Movie theatres present you with many of your fears. Germs, close encounters with other people, sticky floors, public bathrooms…" He looks over at me. "I'm sure you are also concerned with sitting in the theatre seats themselves."

What? He knows that too?

He must once again see something in my eyes that

confirms his suspicions.

"I figured that you'd heard that story about needles in the seats. Almost all OCD patients who list movie theatres as dirty have somehow come across that story."

I don't know what to say. Still. I know I shouldn't be surprised with his magical, all-knowing powers, but I am.

He keeps his miserable eyes on me and seems to realize that I cannot yet talk. That I'm too confused. Too surprised at the extent of his knowledge. His eyes leave mine again, but they don't go far. He looks past me, straight out the passenger side window. And he opens his mouth to talk again.

"My mother heard that story. It haunted her. She wouldn't go to the movies with us as kids." He pauses and forces his mouth to swallow whatever lump has grown in his throat. "She still wouldn't when she underwent treatment in the few years before she died."

Died?

Oh my God.

The despair, the tragic expressions, the sad eyes. Not treating patients like me. Of course. It all makes sense.

I remind him of his mom. And she's gone.

"I'm so sorry." I say the first words I can grasp. He continues to stare past me, out the window.

One. Two. Three.

"I had no idea."

Pause. Nothing.

One. Two. Three.

"I—"

He turns to me and stops me from going on, shaking his head softly. Thank God—I don't even know how I was going to finish that sentence.

Still, he slowly shakes his head. Is he telling me to stop talking? That there really are no words for this situation? Or is it something else entirely?

He tries to form a tiny, perhaps reassuring, smile before he breaks his gaze and goes back to staring out the window.

I don't know how to fix this. Or even how to make it a tiny bit better. *Great, Callie.* You've forced it out of him—now you know why he's so sad all of the time. Probably especially around you. And I just keep pushing him and questioning him and making it worse and worse.

I have to fix this. Now.

I don't even allow myself to count. "Aiden," I blurt out.

His head snaps right to my face at the sound of his name. His eyes are still distressed but also surprised.

Gotta press on. No time for counting or chickening out. "Let's go in."

I watch as shock overtakes most of the misery in his eyes.

"Really?"

I nod quickly. He's not moving so I start to open my door. I can't afford one of his long pauses. If I'm really going to do this, we've gotta move. Now.

He still isn't moving as I step out of the car. His mouth is even hanging open a little.

"Come on," I insist as I begin walking toward the theatre. From behind me, I hear him get out of the car. Then the beeping sound of the car being locked. I don't turn around. I speed ahead toward the movie theatre so that I can try to block out the thought that I'm moving toward a movie theatre. *{And now a little something from Broadway.* "This is the Moment" *from Jekyll and Hyde.}*

My technique fails. I know where I'm going, and

my body is already trembling with anxiety. Before I can turn around and change my mind, he runs up behind me.

"Wait up, Callie. Don't get too excited now."

Callie. He's teasing me. Amused by my taking charge, it seems. I've distracted him.

I know what I have to do. *{Mind-blowing key change.}* As he pushes open the door for me, I count and walk past him into the first movie theatre I've entered in fifteen years.

FUZZY VISION. RINGING EARS. FEATHER-WEIGHT body. I float beside him past the ticket booth (where he presents two tickets for what? And that he bought when?), through the doors to Theatre III, and into the setting of many of my nightmares.

No one is in the theatre. We must be really early. Or else seeing a really lame movie. Or both.

I stand right inside the door, clutching my purse and waiting for him to talk. Just like in his office. Except he is standing right beside me here.

"Good. No one else came early. We should have a little time."

Okay…

"Come with me, Calista."

I force my legs to follow him…probably would have been easier if I weren't wearing boots…

He stops when he reaches the midway point of the center section. Somehow, I get my body there beside him. He moves to the second seat in the row and then digs in his pocket for something. I stand frozen in the aisle.

I watch as he pulls out a pair of gloves and puts them on his hands. Once they are on, he looks over at me warily. I stare back, only able to focus on holding myself up.

"Now, Calista, I know that these gloves will not serve as protection from a needle. They will, however, help me to prove to you that there are no needles in this chair." He pauses, searching my eyes for some sort of reaction.

I don't have a reaction yet. I want to hear more.

He continues. "I am going to run my hands over this entire chair, over the back, the sides, and the cushion. After I do that, you will examine my hands. You'll see that the gloves have no tears, no punctures, and no blood. And you'll know that there are no needles to fear."

"But—" I start to argue.

"I know you have other fears to deal with here. The fact that many others have sat in this chair. The germs. We will be using your relaxation techniques to tackle those."

Right. I'm sure that will work out just fine. I don't voice my reservations though. It'll probably just make him sad again.

I'm sure he already knows about all of them anyway.

He's still looking at me. "Ready, Calista?"

No.

I nod. And then I stand there as he begins to run his gloved hands over the chair. Very slowly, he runs his hands across every inch, every crevice. Making sure not to miss anything. As he smoothly covers, almost caresses, the top cushion one more time, he looks up at me.

Intense, agonized eyes.

He needs me to do this. I said I would at least try.

Holding my gaze, he rises and holds out his hands for inspection. My limbs are tense and there is a piercing ache in the side of my stomach. I realize I'm holding my breath.

But I'm not sure why. Because of the movie theatre? The seat? The looming inspection?

Or is it him? His burning eyes? His need?

One. Two. Three. I force myself to breathe and then drag my eyes down to his gloved hands. He moves them around, showing me every possible angle.

They're clean. Immaculate. No holes. No blood.

No real surprise. I do realize my fears can be absurd. That doesn't stop me from worrying that there is a needle in another seat though. Maybe in the seat behind me. Or maybe in the front row.

Or in his seat.

"Do you want me to check my seat too?"

How the hell does he do it? I manage to keep myself from asking it aloud, and I nod instead. He bends down and begins the slow checking process on his own chair. When he finishes, I again inspect his hands and nod to acknowledge that they are clean.

He turns his body away from me slightly as he pulls off the gloves. He motions for me to move aside and then walks to the trash can at the back of the theatre, talking the entire time.

"Okay, I realize that after I throw away these gloves, it would be best for us if I wash my hands." Of course he knows that. "We can't have you running away, though, so I'm not going to leave you in this theatre alone while I run to a bathroom. Me going into a public restroom and coming back to sit with you is something for another session anyway."

I can't even think about that.

He's walking back toward me now, still talking. "So I've come prepared with a medical strength anti-bacterial wipe. Will this be acceptable?"

He holds up a package I actually recognize. That is a medical strength, insanely powerful wipe. Melanie brought two of these individually packaged wipes home from the hospital after she had Abby. She said that they were in a holder in her hospital room. I've been saving them for an extreme situation because they supposedly remove all kinds of germs, even ones from seriously infectious diseases.

I wonder where I could buy them. Maybe he'll tell me.

Now probably isn't the time for that. He's waiting for an answer so I nod. Yet again.

He wipes off his hands, meticulously cleaning between his fingers, under his nails, everywhere. He then passes me again to throw out the used wipe.

When he returns, I know it's time. To buy a few seconds, I ask him what movie we'll be seeing.

His face looks apologetic. "Well, it's classics night, so we'll be seeing *Gone with the Wind*." Before I even have the chance to tell him that I like *Gone with the Wind*, he spits out more words.

"It isn't my first choice for a movie, but I wanted to make sure that there wouldn't be many people here. So I chose an off night, and I figured this classic showing would be less popular than the recent releases. But if you want to go to another movie, we can. I didn't bring any more gloves or wipes with me, but I can go and—"

"I don't want you to go. It's fine. I really like this movie." *And there is no way in hell that I'm going to move to another theatre with new seats and another checking process.*

He looks relieved. He also looks like he's ready to begin the next part of our session.

As I mentally scramble for something else to say to prolong the next step, an older couple enters the theatre and begins heading down the aisle. Where we are.

This is it.

"We'd better sit," he says lightly, nodding toward the couple and a group of women now entering at the back of the theatre.

I know.

One. Two. Three. Little by little, I move into our row, stopping when I am directly in front of my seat.

Now there is really nothing to do but sit…

One. Two. Three. One. Two. Three. One. Two. Three.

Onetwothree. Onetwothree. Onetwothree. Onetwothreeonetwothreeonetwothreeonetwothreeonetwo—

"Callie." So soft. So concerned.

I have to do this.

Somehow I coerce my legs to bend. Somehow I press the top of my body down into a seated position.

And I'm sitting. Still in my coat. Clutching my chocolate brown purse. Breathing heavily. And sweating. Instinctively, I begin picking at the nails on my right hand.

"Stop."

Stop? Stop the only thing that might keep me together? *No.* I don't even look at him. I scrape the polish off of three fingers in record time.

And then I feel his skin on mine. His hand on top of my hand. And I'm lost. Lost to thinking. Lost to breathing.

My body is filled with tension, and I have no idea how to resume my breathing. But it feels amazing.

{Chantal Kreviazuk is back with “Feels Like Home.”*}*

Simultaneously, my fingers part and his lace through mine. A little pile of fingers right there on my lap.

We sit like that in silence for I don’t know how long. And then—

“Callie? I guess we should talk about a few things now.”

Now? We’ve been holding hands for, I don’t know, maybe four minutes, and he wants to talk about it already? Unrea—

“Your worst case scenario, the odds of that happening, remember? We should go over all of that before the movie begins.”

Oh. Therapy. Right. Nod number 70,302. I shift my eyes from our hands up to his face. His warm, soothing eyes.

“Let’s start with the worst case scenario,” he continues cautiously. “Pretend you do feel a jab while you are sitting there, and—”

I feel my body stiffen all over, and I slide my eyes down toward the floor.

“Stay with me, Callie,” he whispers and tightens his hold on my hand. “Concentrate on the tension, on your breathing.”

Okay. Inhale. One. Two. Three. His hand over mine. His skin on my skin. Heat running through me. *{*“Feels Like Home” *refrain—over and over and over.}*

“Good. I can see the tension leaving you.”

He rubs his thumb back and forth over the top of my hand. *{And over and over and over and over and over and—}*

“All right, keep that focus as we construct your worst case scenario plan.”

I nod and watch his thumb continue its caress of my

hand.

"Okay, so a needle does prick you and—"

Breathe, Callie. His hand. His thumb. *{A special request for the DJ: Please start the song over again NOW.}*

"What will you decide to do?"

Inhale. His warm hand. *{Refrain back on repeat.}* Exhale.

I can't break my concentration to answer his question. I just shake my head to let him know.

"All right, it's too much right now. Let's not push it."

I nod my head in appreciation. His thumb continues to stroke my hand.

"Let's look at this the other way around. Let's think about the incredible odds that your worst case scenario will not actually become reality. Can you do that?"

Another nod. I'll try.

"Good. To start, we proved that your odds of sitting in a seat with a needle are much lower than you imagined them to be. Right?"

Nod.

"Okay, don't freak out, but I have some information about your fears. A friend of mine, who happens to be a doctor, answered some general questions for me. Don't worry—I didn't tell him anything about you or your case to get this information. I want to tell you about some of it to give you some more accurate facts to hold in your mind. Before I do that, however, I want you to promise me that you won't look anything up by yourself because you'll risk reading something that might somehow escalate your fears."

Nod again.

"Good. At any point when you come up with something you want to know, tell me. I will find out and give you information I feel you need, information that I think will help you."

He pauses. "I'll only give you true information. No lies. You are going to have to trust me, Callie."

I do. Quick nod.

"All right, I'm just going to have to jump right in, then, because the previews are probably going to start soon." Pause.

"I specifically asked about AIDS and the HIV virus."

Just as my body begins to scrunch up with painful pressure, he shifts our hands so that his is now under mine and we are holding hands properly. Fingers intertwined completely. The back of his hand resting on my leg. *{The song begins again automatically—no special request needed.}*

The lights in the theatre dim, and a reminder to turn off all cell phones appears on the screen. He leans close to me, so close that I can feel his breath on my cheek, and whispers, "I'm going to have to go through this fast."

Nod.

"One—I'm sure you've already heard that you can't just contract HIV or AIDS by using a public bathroom, touching a doorknob, and so on. Whether you choose to believe that or not."

He already knows I don't believe that.

He goes on. "Two—if a person who is truly infected with AIDS or HIV does bleed and the blood ends up on a physical surface, the disease can only survive in that external blood for a very short period of time. Probably an hour at most, if that."

I did not know that. He continues whispering as a new preview begins on the screen in front of us.

"So, if for some reason you—or another person,

rather—were to accidentally touch a spot of blood, or to be pricked by a—"

As my body stiffens, he pauses and abbreviates.

"Well, anyway, what I'm saying is, the odds are good that any infectious germs that might have been there are already dead and gone."

I will need time to think this over. Later, though, when his lips aren't so close to my face.

He hasn't moved. Well, except for his thumb, which is still rubbing my hand and making me a little lightheaded. I hear "Tara's Theme" and assume that the movie is starting.

He whispers again, somehow even more quietly than before. To make up for that, he moves even closer to me, his mouth only a few inches from my ear. As he tells me that he has one more bit of information he thinks I can use, his breath tickles my ear and heat courses through my body. Almost a warm chill. If that is even possible.

Slowly, he settles back into his seat, saying that he'll tell me the rest later and that he hopes the other information helps.

It does. Or it will. Later. When I'm somehow capable of thinking about anything but him. And his hand. And his lips.

I don't think of much else during the movie. Scarlett professes her love for Ashley. He turns her down. *He's still holding my hand.* Scarlett's first husband dies and she dances with Rhett. *Hands haven't moved.* Scarlett marries another man. He dies. *Hands sweating a little but still together.* Scarlett marries Rhett. *I hope my leg isn't sweating under his hand.* Rhett whisks Scarlett up in his arms and carries her up the stairs. They—

My phone rings.

SHIT.

I have to find it. Stop the ringing. Stop ruining the movie for everyone.

I unceremoniously let go of his hand and immediately begin digging in my purse, quickly realizing that my phone is not in its normal spot. I frantically search every inch but have no luck so I begin ripping items out of my purse and dumping them on my lap. My wallet. My Band-Aids. Keys. Deoder—

I drop my purse on the floor just as my phone stops ringing.

DAMN IT.

Instinctively, I reach down to grab the top of my purse. But I bump heads with him. Because he has the same idea.

"Let me get it, Callie," he whispers, our heads only inches apart.

I let him because I don't even know what to do right now, and it seems a lot less scary to have him make some decisions.

As I try to sit back up in my seat without bumping into him again, I lose my balance and involuntarily grab the top of the seat in front of me.

Oh my God.

I am touching gum. Sticky, disgusting gum that some idiot put on the back of this chair. As I rip my right hand away from the chair, from the gum, I feel something like a dry heave. My body wants to throw up, but nothing comes out.

His questioning eyes look up at me at this point, and I merely nod to the chair in front of me. As he leans toward the chair to investigate, I look down and try to hold my right hand, my fingers, safely away from the rest of my body.

When I look back up, I see my purse suspended in

front of me. He is holding it up for me so I can get my stuff without touching the purse.

I don't argue. Holding my right hand awkwardly up in the air, I dig out the remaining items with my left hand, grabbing my bitch of a phone last.

My lap is now a display case for the contents of my purse. Again only using my left hand, I carefully shove everything into my coat pockets, which are now in danger of spilling over. He then moves my purse aside, assuming that I am finished.

I am. "I have to go," I whisper, not looking at him or at my purse. I have to go home to my bathroom, my shower. Now.

"I know," he says soothingly.

Ugh. Of course you do.

I stand up, and he follows suit immediately, stepping aside so I can walk first to the back of the theatre. I hear him follow me, but I don't turn around. I don't stop until I reach the lobby and hear him call my name.

I slowly turn around. I owe him that.

I'm sure my mouth drops open a bit. He is dangling my purse above the gigantic round trash can sitting by the concessions counter. His raised shoulders and eyebrows ask his question for him: Is this trash?

I nod firmly, once, and turn back around. Seconds later, he is in front of me holding open the door to the outside. I exit, and we walk silently side by side to his car. He opens my door for me before getting in the driver's seat and starting the car.

I vigilantly keep my upturned right hand steady on my lap. Fingers not touching anything. For quite awhile, we ride in silence. What is there to say? Session One: Failure.

"I'm taking you home."

His voice is firm. Resolute. There is no point in arguing with him. Besides, arguing would mean opening my mouth and trying to talk, which would probably also mean crying.

Soon I realize that he's already going in the direction of my house, and he never asked me for directions. I wonder if he really did memorize my emergency form. I also wonder what he expects me to do about my car. I try to work up the strength to ask.

I don't have much success, but it doesn't matter. As he pulls up by my house moments later, he answers my question as though I had spoken it aloud.

"I can come get you in the morning and drive you to your car."

No way. How mortifying would that be? Like some screwed up psychological breakdown walk of shame.

Words splatter out of my mouth. "Mandy will do it." I don't know if Mandy has plans for the morning or if she'll have time, but I'll just figure something else out if she can't.

His response is soft, softer than usual. "If that's what you want."

He sounds hurt. Almost rejected. Oh, God. He's taking this personally somehow.

I don't know what to do. I'm sure I've somehow reminded him of his mother again. Unbelievably, my urge to fix this, to fix him, is almost as strong as my desperation to run into my house, strip down, and take a scalding shower.

I scramble for a quick way to make him feel better as he opens my car door and walks me to the front door of my house. Without taking time to count or think, I look him straight in the eyes and simply say, "Sorry."

He shakes his head, saying, "Don't worry about it,

Callie. You—"

And then the porch light turns on. The door opens and Mandy appears, dressed for bed.

"There you are, Callie. Do you know how late it is? I tried to call you." *Ugh.*

"I, um, was at therapy, and I have to—"

He interrupts me with a firm voice, "Go ahead in, Callie. Take your shower. I'll talk to you tomorrow."

I don't need to be told three times. I give him a quick nod, walk past Mandy, use only my left hand as I carefully unzip my boots to leave them on the towel by the door, and head right up to my bathroom.

AFTER TWENTY MINUTES OF SCRUBBING and rinsing, I am through enough of my sterilization process to be able to think again. I stand still, directly under the showerhead and change the water temperature from burning to just hot. And I think. About the evening. About before my freak out. The movie. Our hands. Him.

What is he thinking now that he's been exposed to even more of my insanity? Will he even contact me to continue treatment?

That's his job, Callie.

But he doesn't normally see patients like me.

I wonder if he treats all of his patients the same way he treats me…

The evening sessions. The hand holding. *Stop it, Callie.*

I shut off the water and get out of the shower to begin my night preparations right away. As I go through my checking routine, I silently pray that I have not contracted any diseases tonight. And then I pray again. And again.

Then I remember his words about my odds of truly catching a disease.

But that was only one disease. What about Hepatitis? Or SARS? And, really, what about HIV? What if someone put that gum there right before we sat in the theatre? And if that person had a sore in his mouth and got some blood in the gum? If my fingers have some miniscule cuts on them that I can't quite see, I could easily have gotten HIV or even full-blown AIDS tonight.

I know that he said the virus can't live very long outside of the body, but, really, where did that information come from? He could have been making it up just to calm—

My phone buzzes on my dresser.

I finish straightening the picture to the left of my bed and go over to check my phone.

A text. From him. Unknown Number.

Count. Open.

`Callie—Please check your email. Right now.`

Jeez. Right now?

I seem to have no self-control so I walk over to my computer and turn it on. I log into my account and click on the email from DA Blake.

Callie,

You are fine. Please do not spend your entire night thinking about a little piece of gum. Don't let this incident take away your whole evening.

I am attaching a list of websites and medical documents that confirm the information I gave you tonight. I really want you to understand that I'm only giving you valid, well-researched facts. Hopefully, you won't feel the need to seek out other websites and articles on your own; reading unfiltered details about diseases may be more harm than help to you. However, if you do feel you must do your own research, please know that I will be available to discuss any questions or concerns that arise. I know this is long (and probably boring), but I really want to help you find some personal value in my information. I'll text you in the morning to set up tomorrow's session. I hope you still want to come.

Good night,
Aiden

I read his email two more times, and it seems to have somewhat of a soothing effect on me. Much like his hand.

I get up from my chair to continue my routine, feeling a strange sense of calm. However, it's unclear if that's because of his words or because I know I'll get to take another shower in about an hour.

After plowing through my routine, I'm back under a cascade of clean water by midnight. Scrub. Rinse. Repeat.

When I feel sufficiently clean (for now), I apply my lotion and flip on the television.

Pizza around the world tonight.

As a petite chef with a heavy French accent describes her pizza making strategies, I write myself a note for tomorrow.

CAR

I've got to talk to Mandy about taking me to campus tomorrow morning. She was asleep when I went in to clean her room so I'll have to catch her as soon as I wake up. I'm sure she won't mind driving me.

I hope not since I already shot down my only other possibility. And made him sad. Again. *{Damien Rice.* "The Blower's Daughter."*}*

I grab my phone from my dresser and start a new message to Unknown Number.

```
Thanks for sending me your re-
search. It does help to know
that stuff, even if it takes me
a while to convince myself to
believe it. I will see you to-
morrow for Day 2 of treatment.
Good night.
```

One. Two. Three. Send.

Chapter 16
day two

ON TUESDAY MORNING, I WAKE up one minute before my alarm rings. My car pops right into my head so I bolt over to Mandy's room. She is surprisingly awake, furiously typing a paper that must be due at her 10:30 a.m. class today. She doesn't even look up as I stand in her doorway.

"Hey, Mandy. Sorry to interrupt, but do you mind driving me to campus today? My car is—"

"Already taken care of, Callie." She looks up with a cheesy smile. "That hot doctor boyfriend of yours told me all about it so we picked up your car last night."

She did? They did? He drove her back to my car while I was—

"He was all worried about you, Callie. First he was worried that you wouldn't make it to campus in time. Then he was worried that you would be worried. So I just decided to help him." She pauses, looks at me, and breaks out another toothy grin. "Believe me, it wasn't that much of a sacrifice sitting in a leathery Lexus next to him in silence. You know, having nothing to do but stare at his muscles and that super intense look on his face while breathing him in. The man smells like the freaking pages of a fashion magazine, like one of those high-end cologne samples. Delicious."

She winks at me this time as she smiles. "Good choice, Callie."

"I-I'm not dat—"

"I know. I know. There's nothing there, right? The late night appointments, trips in his fancy car, and terribly concerned looks on his face are all just part of your treatment package, right?" She rolls her eyes dramatically and then holds up a set of keys. My spare keys. She must have taken them from the kitchen drawer before leaving with him last night. She tosses them to me.

"Do you have another 'session' tonight?" Her voice is rather suggestive.

"Yes, well, I do, but I don't know where or when yet."

"I bet you'll find out something soon," she says before turning back to her laptop.

"What is that supposed to mean?"

"You'll see." She doesn't turn back to me as she talks. Clearly, she won't be saying any more about it.

After thanking her, saying goodbye, and leaving her room, I get to work on my routine right away. Can't be late for my 11:00 a.m. class.

10:40 a.m. When I get into my car, I see it right away. Positioned carefully on top of my steering wheel is an envelope with my name on it. Taped to the envelope, a yellow rose.

I know that it's from him. And that he obviously had some help from Mandy.

But where did he get the rose? When? And why did he remember that little bit of accidental information about my favorite flower? *{The opening chords for Bette*

Midler's "The Rose" *begin to play.}* I can't wait any longer so I tear open the envelope.

Count. Unfold. Read.

Dear Callie,

I'm sorry our first session ended the way it did. Whether you realize it or not, we definitely made some progress. You entered a movie theatre for the first time in many, many years. You sat down in a theatre seat. And you made it through a pretty large portion of the movie (and let's face it—Gone with the Wind is a LONG movie). Please start Day 2 by focusing on these accomplishments. I'll contact you soon with more details for tonight.

-Aiden

My phone buzzes in my purse, my newly-filled tan leather purse.

This time I find the phone right away. *Of course.*

Text from Unknown Number.

Count. Open.

I'll meet you at your house after your night class. I know you often get out early so I'll get to your house around 8:30 p.m. Don't rush. If class runs long, I'll just wait. We'll be eating dinner…so save some calories for me. Have a good day.

My eye catches the time on the text. 10:46 a.m. *Shit.* Gotta get moving.

Throwing my phone back into my purse, I start my car and head to class. Unbelievably, I manage to arrive two minutes early. I pull out my phone to reply to his text so he knows that I haven't chickened out. Yet.

Count. Reply.

I'll be home tonight as soon as class ends.

Hmm...not done yet.

Thanks for the rose.

One. Two. Three. One. Two. Three. OneTwoThree. Send.

DR. EMERY BEGINS CLASS A few minutes late. As usual. She reminds us that our first poetry portfolio is due next week. We are supposed to make a collection of our best poetry from each weekly assignment.

I clearly have a lot of work to do for my portfolio. I didn't like a single poem from last week's fruit bowl fiasco. My poems about an open field from the week before aren't much better.

And this week's subject…da da da duuuhhh…rainbows. *Ugh.* Dr. Emery starts prancing around the room as she hangs up different pictures of rainbows in various locations. It's nauseating. Isn't this supposed to be a graduate level class?

We have an hour and a half to ponder, reflect, and create, as Dr. Emery explains it.

"Begin now," she says with her hands clasped by her chest and her eyes closed. An attempt at inspiration? "Follow your rainbow." *Oh dear God—did she really just say that?*

Okay, rainbows… *{Kermit the Frog asks a stream of questions as he sings* "The Rainbow Connection."*}* During the next hour and a half, at least half a dozen rainbow songs run through my head. They'll probably stay there for a week.

I really do try to think about rainbows, but my mind keeps conjuring images of pots of gold and tiny little leprechauns dancing around. Soon, I'm thinking about the little leprechaun in the commercials for Lucky Charms, and before I know it, I'm trying to calculate the number of calories that would be in a big bowl of cereal.

Needless to say, I'm pretty hungry by the time class "sharing" begins. Luckily, there are enough volunteers to "share" and plenty of follow-up questions; I am able to avoid going up in front of the class with a growling stomach.

I leave class uninspired by the shared poems and unfortunately humming the theme from *Reading Rainbow.*

When I get to my car, I check my phone.

He wrote back.

```
Glad you liked the flower. No
dirt. No thorns. Just to look at
and smell. See you tonight.
```

Ugh. More evidence suggesting he really did memorize my email responses. Nonetheless, his text makes me smile as I put away my phone and head home for a few hours.

When I get home, I take the plastic water container off the stem of my yellow rose and put the flower in a vase on my dresser. I then repaint my nails and work on my paper for *The Scarlet Letter.* Some notes taken. Some articles highlighted. I have a snack as I work, saving seven hundred calories for tonight. Once again I don't know what to wear for my late evening therapy session so I get dressed in jeans and a long-sleeved tee. Just in case, I throw a sweatshirt in my bag.

5:58 P.M. I'M BACK IN A classroom, ready to sit through another publisher presentation. Tonight's speaker writes children's books. Some of the books are cute, but I don't really see the point. How is this presentation going to help me publish a piece of literary criticism?

The presenter spends a lot of time reading her books out loud to us. After taking questions, she dismisses us around 8:10 p.m. I bolt out of the classroom, wondering if he'll already be at my house when I arrive.

He is. And it's only 8:26 p.m. I pull in around his car, turn off my engine, count, and head toward him. He actually gives me a little smile as he stands at the passenger door waiting to let me in. I find myself smiling back as I thank him and slide into my seat.

As soon as he gets in the car, he looks right at me. "How are you tonight? Are you ready for this?"

Even though I don't know what this is, I nod and tell him that I'm fine.

And we are off. To where, I don't know. We pass campus buildings, apartments, restaurants, town shops, and so on. *{Big Muppet day today. Kermit and Fozzie jump into* "Movin' Right Along."*}*

He glances over at me, catching my eye and giving me a little smile. He's probably afraid that I'm going to spontaneously freak out or something. I give him a small smile back to try to give him some reassurance.

He keeps looking over with that smile every three minutes or so. Almost as though he's afraid I'm going to disappear—like that little boy version of him in the picture with his mom.

CALLIE! I scold myself. Somehow I always manage to bring up the painful subject of his mother. At least I didn't do it out loud this time.

When he looks over the next time, I give him the most confident smile I can manage. Smile. Smile. Smile. *No, Aiden, I wasn't thinking about your mother.* Smile. Smile. Smile. *Please, oh please, don't get that devastated look in your eyes.* Smile. Smile. Smile.

He doesn't. But he does continue his little looking and smiling routine like clockwork.

I almost feel like I've pulled one over on him. Finally, I've had a thought that he didn't hear or predict in advance.

Twenty minutes pass in silence. Where exactly are we going for this dinner? *{Kermit and Fozzie continue to sing.}* When I notice that twenty-five minutes have now passed, my curiosity wins, and I interrupt the silence in the car.

I blurt out, "Where are we going?"

He doesn't look over as he says, "Pittsburgh."

"Pittsburgh?" I probably say it louder than I should.

"Well, Oakland, actually." He sounds nervous. Perhaps because Oakland is busy, noisy, and far less than overwhelmingly clean…

I know these things. I spent plenty of time there when I was younger since it was only about twenty minutes from home. We ate dinner there once in a while, and I went to some campus events there when Melanie was in college. That was back when I had a tiny hint of a social life. Back when I had time for friends. Back when it was a little easier to get myself out of the house.

I push those thoughts aside and try to calm his nerves a little. "Oh, I used to go to Oakland quite a bit.

When I was younger. Not in a long time though." But why are we going there now? Why are we driving an entire hour just for dinner?

"I sort of assumed that, with your parents living so close by."

I don't remember telling him where my parents live. The information is probably somewhere on my patient ID card though. If he ever has to take a quiz on my contact information, I'm pretty sure he'll get a perfect score. No problem.

"Maybe you've also been to the restaurant where I'm taking you," he continues. "Dawson's Grille."

I love Dawson's Grille, but I haven't been there in ages. I tell him, "I've been there many times, sometimes with friends in high school and also with Melanie when she was in college."

He looks over and smiles. "Good. I hope you like it there. It was the only place somewhat nearby where I could find nachos with melted cheese. Most places just use nacho cheese."

So he really has memorized my emails.

It seemed like a strange but general therapy question when he asked me what I would eat if calories didn't matter. Clearly it was more than that…seems to always be that way with him.

I tell him what I'm sure he's already realized. "Those are the exact nachos I was talking about."

"Good." His smile gets bigger. He looks a little surprised, a little relieved, and more than a little proud of himself.

As he continues, concern joins the other emotions on his face. "So you are okay with going to a restaurant?"

"Well, yes, as long as stuff is clean. You know, the table, the dishes, the waiter."

"I hope, then, that all of that meets your expectations tonight." He does? Isn't this therapy supposed to be challenging?

"I don't want to make tonight's exercise any more difficult than it needs to be." He pauses, glances at me warily, and continues quietly. "That gum really threw me last night. I would never—"

"Stop," I interrupt. I know he didn't arrange for that gum to be there or secretly know of its existence, and I don't want him to try to apologize. In fact, I don't want to talk or think about that gum at all. I've tried to avoid thinking about it all day.

"I just—" he tries again.

"Don't," I say firmly. "It wasn't your fault. And I don't want to talk about it. Not if you want me to make it through tonight anyway."

He nods, giving in rather swiftly. He must really want me to get through my challenge tonight, whatever that is.

"What's tonight's challenge anyway?" I brave the question spinning through my mind.

"The nachos," he says simply.

"What—is someone going to spit in them or something?"

"No. You are going to eat them. All of them."

Shit. Seven hundred calories are not going to cover this. Not even close.

"Oh."

"You like them, right?"

I love them. I just don't love them adding pounds to my body.

"Yeah."

"Well, it's time for you to splurge a little on your eating. Your fourteen hundred calories a day have just become another routine, another obsessive way to have control. I want you to realize that taking a night off from counting every now and then won't be the end of the world."

{Two female voices initiate the opening dialogue of "Baby Got Back."*}*

"Are you okay?" He shoots a concerned glance my way.

I nod but probably not very convincingly. I can't remember the last time I went even slightly over my calorie count. This will be way over.

"Do you want to turn around?"

Oh, God. I've already put the sadness back in his voice, and dinner hasn't even begun.

"No, I want to try," I blurt out. I do want to try. I'm just not sure that I can do it.

He looks at least somewhat placated. Placated enough to continue driving. *{Sir Mix-a-Lot's turn.}*

Before I know it, we are in Oakland.

It's been so long since I've been here. As we get out of the car and start walking the city streets, I can't help but remember a time long ago on these very streets when a passerby spit and the spit hit my leg. Unbelievable. I lost at least a week of my life in the aftershocks of that one.

I try to push the thought from my mind, but it doesn't work. Luckily, we have just arrived at Dawson's Grille. He grabs my hand as he navigates through the crowd to our table. I hold my breath during the entire journey. Because the area is hot and sweaty. Because there are people swarming all around me.

Because he is holding my hand.

Fortunately, our table is in the downstairs area of the restaurant. There are only a handful of tables down here, and only one of them is already occupied. He selects the farthest spot from the other people. After methodically examining the table and chairs, he motions for me to sit. Our table is spotlessly clean. My seat also passes my personal inspection.

We naturally drop hands as we sit, and my hand feels suddenly empty. The bubbly waitress gives us menus, but I already know what I'll be having. What I'll be trying to have.

"So…what is good?" he asks after the waitress takes our drink orders and leaves us to look at the menus.

"I've only ever had the nachos here."

"Seriously?" He looks up at me.

"Yep. The first time I came here, a high school friend ordered them. Nachos with melted cheese and tomatoes. They sounded delicious so I ordered them too. And our love story began." I smile up at him. His returning smile is boyish, almost carefree.

Wow. {Back to you, Damien Rice.}

Our waitress comes back to take our order. He nods for me to go first so I order my favorite nachos for the first time in years. He also orders the nachos but with every topping imaginable.

The waitress leaves to place our order of around ten million calories.

"When was the last time you were here?"

I remember exactly. "Christmas break during my freshman year of college."

"That long ago?"

About six years. "Yep."

"Why?" he asks as he takes a sip of his soda.

Where do I begin? "It's a bit complicated."

"Psychologists kind of expect that."

True. I'm sure he's going to wrench this all out of

me at some point. And then probably memorize it. *Just get it over with, Callie.*

One. Two. Three. GO.

"It was a, um, rough night the last time I was here."

He nods, encouraging me to go on.

"As I said, I was home for Christmas break. And I was out with my then boyfriend." As I pause to drink, I notice a shocked look on his face. I can't really blame him. It was so long ago, and I haven't dated anyone since…that relationship seems pretty surreal to me too.

I go on. "We dated for about a year in high school and then tried the long distance thing during college. I was at Pierce, and he stayed home and went to school here. Over break we were finally able to spend some time together."

"And you came here. For nachos."

"Right. We'd done that many times before in high school. But it was different this time. Everything was different."

"How so?" He says it in a way that makes me feel like I'm on the couch in his office, spilling out my problems.

"Well…college really changed him. Half a year of it, and he was totally different. Different priorities. Different interests." Pause. "Different thoughts about me."

"Different in what way?"

As I take a prolonged sip of my drink, the waitress arrives with our food. Already. The people upstairs must be doing a lot more drinking than eating.

My first bite tastes just as I remembered. All two hundred calories of it.

He starts to eat his nachos too. After he swallows, he leaps right back into our conversation. "Okay—how was he different with you?"

One. Two. Three.

"He, um, Tony, wasn't the generous, patient guy from high school anymore. I started to realize this during the few times he came to visit me at college, but I tried to ignore it."

He continues to eat but keeps his eyes on me. Concerned. Patient.

"I think he'd had it with my whole OCD thing. In high school, he actually seemed to find it somewhat endearing, cute or something. Maybe he thought I was just making it up for his benefit—I don't know. But he had infinite patience with me back then." I pause to decide where to go next with my story, and he jumps in quickly.

"Eat, Callie. Please. I want to hear all of this, but please don't forget to eat too."

I nod and pick up a small pile of nachos, tomatoes, and melted cheese. Another couple of hundred calories, no doubt. He smiles his appreciation and nods for me to continue talking.

"When he came to visit me for the first time at Pierce, we fought most of the time. It was weird because we had spent months planning and looking forward to his visits, looking forward to being alone and being on our own, away from our parents. I never would have thought that our freedom would ultimately break us up."

He nods his head toward my plate, and I obediently take another bite.

"We broke up shortly after that last trip to this restaurant," I say in closing.

"I'm having trouble seeing how your trip here was instrumental in ending the relationship." Well, that sounded rather doctory. "Callie, I'm glad you have been able to open up a little, but I need more so I can help you better."

Fabulous. Should've kept my mouth shut.

"Can you do that?"

I nod. Reluctantly.

He smiles. "All right. Why don't you take another bite, a big one, and then tell me again about your last visit to this restaurant? No glossing over important details."

UGH. I have to talk AND eat. Aren't we tackling too many things at once?

He's still staring at me so I acquiesce. I said I would try. I take a slightly bigger bite than the last one, knowing I'm way over my calorie count now. After swallowing, I begin again, forcing myself to think back to my last few weeks with Tony. *{Next up, we have Gotye with* "Somebody That I Used to Know."*}*

"Like I said before, Tony really changed when he went to college. He met new friends who I really didn't know but knew I didn't like. From what I could tell from the stories Tony would tell and the new phrases he used, this group was pretty judgmental about people who were different from the norm. Their norm. Or what they thought the norm should be, I guess.

"They made not just little jokes but really cruel comments about people who didn't fit into their vision of normal. Gay people. Overweight people. People who weren't overly smart. And the list goes on. God only knows what they would've thought of me if we had ever been introduced."

I take a sip of my diet soda. "Well, I guess I do know. They probably would have seen me the same way Tony had started to see me."

"How was that?" he prods while simultaneously nodding toward my nachos.

I force another delicious two hundred or so calories into my mouth, chew, and swallow before continuing.

"He all of a sudden despised any part of me related to the OCD—and that equaled out to be, well, almost all of me."

He finishes his nachos and leans back in his chair, all attention on my little fairy tale.

I continue. "I wasn't even that bad back then. I mean, not like now. But it was still too much for him.

"During those couple of trips to Pierce, Tony tried to 'fix' me." I meet his eyes with a small smile. "His immersion treatment consisted of screaming at me when he saw me checking something, reading me articles to try to disprove my religious beliefs, purposefully messing up spaces and items that I'd cleaned and telling me I needed to go to bed or leave my dorm room without fixing them…that kind of stuff.

"Oh, and making biting, sarcastic comments about my OCD in front of my roommate, friends, and family. He was bashing me, bullying me, to try to cure me. It was ridiculous."

"How did your family and friends react to that?"

"You have all the right therapist questions just waiting to burst out of your mouth, don't you?" I blurt out without thinking.

Stupid. Stupid. Stupid. He looks melancholy again.

I smile as quickly as my face will allow to show him that I am only teasing.

He smiles back.

Whew. Quick fix.

"I'm pretty sure my family and friends didn't like him. When Tony would start with the malicious OCD commentary, they would often try to change the conversation. Or at least lighten it up a bit."

He looks confused.

"We've always laughed about my OCD. My parents, my friends, me most of all, probably. I think we have to laugh about it because we all know that some of the stuff I do is ridiculous. Again, probably me most of all."

He still has a confused look on his face. I'm guessing he never found a lighter way of looking at his mother's condition.

I can't say that I'm very surprised.

"Come on," I say with a grin. "It is ridiculous. Washing my hands until they bleed. Being afraid that I'll catch diseases through the cuts on my hands. Washing my hands more to try to stop thinking about the diseases. It's an ugly cycle. Absolutely ludicrous."

He is still listening, seemingly surprised by my words.

I continue my list of absurdities. "The checking, the routines. I know they don't make sense. But I also know that I can't do anything else unless I go through them. So I have to do them."

When I look at his face again, I can't say that all of the confusion is gone, but he is smiling again. He also reminds me to keep eating.

I eat another mouthful of nachos before continuing.

"If you think about the ridiculousness of it, it really is a little funny."

"It is," he says slowly. "I just haven't had too many patients who see it that way. Or at least I don't get that impression from them."

Yeah. But you don't treat patients like me.

Thank the Lord my mind filters that thought before it heads to my mouth.

"I have to look at it that way when I can. If I took it seriously all of the time, I think I might actually go insane. The whole way."

"It's something for me to think about, I guess," he says before AGAIN pointing to my nachos. "But for now, let's get back to that charming ex-boyfriend of yours."

I look him in the eye and pretend to gasp. "Dr. Blake, did you just make a joke about my situation?"

And he smiles at me. With his mouth *and* his eyes.

It feels like freaking Christmas morning. No—better.

{Damien—again.}

"You aren't the only one learning during this therapy, Callie." He pauses. "Now, tell me about this guy." He pauses again. "After you eat another bite."

"Aren't you bossy tonight?" I shoot back. But then I take another bite and delve back into my past.

"Tony wasn't teasing or laughing. He was ridiculing, chastising. As though he thought I had the control to simply stop the checking, the routines, the thoughts."

More soda. "He didn't get it. That was very apparent during his visits to Pierce. It was also apparent that he was embarrassed by me." *{Back to Gotye—the refrain now.}* "Looking back, I wish it would have ended then, before our holiday break. Because it only got worse."

"How so?" he says while looking pointedly at my food.

I pretend not to notice his glance and try to answer his question. "Well, a lot of things were bad. He tried even harder to cure me, as he called it. He kept telling me that I needed to loosen up. I guess he was trying to make me as presentable as he could before introducing me to his new friends. That meeting never happened anyway."

"More eating."

As I begrudgingly take another nacho, he says, "Tell me what happened the night you came here."

One. Two. Three. *Get it over with, Callie.*

"Okay. It wasn't the first time he did something like this, but it was the most memorable. Like I said before, his new friends were all concerned about being 'normal' and keeping up with their images."

I take a minute to swallow the handful of rocks creeping into my throat, realizing that I've never actually said this aloud before.

Picking at my fingernails (secretly—under the table), I continue. "He was always talking about new college students gaining the 'freshman fifteen.' He'd even point out people around my dorm who looked bigger to him than they did during a previous visit. Sometimes, he also told me about running into friends from high school who'd gained some weight.

"I just kind of brushed it off when he mentioned it because I didn't gain any weight during my freshman year. I weighed the same as I did in high school. And I wasn't really concerned about weight back then because I was pretty thin, not a size zero or anything, but nothing to worry about.

"I guess I just ignored his comments because I assumed he was only making small talk about other people. Just strange, kind of obsessive conversation."

The nail polish is gone on my left hand. I start on my right hand immediately.

"That night, though, the last time I was here, it seemed like a lot more than small talk. To me anyway."

Here goes. And with only four more nails to pick.

"We were here with two other couples, friends from high school. They had all gone to nearby colleges so they stayed home and basically continued living as they had in high school. No long distance. No weeks and months apart. No growing completely apart from one another.

"We sat at a table upstairs. Tony and I were on one

side with Kim while Jess and Luke were on the other side with Matt. Luke had his arm around Jess throughout the entire evening. Kim and Matt held hands across the table. Tony and I sat side by side, once in a while accidentally bumping arms or feet.

"When I ordered my nachos, like I always did, he stopped me. Right in front of four friends I hadn't seen in months. With the waitress standing there taking our order. 'Callie,' he said, 'are you sure you want to order those?' Then he nudged me and used a singsong voice to say, 'Don't forget the freshman fifteen.'"

Only one finger left with nail polish on it. Gonna have to work at it slowly.

"I brushed it off as I always had and ordered my nachos. I was somewhat irritated, but I assumed he was just being stupid and trying to make the other guys laugh.

"The others didn't laugh though, and Tony didn't stop. After the waitress left, he elbowed me again and said, 'Can't have my Callie getting fat.'"

I pause. "Then he—" Deep breath. Nail polish is gone. Count. One. Two. Three. One. Two. Three. One—

"Callie? Do you want to stop?"

I shake my head, keeping my eyes down on the table. I want to get this over with, not start it all over again at a later session.

"Callie." He says it again, even more delicately this time.

His hand appears in my line of vision. Upturned. Waiting for my hand. *{Your turn again, Mr. Rice.}* I move my hand out from under the table and place it in his hand. His thumb immediately rubs over my thumb nail and then pointer nail.

He knew I was out of nail polish. Of course.

"Go on, Callie."

One. Two. Three.

"Then he, well, he pinched at the skin on the side of my stomach, as though assessing whether or not he needed to worry about fat on my body. He then made a sort of 'tsk tsk' sound to imply that, I don't know, that he wanted me not to order nachos? To stop eating altogether?

"I really don't know what he meant for sure. I was too busy being mortified. The girls with me, Kim and Jess, had incredulous looks on their faces. There was also some pity in their eyes, but I'm pretty sure there was something else too. Anger. They both looked really pissed.

"I didn't blame them. They were both about my size."

He squeezes my hand as he asks, "What did you do?"

"Nothing. Kim introduced a new topic of conversation, and I tried to ignore the whole situation. I sat a little farther away from him during dinner, and I didn't eat more than three nachos."

I pause, but I don't look up. I don't want to see what is in his eyes. Not yet.

"I made it through the evening without losing it. When I got home, I stared at myself in the mirror from every possible angle. Cried a little too. But then, like I said, we broke up soon after."

"Who broke it off?"

"He did." Pause. "But I should have. Every time he touched me after that night, all I could feel was him pinching the skin on my stomach."

"And then you started the fourteen hundred calories a day thing, because of him?"

"Sort of. I guess I went a little extreme at first. Much less than fourteen hundred."

"Like eight hundred?"

My head springs up before I can think to stop it. "Yes. Exactly."

I search his eyes for an answer to my unspoken question, but I find no response. So I ask. "How?" *How do you know about this?* Did I write this in one of my emails and forget? Doubtful. Did his mom have this problem too?

"Your medical reports from the last ten years were sent to me."

"Oh." No magic. No deep insight. This time. I let my gaze fall back down to the table.

"The report from February of, I assume, the year of your break-up was pretty intense. Eight hundred calories a day. Purging. Late period. Pregnancy test."

My head snaps up as I snatch my hand away from his. I feel my cheeks turn insanely red. "The nurses at the college health center insisted I take that test. They must see a lot of potential pregnancies come through or something."

I put my head down again, urging my cheeks to cool off.

"But it wasn't a—you weren't. Pregnant." He sounds almost as flustered as I feel but continues. "The report said the test was negative."

"Of course it was," I cry out, probably in a much angrier voice than necessary.

I peek up at him. He looks broken again.

Damn it. Shit. Damn it.

{R.E.M. cuts in with the melancholy "Everybody Hurts."*}*

"We didn't, um, we never—" I try to explain. "I had no need to take that test."

"Oh." His eyes go from wounded to shocked. I

guess that is better.

For him anyway.

"I-I'm sorry, Callie. I just read the report. I didn't mean to bring up—"

"Don't worry about it," I force out the words as I look back down at my plate of half-eaten nachos, unsure of where to go from here. Well, at least he probably won't force me to eat any more nachos.

"Callie."

I can't look up at him. Not yet.

{R.E.M. continues, slow and solemn.}

"Callie."

Still not ready.

Before I can even really register the fact that he is moving, he's beside me.

"Callie."

As my eyes begin to fill, I close them and push my head down even further. *{The refrain begins pounding.}*

He covers my hand with his and tugs it to his lap.

"If you want to talk about this now, I'm here. I hadn't planned to hit such serious topics until later in our treatment, but since it seems there's some overlap here with the eating thing, it's fine."

My hand is in his. On his lap. And he wants to talk about sex. The sex I didn't have with Tony.

"Callie?"

Clearing my throat, I try to answer. "Um…I don't mind going through this with you for, uh, our treatment, but, um…I'm not sure if…if I can say it all here. It's, well, pretty humiliating." I keep my head down, waiting to hear his response.

He responds with his hand before his voice, squeezing and again rubbing his thumb over the top of my hand. Back and forth. Back and forth. Back and forth. *{"The*

Blower's Daughter." "The Blower's Daughter." "The Blower's Daughter."}

"Callie, I know it's the cliché doctor thing to say, but there really is nothing to be embarrassed about."

Back and forth. Back and—

"Yes, you have some problems that complicate your life, but it sounds as though this relationship had entirely unrelated issues. It sounds like this guy had quite a few issues of his own."

Yes, yes, and yes. My head nods a little.

"However, I know that these things can be challenging to discuss, especially to say aloud. So, because we do need to finish this conversation in some way for your treatment, I'm going to add it to tomorrow's plan."

So now I have twenty-four hours to obsess over it? *Fantastic.*

"Tomorrow you will have a full day of assignments but no face-to-face session. This personal day of work is essential to your treatment because you do have to be able to do some of these things on your own when no one else is watching.

"Now, I'm not talking about major things here. We'll just be concentrating on little fixes that you can make as you go through your day, small exercises to try to improve the quality of your everyday life."

While I am glad that it sounds like I won't be having a personal picnic on the floor of a public bathroom, I'm still not sure what he means.

"So what will I be doing?" My emotions are all pretty much under control so I look up as I say it. His eyes are patient, concerned. Still pretty intense, as usual.

His thumb continues to massage my hand as he answers, "Well, there are some minor tasks you can complete. One thing that really struck me from our email conversations was the fact that you really don't have much spare time. This makes sense because of the time you put into your routines and checking. However, you need to teach yourself how to relax, how to have spare time without making it worry time. This will take some work so we are dedicating tomorrow's entire session to it."

"But I have to work at—"

"I know, and you'll still go to work. In life, that's what many people do—they spend half of a day at work and then get some spare time to relax during the other half of the day. I know you have the work part down. We just need to add the relaxing part.

"During your down time tomorrow, you are going to participate in some activities that are generally considered to be fun. You'll be watching a movie, playing a game, reading in the bathtub. Oh, and chatting online.

"That's where I will come in. We'll chat online tomorrow evening and discuss tonight's activity, your worst case scenario and odds. Then we'll also talk about all of this stuff that came up. I think it might be easier for you to write or type it, if I remember your first appointment correctly." He smiles. "Does this sound okay?"

It's worth a try. Nod number 603,969.

"Good."

He squeezes my hand and moves his own to pick up the check, leaving my hand right there in his lap. Instinctively, I begin to pull away, but I don't get very far. He grabs my hand and puts it back in the same spot in his lap. He gives it a firm squeeze this time before again moving to pay the bill.

I don't move this time, and his hand joins mine again moments later as I thank him for dinner. Neither of us lets go as we get up from the table. Or when we leave the restaurant and head for his car.

Inevitably, the moment comes when we have to separate to get into the car, but he takes my hand again the second we are settled. Our hands rest in the leather area between our seats.

The ride home flies by. He occasionally breaks our silence to give me some instructions for tomorrow. Putting Words with Friends on my iPhone. Trying to remember my password for the Facebook account Mandy set up for me years ago. Figuring out how to "friend" him so we can chat tomorrow night. He also wants me to try to omit one item from each of my routines tomorrow. I'm not sure what I'll do about that, but I'll have to think about it later. When we aren't holding hands.

Way too soon, we arrive at my house. He turns off the car and looks over at me. Calm, almost relaxed eyes.

His eyes don't leave mine as he lifts my hand up to his lips. Waterfalls of heat course through me as he places a soft, lingering kiss on the top of my hand. Slowly, he turns his head to rub my hand against his cheek and jaw line. One more kiss, this time on the palm of my hand, a searing gaze, and he places my hand in my own lap.

He comes to my side of the car, walks me to my front door, and says good night. Once his car is out of sight, I close my front door, take off my shoes, and breathe.

Chapter 17
day three

MY DAY OF RELAXATION BEGINS with exhaustion. I could not have slept more than three hours. That means I spent at least three other hours thinking about nachos. And calories. And clothes that might not fit me anymore.

Before I even get out of bed, I make two very important decisions. One: I am not weighing myself this morning. I can't face it right now. I will simply count that as the item removed from my morning routine. Two: I am not eating today. That should balance things out from yesterday. I'll weigh myself tomorrow and everything should be fine. And if it's not, I can fast tomorrow too.

Confident with my plan, I get out of bed and start my day.

AS I'M PUTTING MY HAIR dryer away, my phone buzzes.

Him.

Count. Open text.

```
Good morning, Callie. I'm sure
you are almost done with your
morning routine. Ready to re-
lax?
```

Smile. Count. Reply.

```
I guess so.
```

Seconds later, my phone makes an unfamiliar sound. It is coming from the Words with Friends application I downloaded last night. DA Blake has invited me to play a game.

Count. Accept.

He has already used a double word tile and earned eighteen points with the word "broth." *Ugh.* After at least seven minutes of thinking and maneuvering my letters, I come up with twenty-four points for the word "booth."

I go back to the bathroom to straighten my hair. Around ten minutes later, my phone buzzes again. He took another turn.

I play, finish straightening my hair, put on some comfortable clothes, and hear my phone buzz again. This time, there is an alert that I have a turn and a message as well. I didn't even know I could send messages through a game.

It takes me a few minutes to play a word and another few to figure out how to read his message.

`Movie time?`

That is all it says. It's 11:15 a.m. I guess I do have time now before work. I reply.

`Sure.`

For the first time in an eternity, I change the channel on my bedroom television. I find the cable menu and search for movies that can be viewed instantly. *Pretty Woman* catches my eye, and moments later, the movie begins.

My phone buzzes again. Another turn played. I push pause on the movie and come up with my response, pleased that I'm now beating him by thirty-eight points. I send him a fast message before putting down my phone.

`Hey! You are interrupting my movie!`

I add a small smiley face at the end of my message, hoping it might prevent putting a sad face on him.

Two minutes later, another buzz. Movie back on pause. He's played AND sent a message.

```
The kids are doing both nowa-
days. And more. Watching movies,
playing games, texting, eating,
talking on the phone—all at the
same time.
```

The kids? Yes, maybe thirteen-year-olds have time for all of this, but—

But I promised him I'd try.

So I play my turn, unpause my movie, and settle back on my bed.

After about twenty minutes of taking turns in our game and staring at Julia Roberts, I realize that I have been picking at my nails in between turns. I'm probably not supposed to be doing that.

It really is hard to sit here when I have so much to do. It doesn't help that my stomach keeps growling. I grab my notes for my paper on *The Scarlet Letter*—to fill in the time between turns.

I get a pretty smooth system going. Listening to the movie, writing down ideas for my paper, and playing my turns. I even decide to throw repainting my nails into the mix.

"What are you doing?" Mandy asks from my doorway. I didn't even hear the door open.

"Relaxing," I answer simply.

"Sure—it really looks like it," she says, laughing. "Hey—I'm heading out. I'll see you after work?"

"Yep." I'll be home tonight. Chatting on Facebook about sex. Can't wait.

"Careful, Mandy."

"Okay. Bye, Callie."

"Bye." I return to my relaxation routine, putting on a second coat of nail polish after taking another turn.

{In honor of my day, Bruno Mars sings "The Lazy Song."*}*

AT THE END OF THE movie, I have freshly painted nails, pages of notes written for my paper, and a 41-point lead in Words with Friends. Not bad.

And I feel pretty good—I haven't had any time to worry in the last two hours. Maybe I can get used to this relaxation thing.

My phone buzzes, this time with a text message.

`Ready for your next activity?`

It's 1:30 p.m. I guess so.

Reply.

```
Yep. What's next?
```

Seconds later, he writes again.

```
A long bath. For relaxing, not
scrubbing. Check your email for
your tub activity.
```

A tub activity?
Buzz. Another text.

```
Oh, and don't forget to bring
your phone.
```

Reply.

```
To the bathtub?
```

Buzz.

`Yep.`

All right…

I go to check my email. Some junk, a note from Dad making sure we are still shopping on Thursday, lesson plans (and date plans) from Dr. Gabriel…

Buzz. My phone again.

`Did you get it?`

Reply.

`Hold on, I'm getting there!`

I add another smile before sending.

Okay…the other emails will have to wait until later. I click on his email. He's sent me an electronic gift card to Amazon. He wants me to buy a magazine on my Kindle for my tub activity. So now I'm taking two electronic devices into the bathtub with me? That ought to be good.

He has included a list of suggested magazines. I recognize two of them as literary journals because I've read issues of both before. Under these titles, he's written, "If you find it difficult to leave your zone of comfort."

Next, he has listed two celebrity gossip-type magazines, just like the ones my mom subscribes to at home. Under these, he's commented, "I hope you pick one of these. It's easy to relax and escape your own life while reading about other people and their problems."

Lastly, he has included the title of a gourmet cooking magazine, under which he has simply typed a smiley face.

I take a moment to marvel at the fact that he understands my real connection to cooking well enough to joke about it after only knowing me for a couple of weeks while Mom and Dad will no doubt buy me yet another set of hardcore pots and pans for Christmas this year.

BUZZ.

`What did you pick?`

Reply.

`The celebrity nonsense :)`

Send.
Buzz.

```
Good.
```

I get ready for my bath after downloading the magazine on my Kindle. Oh so carefully, I step into the bubbly water and place my phone and Kindle on the ledge of the bathtub. I read. And take turns in Words with Friends.

When I start to get overly wrinkly and begin to think about getting out, I do feel rather relaxed. This celebrity gossip really can be pleasantly mind-numbing. Maybe that is why Mom likes it so much.

I get out around 2:40 p.m. Jeez.

My phone buzzes yet again.

```
Almost time for your leaving
preparations. Don't forget to
skip something! I'll chat with
you tonight.
```

Reply.

Sounds good. Thanks.

I get dressed, and thankfully, my purple and black color-blocked dress still seems to fit just fine.

3:00 p.m. I'm ready to begin my leaving preparations. I'm not quite sure how to omit one of my thirty-three checks. Then the numbering will be all out of whack, and something serious might happen as a result. To a family member. To me. To him.

This is ridiculous. Why take one thing out just to say I did and then end up messing up something major?

I could always omit three different checks, taking me down to thirty, but how would I even choose? What if I overlook something serious and my house burns down? Or floods—especially now that I found out that flooding isn't covered under normal homeowner's insurance.

Now it's 3:10 p.m. My fresh coat of nail polish is already gone. As I finally allow myself to begin my checks, my stomach makes a loud, angry noise. This, accompanied by the painful sensation I'm experiencing, must mean that my stomach is eating itself.

Good. Maybe I'll be back to normal by tomorrow.

Still focused on my rumbling stomach as I start my second round of thirty-three checks, I come up with a loophole for my predicament. I usually grab a cereal bar or snack before I go to work. I won't be doing that today. That can count as my omission, can't it? If he asks, I can truthfully say I left something out.

Pleased with myself, I finish my rounds of checking. And then I'm off to work.

THERE MUST BE A LOT of writing assignments floating around campus this week. Most of the computers are taken when I arrive at the writing center.

Brittany is here and that Luke kid is sitting right beside her tonight. They lean over to help each other or make comments or something every once in awhile. They look pretty comfortable. Maybe they are dating now. Love at first sight in the Pierce Writing Center.

Most of the other students keep to themselves, typing away intently. I get more tickets than usual, but I still have plenty of down time to get my own work done.

After typing a few pages of my paper on *The Scarlet Letter,* I decide to check my silenced phone. Just in case he's written. Making sure no students are looking my way, I slip the phone out of my purse. It's my turn in our game. I happily increase my lead to fifty-two points.

Ten minutes later, I reach for my purse to get a piece of gum. A few calories to settle my stomach a little. I slide out my phone and notice that he has played. He's also sent a message.

I look around. Everyone seems to be working.

Count. Open message.

`Aren't you supposed to be working?`

Count. Reply.

```
Aren't you? :)
```

Seriously—doesn't he have patients today? Where do they fit in with all of this texting and game playing?

He's written back already. Look around. Open.

```
I am working. I've dedicated my
day to spending some relaxation
time with a VIP patient.
```

Wow.

I don't know how to reply to that. I settle with a simple thank you. Seconds later, he sends another message—a colon and a parenthesis. A smile from the man who wouldn't even look at me during most of our first appointment together.

Another ticket comes in. More proofreading to do. Reluctantly putting my phone back into my purse, I get back to work. The students in the lab keep me busy with a steady stream of tickets, and soon it's time to go.

HIS NEXT MESSAGE COMES AROUND 8:00 p.m. I am already home and dressed in sweats.

`Ready to chat?`

I text back a yes and head to my computer. After logging in to Facebook with the password Mandy reminded me of last night, I also pull up the latest version of my paper.

HOURS LATER WHEN I TURN off my computer, I haven't touched my paper. I complete my night routine (in its entirety) in a daze and am in bed at 1:30 a.m. with a printout of tonight's chat session. Two chefs are on TV preparing some sort of Beef Wellington dish, but I don't really hear them as I begin reading through our night's discussion.

DABLAKE: Stop beating me in Words.

CALISTAROYCE: Stop playing sucky words, and maybe you'll win.

DABLAKE: I'll try...

DABLAKE: Ready to get started with our chat?

CALISTAROYCE: Yep.

DABLAKE: Okay, let's start with our nacho exercise reflection.

Stupid doctor terms—reflection sounds a lot like sharing.

DABLAKE: Let's talk about the odds of your worst fear actually coming true.

CALISTAROYCE: Okay...

DABLAKE: I assume your worst fear would be gaining a large amount of weight?

CALISTAROYCE: Well, gaining weight in general, yes.

DABLAKE: Okay. Can you think of some reasons why that isn't likely to happen after one night of eating nachos?

CALISTAROYCE: Because it can't. I

won't let it.

DABLAKE: Well, right. I'm sure you would do specific things to prevent it from happening. Like, I'm sure you went back to your structured eating routine today, right?

CALISTAROYCE: I definitely made sensible eating choices today.

DABLAKE: So you know that you have the willpower to go back to your eating plan after a day of splurging, right?

CALISTAROYCE: I guess so.

DABLAKE: So maybe it's okay to splurge once in awhile.

CALISTAROYCE: I don't know…maybe.

DABLAKE: Okay, let's talk about your worst case scenario, what you would do if your worst fear came true.

DABLAKE: What would you do if you did gain some weight?

CALISTAROYCE: I can't…I won't.

DABLAKE: But you worry about it nonetheless, so what would you do? Buy some new clothes, maybe?

CALISTAROYCE: No. It won't happen.

CALISTAROYCE: I can't think about that right now.

CALISTAROYCE: Sorry.

DABLAKE: It's okay. We can move on for now.

CALISTAROYCE: Thanks.

DABLAKE: Now…Tony. Do you want to start where we left off?

CALISTAROYCE: I guess so.

DABLAKE: Let's move beyond the night with the nachos—what happened next?

CALISTAROYCE: Oh…well, I started the 800 calorie thing, like I said last night.

DABLAKE: Did Tony know about that?

CALISTAROYCE: No. I didn't talk to him about any of it. I didn't eat in front of him after that either.

DABLAKE: How long did you keep that up?

CALISTAROYCE: The 800 calories? Until that trip to the health center.

DABLAKE: Why did you go to the health center that day?

CALISTAROYCE: I was scared.

CALISTAROYCE: I hadn't had my period in a couple of months.

I cannot believe I wrote that. Look at me getting all brave when protected by a computer screen.

CALISTAROYCE: I thought that I had completely screwed up my body. Irrevocably. I figured I would never go back to normal, never be able to have children...

CALISTAROYCE: It turned out that I stopped having a period because I had stopped eating all foods that contained any fat whatsoever. Apparently, the amount of fat you consume somehow has something to do with your period...or something.

DABLAKE: That's true. Did the nurse at

the health center talk to you about that?

CALISTAROYCE: Yes. AFTER my pregnancy test came back negative.

DABLAKE: Right. I guess she just figured that would be the most obvious explanation for your problem.

CALISTAROYCE: Yeah, I guess.

DABLAKE: But it made you angry.

CALISTAROYCE: Yeah, it did.

CALISTAROYCE: It was a pretty touchy subject at that time.

DABLAKE: Why was that?

DABLAKE: Callie?

DABLAKE: Callie?

DABLAKE: Are you still on?

CALISTAROYCE: I'm here. Sorry—Mandy came in to borrow a suitcase.

That was pretty good timing, Mandy.

DABLAKE: Oh, is she going somewhere?

CALISTAROYCE: She is going to go visit her boyfriend in Pittsburgh on Friday.

DABLAKE: So no Girls' Night on Friday?

CALISTAROYCE: Nope. Not this week.

DABLAKE: Couldn't you do it tomorrow night?

CALISTAROYCE: Nah. Melanie is leaving town tomorrow. And Mandy goes out every Thursday night.

DABLAKE: Oh.

DABLAKE: And you?

CALISTAROYCE: And I have therapy after class, right?

DABLAKE: Right. But I would've postponed for Girls' Night...

CALISTAROYCE: No big deal.

DABLAKE: Okay. Back to tonight's therapy.

DABLAKE: Why did that test make you so mad?

CALISTAROYCE: Because of Tony, I guess.

CALISTAROYCE: We weren't even dating at that point, but I couldn't get the whole thing off of my mind.

DABLAKE: What "whole thing"?

CALISTAROYCE: The relationship. The weight thing. The arguments. The breakup.

DABLAKE: Arguments about?

CALISTAROYCE: Sex mainly.

DABLAKE: Okay…

CALISTAROYCE: He wanted to have sex, obviously. I mean, he was a 19-year-old male. We'd been dating for a long time. And we were in college. It wasn't really a farfetched idea. For most people.

DABLAKE: But…

CALISTAROYCE: But I wasn't every other college girl. I've never been every other girl. Obviously.

Or we wouldn't have had to conduct this unconventional late night therapy chat session.

DABLAKE: And Tony thought you could be?

CALISTAROYCE: No...I don't think so. I think he thought he could change me. Or "fix" me, as I said before.

CALISTAROYCE: When that didn't work, he tried to manipulate me. Especially near the end.

DABLAKE: How?

CALISTAROYCE: He used my feelings for him. Tried to twist them around for his own benefit.

DABLAKE: How?

You already used that question, Doctor.

CALISTAROYCE: He talked about having a future together. He told me he thought that he was looking at the rest of his life when he was with me. I knew I didn't feel the same way.

CALISTAROYCE: I also knew he was lying.

DABLAKE: You didn't feel the same way?

CALISTAROYCE: Not really. I mean, I thought I loved him, and I was terrified of the idea of him breaking up with me. But I didn't trust him at all.

CALISTAROYCE: And I couldn't see how I would ever be able to share a home and have a family with someone who refused to understand the OCD thing, someone who antagonized me about it.

You used the word "share," Callie. Way to sound like a tool.

CALISTAROYCE: Oh, and the weight thing. After the nachos, I couldn't even have him touch me without cringing. That couldn't be the rest of my life. It couldn't.

DABLAKE: How did he react to the whole cringing thing?

CALISTAROYCE: I doubt he even noticed. And if he did, he would've just blamed it on the OCD. Never on himself.

DABLAKE: All right, so you just kept saying no to him about furthering the relationship physically?

I was right. He does spell "all right" correctly. *Figures.* The chefs on television have just plated their Beef Wellington. My stomach growls. *{Jimmy Buffett takes that as a cue to sing* "Cheeseburger in Paradise."*} Stop, Callie.* Back to reading.

CALISTAROYCE: Well, kind of. I did try to come around.

DABLAKE: How?

CALISTAROYCE: Well, I told him my conditions.

DABLAKE: Conditions?

CALISTAROYCE: Yes. Obviously, I was pretty worried about a couple of things. Pregnancy. Diseases.

DABLAKE: Pregnancy, I understand. But diseases? Weren't you two together even in high school? I had the feeling that you guys hadn't really dated seriously before each other.

CALISTAROYCE: We hadn't. But remember, I didn't trust him. What if he had slept with some other girl when he was out with his new obnoxious friends? What if he started doing drugs with those friends and shared a needle or something?

CALISTAROYCE: The numbers started to add up in my head. If he had slept with one girl, and she had slept with two other guys, and if they had each slept with three people…

CALISTAROYCE: Or…if he had shared some sort of needle with two other people, and they had each shared one with five other people…you can see how fast this all added up—just like in the old public service announcements about sex.

CALISTAROYCE: By the end of my calculations, he had approximately every single contagious and sexually transmitted disease.

CALISTAROYCE: And soon I would too.

DABLAKE: But you weren't going to let that happen.

CALISTAROYCE: Of course not. I got the most heavy duty looking condoms I could find after going on the pill.

DABLAKE: And he didn't agree to using a condom? Seriously?

CALISTAROYCE: No, he did. But I wasn't done yet.

CALISTAROYCE: I wanted him to get tested for Hepatitis, AIDS, everything.

DABLAKE: Oh.

DABLAKE: And he wouldn't do it?

CALISTAROYCE: Well, he fought it for a while. He told me that I was ridiculous and paranoid.

CALISTAROYCE: And I was, of course. But I still needed him to go through with it.

CALISTAROYCE: So eventually he did.

DABLAKE: Well, good. What happened?

CALISTAROYCE: According to the tests, he didn't have any diseases.

CALISTAROYCE: So we planned to spend the first weekend together when break ended and I went back to school.

DABLAKE: So he came out to Pierce that weekend?

CALISTAROYCE: He did. For the last time.

DABLAKE: You broke up?

CALISTAROYCE: Yes, he ended it after I didn't really sleep with him.

DABLAKE: Didn't really?

CALISTAROYCE: Well, we were pretty close. Clothes off. Me feeling like a whale. Condom on, lights off, and him just closing in. And me pushing him away just in time.

DABLAKE: Why?

CALISTAROYCE: It had been over a

week since his blood test and I couldn't stop wondering if he had slept with someone or done something since then.

CALISTAROYCE: He just wasn't clean to me.

DABLAKE: Mom always used that phrase—people that were and were not "clean to her."

CALISTAROYCE: I guess the terminology just comes with the disease. Like a package deal.

DABLAKE: I guess so…

DABLAKE: So he wasn't clean to you?

CALISTAROYCE: No.

DABLAKE: Was he ever?

CALISTAROYCE: I don't know. I guess it seemed so at first when our relationship was young and I thought I knew him. But once college started, and he had his new friends and new ideas, that all changed. Or became more clear maybe.

DABLAKE: So what happened next? After you pushed him away?

CALISTAROYCE: He exploded. About everything. He said that he was done trying to put up with me, that he couldn't "fix" me. So he left. And that was it.

CALISTAROYCE: I haven't seen him since.

DABLAKE: Wow. I'm sorry.

CALISTAROYCE: Don't be. I'm not anymore.

DABLAKE: But you were in the moment?

CALISTAROYCE: Of course. But not like you'd think.

CALISTAROYCE: Even though we didn't really do anything, I, of course, figured I was pregnant and diseased.

CALISTAROYCE: So I spent the next month taking over-the-counter pregnancy tests and trying to get myself to schedule a blood test for STDs.

CALISTAROYCE: Obviously, I wasn't pregnant. No immaculate conception for me. I did do some weird jumping up and down routines and some hitting of my abdomen to make sure no imaginary sperm somehow entered my body through a cut on my hand or something and managed to work its way through my body to impregnate me weeks later. Then I spent days feeling guilty about that. And I never did get myself to the doctor for a blood test.

DABLAKE: You realized you couldn't possibly have gotten an STD?

CALISTAROYCE: No. I still have to convince myself of that on bad days.

CALISTAROYCE: But I couldn't force myself to go to a doctor's office. I couldn't let someone stick a needle into me. Too many what ifs.

DABLAKE: What ifs?

CALISTAROYCE: What if the needle was dirty? What if the person who sat in the chair before me had a serious disease? What if the person bled on my chair?

CALISTAROYCE: What if I ended up getting a disease during the test? What if the test came back positive?

CALISTAROYCE: To name a few...

DABLAKE: Gotcha.

DABLAKE: So you were already pretty convinced that you weren't pregnant by that appointment in February?

CALISTAROYCE: Yeah. And I knew what I was (or wasn't) eating. I figured I was somehow causing what was happening to me.

DABLAKE: But you got better? You... it...started again?

CALISTAROYCE: It did. After a few months of eating some fat again, my whole cycle returned to normal. No permanent damages, thank God.

DABLAKE: Good.

DABLAKE: Callie?

CALISTAROYCE: I'm here. Just looking at your lame Facebook page.

DABLAKE: Lame? How so?

CALISTAROYCE: It's empty. You don't even have one picture posted.

DABLAKE: Oh—like yours is any better?

CALISTAROYCE: I at least have a picture up.

DABLAKE: Yeah, one. And you must be, what, thirteen in it?

CALISTAROYCE: Probably…

I really should change that picture. It's the one Mandy put up when she set up my account. Us as kids.

As my stomach groans yet again, I glance at the clock. 2:20 a.m. I should probably get some sleep soon. *{Jimmy Buffett exits, and Kelis comes in with* "Milkshake."*}*

DABLAKE: Is there anything else you want to cover tonight?

CALISTAROYCE: Not that I can think of.

DABLAKE: I have one other question then.

CALISTAROYCE: All right…

DABLAKE: Am I clean or dirty?

CALISTAROYCE: You are pretty clean.

DABLAKE: Clean enough to maybe dance with you tomorrow?

My breath catches just like it did the first time I read it.

CALISTAROYCE: We are going dancing tomorrow?

DABLAKE: You'll see...but am I clean enough?

CALISTAROYCE: Yes, I think so.

DABLAKE: Good.

DABLAKE: Then I'll let you go to bed. We're going to have a late night tomorrow.

CALISTAROYCE: Okay...

DABLAKE: Good night, Callie.

CALISTAROYCE: Good night.

I put the copy of our chat on my nightstand before settling into bed. As I lie down, I try my best to sleep, but

I am distracted by the cartwheels my stomach is making. I'm pretty sure they have nothing to do with hunger this time.

Chapter 18
day four

WHEN MY ALARM RINGS AT 6:00 on Thursday morning, another dream about him is cut short. In this one, we jousted for a while but then eventually the jousting turned into dancing.

I don't think I need to consult a dream reader about it.

6:10 a.m. My phone buzzes just after I sit down with a 250-calorie bowl of cereal.

Him. Already.

```
Day 4 Assignment 1: Try to post-
pone your grocery trip for a few
hours. Mix things up and go lat-
er in the day. Think you can
handle that?
```

Ugh.

Count. Reply.

I'll try…

Buzz. Open.

Good. More later.

Why does he have to mess with my grocery shopping? Especially now that I have my timing down to a science. Especially after my little fast yesterday worked and brought my weight back to normal…

I finish my cereal and begin my morning procedures. All of them.

Melanie calls around 7:30 a.m. She's leaving for Ohio in a few hours. Checking to see if I'm going to be okay. I say I will be. She doesn't believe me. Pretty standard. She tries to change the subject. Probably so she can jump back into it in full force later.

She talks for a bit about Mom's present and my shopping trip with Dad. Then she wants to know when Mandy is leaving. I'm not really sure. Sometime tomorrow, I guess. I'm sure this is somehow part of her build-up back into the "okay" discussion.

Yep. She's back into it full swing, telling me that I should just go with Mandy to Pittsburgh and then have Mom and Dad get me so I can spend the weekend with them. And then she or Mandy can drive me home, and—

This plan is clearly premeditated.

"Melanie, I have work to do this weekend. A big paper and a poetry portfolio. And I haven't even gotten Mom's gift yet."

"But you can—"

"No, Mel. I'm going to stay here. I'll be fine. Really."

"All right…if you're sure."

That is code for she'll have Mandy try to convince me to agree to the plan later. But I don't call her on it.

"I'm sure, Mel. Have a fun trip and be safe. I'll see you on Sunday."

"Okay. See you then. Bye, Callie."

We hang up. I'm sure she is already dialing Mandy's number. Too bad Mandy has an 8:00 a.m. class and her phone is probably on silent…

I finish my routine a little after 9:00 a.m. and then spend approximately twenty minutes picking at my nails and wishing I could go to the grocery store. If I go later, there will be people everywhere. Workers will probably be stocking shelves. Aisles will be crowded. Lines will be long. The parking lot wi—

No, Callie. You are going to wait. At least try to wait.

Or…I probably have enough food to last a little while. I could just go at 9:45 a.m. on Tuesday before class. I'm sure it will be pretty much like 9:45 a.m. on Thursdays. At least it will be better than going over the weekend when everyone has plenty of time and money from new paychecks to spend. And it will definitely be better than going later today.

Committed to my plan, I settle down to work for a little before my shopping trip with Dad. I pay some bills.

Try to write some poems about fields and rainbows.

My phone buzzes around 10:30 a.m. Unknown Number.

`Did you wait to go?`

Count. Reply.

`Yes, I am waiting.`

One. Two. Three. Send.

Back to writing stupid poems.

{Billy Joel's "Honesty" *chastises me quietly.}*

I don't know how I'm going to get a good grade on this poetry portfolio. I currently have a total of zero acceptable poems.

My phone buzzes again.

Him.

`Therapy tonight after class. I'll wait for you at your house just like Tuesday. Take your time.`

Reply.

`Sounds good.`

Send.
Reply again.

`Are we dancing?`

Send quickly.
Buzz.

`Maybe...`

Smiling at the phone, I put it on my dresser and go back to work.

I GET TO THE MALL at 3:00 p.m. and find Dad before I even get to our meeting spot. He's examining an iPad like he's never seen anything like it before. He probably hasn't. This gift shopping for Mom is the only shopping he ever does. It's normally quick and always at this little local Pierce Mall.

"Hey, Cal," he says as he gives me a hug.

"Hi, Dad. Thanks for driving to meet me."

"No problem. Thanks for your help. Have you ever seen one of these iPads before?"

"Yes, Dad. They are kind of a big thing right now."

"Oh. Do you think your mother would like one?"

"Um. Sure, I guess she could use it on trips and to chat with Abby and stuff."

His face is blank. "Well, all right. Let's get it then if you think she'll like it."

"Sure, Dad."

Ten minutes later, he has purchased an iPad, added a protection plan, and found a gift bag. Already freed from entering a mall until mid-December.

As we sit down for a late lunch, I reassure him that she will really like the iPad. She will, but she'll love the homemade card he'll make to go with it even better. She always does.

We talk about my classes, about Abby, about Jared's new girlfriend, and so on. He dances around the therapy subject, but I don't "share" any information. Not ready yet.

After he gets on the road, I make a quick run back to the mall where I pick up a sparkly iPad case, a protective cover, and an iTunes gift card.

Birthday gifts: check.

I only have a little time at home before class so I begin to pick out an outfit for this evening. I settle for jeans and a fitted scoop neck tee. Simple. Versatile. *{Michael Bublé steps up to an old fashioned microphone to sing* "Sway."*}* I waste a little more time writing crappy poetry and then start my leaving routine around 5:00 p.m.

Thirty-three checks done once.

Twice.

Three times.

Out the door.

TONIGHT'S PRESENTER PUBLISHES PHOTOGRAPHS APPARENTLY.

Seriously? I know all that stuff about a picture telling a story and everything, but really? Seems like my professor has run out of ideas…or maybe out of volunteers…

We begin watching a slideshow of pictures, stopping on every photo so Mr. Photographer can "share" his experience of getting each one published. Despite my original misgivings about the published material itself, the presentation is pretty interesting. After the slideshow ends, our presenter gives us a few pretty decent publishing tips, holds a very short question and answer session, and then lets us go.

As I walk to my car, I check my cell phone. It's only 7:45 p.m. I wonder if he'll already be waiting for me at my house. It is pretty early. And Mandy won't be there to let him in or anything so he'd just have to sit in the car and—

Well, I assume Mandy won't be there since it's Thursday night. But she hasn't sent me a text invite.

Maybe she's taking off this week to pack for her trip tomorrow.

I turn into my driveway around 8:00 p.m. He's already there. I park, turn off the car, and sit for a few counts of three. *{Faith Hill picks a suitable time to serenade me with* "Breathe."*}* And another few counts. The last time that I saw him, he kissed my hand. That was before he knew my whole non-sex history though.

A hand, his hand, is knocking on my window. Guess my counts are up.

I slowly push open my car door, and he takes a step to the side. Before I can even get one foot on the driveway, his open hand appears before me. I take it, letting him help pull me out of the car to a standing position only inches away from him.

"Hi." He's all twinkly eyes and flashy smile when he says it. *Wow*. The best mood I've seen on him. Before I can say anything back, he continues, losing a little bit of the razzle-dazzle on his face.

"What was wrong back there? In your car."

I look down. "Oh, I, um, was worried about Mandy," I improvise, noting that her car isn't in its spot. *Where is she?* Now I really am kind of concerned. She didn't text or call. Very unlike h—

"Why?"

"I haven't heard from her tonight, and normally on Thursdays she—"

"—texts you to go out for drinks even though she knows you'll say no."

"Well, yeah."

"I know where she is."

My head swings up. "You do?"

"Yes, because we are meeting her there."

Oh. Right. The dancing. Going out to a bar—one

of the items on my "dirty" list. Surprisingly, I feel some disappointment rise inside of me, and I have to quickly pound it down.

"Is that okay?"

"Sure." I recover in a second, pushing away the image of the two of us slow dancing at a quiet, private restaurant. That wouldn't make sense, I realize, as we walk with linked hands to his car. He's not trying to cure me of a debilitating fear of immaculate, exclusive restaurants.

Too bad.

The trip to the uptown bar is fast. Silent as usual. When we get out of the car, he takes my hand to lead me inside. I'm sure Mandy will just love seeing this.

Please don't embarrass me. Please don't embarrass me. Please don't embarrass me, I mentally plead with her.

We are stopped by someone who I assume is the bouncer. I feel pretty out of my league, having never really done the whole going to an uptown bar thing before.

"Relax, Callie, and get your ID out."

I do as I'm told and reluctantly give my ID to the sweaty bouncer who runs it through some scanning machine. I guess that's how things are done at a college bar…a way to check that college students aren't lying or doing something stupid. A tradition much like the health center's pregnancy test custom…

I really wish he didn't have to touch my ID. I really wish he wasn't so sweaty…

"It's okay, Callie. Release the tension and remember your relaxation techniques." I try to focus on my breath as I watch him take my ID and shove it into his own pocket.

"I'll give it back to you after an hour or so," he says to answer the question on my face.

Oh. After an hour—when all potential (and imaginary) disease germs on it have died. Good call.

We get into the main part of the bar, and it's not quite as crowded as it is in my scary visions (pick any scene from *Coyote Ugly*), but there are still way too many people.

My hand secure in his, I follow him through tables, past dancers, and around waiters, and I pray that I don't bump into any bodies or objects on the way. He seems to know exactly where he is going. He does. We end up at a table in the back corner where Mandy and some of her sorority sisters are seated. Hillary, the redhead who spent a night throwing up in our downstairs bathroom about a year ago, sees us first.

"Callie!" she screeches as she stands. "It's been too long."

Please don't hug me. Please don't hug me. Please don't—

In a super smooth maneuver, my hand is dropped and an arm circles around my waist. His warm, strong arm. *{An unidentifiable voice sings the opening of Gershwin's* "Someone to Watch over Me."*}* It does the trick. Hillary is distracted by the gesture, and she quickly nudges Mandy. Hug averted.

Mandy's eyes linger for only a moment at his hand around my waist, and she quickly welcomes us over, showing us two empty seats. We walk over, and he releases me to pull out my chair. Actually, he pulls out both chairs and quickly inspects the seats and backs. *{The song continues, louder now.}*

"Your chair, my lady," he says with a silly smile, gesturing for me to sit.

Adorable.

We both sit down and I nod my hellos to the girls

around the table. Most of them are looking to my left, at him. *Vultures.* I look over at him. He doesn't acknowledge their looks. Because he is looking at me.

A waitress shows up almost right away to take our order. She stands only inches behind us, so close that I think I can feel her breath on my neck. I hope she doesn't accidentally spit while she's talking.

"She'll have a margarita, and I'd like a Jack and coke, please," he says before I can even think about what to order. "Wait—Callie, do you want salt?" He looks at me intently.

I nod and mouth a thank you before he turns to the waitress to tell her. *{And even louder.}* Mandy's sorority sisters have about three different conversations going on among the six of them. I can hear all of them and none of them at the same time. It's kind of nice—not unlike my cooking show white noise.

My margarita arrives in a fancy (and clean) glass, and he leans over to whisper in my ear.

"Try to enjoy your drink, Callie. You can even go over your one drink limit tonight, if you want…"

His breath feels like…I don't know. There isn't a word good enough.

I guess he takes my silence as resistance. He goes on.

"It will be fine either way. You aren't driving. You have no one you need to take care of tonight." He grabs my hand on my lap. "And I'm here to take care of you."

That. Sounds. Perfect.

I squeeze his hand and nod. And then I take a sip of my drink with my other hand. We sit like that for a while, silent amidst all the chatter at the table.

Eventually, he leans over again, whispering, "How is the bar experience so far? You okay?"

I nod. Oh so close to his mouth.

This bar is much better than I expected. I have breathing room. A clean seat. No one touching me.

Well, no one else touching me.

I smile at the thought as I take another sip of my drink. Surprisingly, there isn't much left to sip. He notices too, and before I know it, I have another drink in front of me.

Probably ought to slow down, even though I don't really feel any different. Just a tad calmer than usual, maybe.

"Are you okay to drink this?" he asks quietly, even though he is the one who ordered it for me. "I don't want you to feel any pressure if you don't want—"

I shake my head with a smile. "Nope—I'm fine for now."

"Thank you," I add in a quieter voice.

He squeezes my hand, which has been all entangled with his for quite some time now. For one entire drink anyway…

I'm just starting my second drink when Mandy begins reading directly from Melanie's script.

"Why don't you come with me to Pittsburgh tomorrow, Callie?"

Before I can say a word, she continues.

"Mom or Dad will pick you up on campus, and you can hang out with them and already be there for Mom's dinner on Sunday."

Jeez. You'd think Melanie would have taken the time to change up the monologue a tiny bit. Didn't she think that I might recognize it?

"Well?" Mandy prompts, shrugging up her shoulders a little and raising her eyebrows.

"Thanks, Mandy, but no. I have so much work to

do…a paper due Monday and an entire poetry portfolio to do before Tuesday." And a therapy session tomorrow night.

"You could bring your work with you."

"Yeah, and get it done at Mom and Dad's house?" I throw back with a smile.

She doesn't say anything because she knows I'm right. There will be neighbors Mom wants to visit and shopping to do and dinners out. And no time for paper writing. For sure.

"Okay…I guess…but if you change your mind, I'm not leaving until after my classes tomorrow."

I can't believe she gave in that quickly. Melanie would be pissed. Lucky for Mandy, I'm too grateful to tell on her.

Mandy goes back to texting something on her phone (to Melanie?), and I try to lose myself in her friends' garbled conversations again. All of a sudden, one of them (a pretty, toothy blonde—I don't remember her name) jumps up and starts grabbing the hands of the girls sitting on either side of her. Apparently, some important song is playing. From what I can make out of their jumbled sentences, it is "badass" and "totally sick." I don't recognize the song. Nor do I fully understand their verbal description of it.

Mandy, who seems to understand the significance of the song, starts to move with them toward the dance floor. She takes a few steps away from the table before turning back to me, making a motion for me to join them. She doesn't have time to wait for my response though because the excited blonde is tugging at her arm and shouting something with her insanely white teeth.

"What do you think?" he asks with a grin. "You wanna dance to this 'sick' song?"

Smiling up at him, I give him my nod.

We stand up and he leads me to the dance floor, definitely taking the path least traveled. We end up in the corner with Mandy's group. She and her friends are dancing in a circle, which they immediately enlarge to let us in. We have plenty of room, really. No one is brushing up against me or touching me.

Unfortunately, he isn't even touching me right now. We sort of dropped hands as we joined the circle and started to dance. He does keep looking over at me, checking on me every two seconds. Even when he's surrounded by all of these bouncy girls—girls who won't stop staring at him. I can't even blame them.

He looks pretty natural here. Who knew he could dance? It looks like he's even holding back a little. Probably so he can keep an eye on me. But I'm not going to pass out or throw up or anything anytime soon. I don't think.

I feel pretty good. A little buzzed from my one and a half margaritas and moving in a circle of people on a dance floor in a bar. Pretty unbelievable.

The all-important song ends, but we stay in our dancing circle as, I guess, less exciting songs are played. In the middle of a song, he stops dancing suddenly and reaches into his pocket, pulling out a pager.

I can't believe doctors still use those. Do stores even sell them anymore?

He glances down and then looks at me. All worked up. Completely distraught. *{Cue Damien Rice. Cue Damien Rice. Cue Damien Rice.}*

"I have to make this call. Tell me what you want me to do. Do you want to come with me outside or would you rather stay here with Mandy?"

I weigh my options. I'm here in this circle with

people I know (or kind of know—Mandy knows them at least), not bumping into anyone. Walking outside means walking through the crowd, having to pass the sweaty bouncer again, standing on a dirty sidewalk in the dark where I'm sure people have dropped all kinds of trash and—

"I'll stay here."

He looks surprised. "Really?"

Nod number 999,999.

"Look at you," he says with a smile. "I'll be right back."

He will be right back. I know that. So I keep dancing.

Mandy throws a smile my way as she spins around with her arms up. She looks proud. Like her big sister is so brave, dancing in a bar without her psychologist. I smile back and keep moving until the song ends and the first slow song of the night (or at least since I've arrived) begins to play.

Shit.

Mandy and her gang decide that it's a good time to take a break and get another drink. That means I need to make my way back to our table.

Shit. Shit. Shit.

I feel a soft tug at my hand. *Too soft to be him.* I look up, and it's Mandy. I mouth thank you over and over as she guides me off the dance floor. After several steps, I feel a tug at my other hand. *Too harsh this time.*

Oh my God. I turn and try to free my hand, but I feel myself being pulled away from Mandy. The hand dragging me is rough. And sweaty. When I look up to see its owner, I again think rough and sweaty. No idea who he is.

"No need to waste a slow song, beautiful," the

stranger slurs as he turns toward me, still pulling me further back onto the dance floor.

I freeze as tension rips through my body. This man, this mass of germs is going to pull me nearer to him. Any second now.

"Oh—you wanna dance here? Thought you'd want to be closer to the speakers."

This is it. He's twisting my hand out, trying to force our bodies closer together.

I can't get away. I can't convince my limbs to move. And our bodies are going to be smashed together in three, two, on—

Other arms encircle me, smoothly pulling me back, back, back against a hard, tense body. *His body.*

"What's going on here?" he asks in a loud, angry voice that I've never heard from him before. He keeps his arms around me, one slung loosely around my neck and the other firmly around my waist.

"Just trying to have a little dance," Rough-and-sweaty drawls.

"Well, it's not your dance to have." He pulls me back even further, our bodies completely molded together. My would-be dance partner holds his hands up in the air (Meaning he gives up? Or he's sorry? I don't know) and walks away.

I don't move. After a moment, he carefully turns me around to face him.

"I'm so sorry, Callie. I'm so, so sorry."

I meet his eyes. He is that sorry. And miserable.

He doesn't move his eyes as he reaches into his pocket, saying, "Where did he touch you?"

I look down at my rigid hands, which are still hanging awkwardly in the air in front of me, touching no other part of me.

I watch him rip open a packet, one of those super germ-eliminating, disease-preventing wipes and remain still as he thoroughly cleans my right hand and then my left. I don't move. A moment later, he rips open another package and repeats the process. And then he does it again with a third wipe.

After he opens the fourth packet, he cleans his own hands systematically. He then pulls out a plastic bag from his pocket and deposits all of the used wipes and empty packaging before tying it shut.

When our eyes meet again, he is questioning me silently. Did he do enough? Should he—

"What is going on?"

Mandy.

"Where did you go, Callie? What happened—"

"I'll take care of her—don't worry," he answers for me without moving his eyes.

"Oh, great. I just—" Mandy begins.

"Don't worry," he says again, hesitantly moving his eyes to her. "But hey, do you mind throwing this out for me?" He hands her the plastic bag, and she takes it immediately before turning to go.

"Thanks," he calls after her.

And then he's looking back at me, questions hanging in his eyes.

"Thank you," I somehow get out.

"Is there anything else I need to do?"

I shake my head. "No—you took care of it just like I would have. Even better. I don't have easy access to those wipes."

He smiles as relief fills his eyes.

"We'll go soon," he says. "I have to call that patient for an emergency phone session in an hour."

I nod.

"We can go right now if you want," he continues.

I shrug my shoulders as I shake my head. "No, it's fine. Whenever you are ready." My voice is shockingly calm; somehow I must actually mean what I am saying.

He smiles. "Then how about that dance with me?"

A dull ache, his dull ache, begins surging through me. I manage to nod, and he's moving closer to me, pulling my body into his. Arms touching. Hips touching. Everything touching. My head resting on his lower shoulder. His hand on my upper back.

A song is playing, I'm sure, but I can only hear the sound of his breathing.

It might be a slow song. I don't know. It doesn't matter. We move back and forth, back and forth in our own rhythm.

I feel his lips on the back of my head as his hand slides from my back up to my hair. Gradually, I turn my neck so I now face him when I place my head back on his shoulder. Inches from his neck. *{A song is playing, I'm sure, but I can only hear the sound of his breathing.}* He rubs his head against mine, and the throbbing in my stomach overwhelms me. Turning my face up to his, I have to wait no more than a blink and his lips move right to mine. An extravagantly slow, gentle kiss. I don't know how long our lips move together or who pulls back first so we can each take a breath.

He trails kisses across my cheek as he pulls me even closer in to him, mumbling, "Callie." I put my head back on his shoulder and crush myself against him.

And then his pager goes off again. Of course.

As he pulls back a little to grab the device from his pocket, he looks up at me quickly, his hair disheveled, his eyes scorching.

Another beep comes from his other pocket, and he

soon has to steal his eyes away to read the text on his cell phone.

"My emergency phone session is now an urgent hospital visit. We have to go."

I nod into his intense eyes. They haven't yet lost all of their fire.

Grabbing my hand, he carefully navigates us back to our table so we can pay our bill. Mandy is there shrugging on a sweater.

"Oh, you guys are going?"

I nod as he says, "Patient crisis." He flings some cash into the bill holder and hands it to Mandy, asking if she minds taking care of it.

"No problem," she says. And then, "Why don't you let me take Callie home? I was planning to go soon anyway so I can pack for tomorrow."

" No, I want to—" he starts.

Mandy breaks in. "Get to the office or wherever you are going. Really. I only had one drink tonight, and that was a couple of hours ago. I am fine to drive, and you really need to go."

He looks at me.

"I'd really like to take you—" he whispers before his phone beeps again.

He reads another text and looks up at me regretfully.

I nod and say, "Go. I'll be just fine."

"We'll even walk out with you," Mandy pipes in, adding some cash to the bill holder and turning it over to the other two girls at the table.

I grab my purse off the back of my chair before he grabs my hand and leads me outside to Mandy's car. Mandy jumps into the driver's seat, and he opens my door.

"I'll text you when I get home," he promises as he

squeezes my hand. "It might be really late."

Nod. Smile.

"Bye, Callie."

"Good night, Aiden."

Chapter 19
day five

MY FACE IS STILL SMILING when I wake up on Friday morning. Last night starts rushing through my mind before I even open my eyes. Our dance. His lips. Warm trembles throughout me. The heat in his eyes. *{Damien Rice starts AGAIN.}* Mandy's teasing in the car. Her endless stream of questions. Her comments about his designer-smelling cologne. The fact that I could still smell it on my skin before my shower last night…

His late night text. How sorry he was about having to leave so suddenly. Still having my ID. How he had a great night. That he'll talk to me tomorrow.

{He sings louder and louder. Over and over.}

Now that it's tomorrow, I should probably get moving. I do, unfortunately, have class with Dr. Gabriel in a few hours.

Morning preparations. Let's go.

10:00 A.M. A TEXT COMES JUST as I am putting my steam mop away. I run right to my dresser to check the message.

`Good morning, Callie. Hope you slept well. Therapy today around 8:00 p.m. I can pick you up at your house. Sound okay?`

I write back.

`Sounds good. See you soon.`

Soon. Does that sound too eager? Desperate? 8:00 p.m. is ten hours away, after all. Not really soon.

Erase text. Start again.

`Sounds good. See you then.`

Too informal? Like I'm not looking forward to seeing him? I did say that I had a good time when I replied to his text last night, but this is today. I don't want to sound indifferent. Or cold.

Erase text. Start again.

```
Sounds good. See you then. :)
```

Good, I think.

One. Two. Three. Send.

I head to the shower and then complete my morning and leaving preparations. Before I leave for class, I say goodbye to Mandy. Tell her to have a safe trip. To have fun. That I'll see her on Sunday.

She tries one more time to convince me to go with her and tells me to call or text her if I change my mind before she leaves when her class ends at 2:00 p.m.

Smiles. Hugs.

I leave for class, hoping that the murderers won't be waiting for me when I return to the Mandy-less house. I am also hoping that by some miracle Dr. Gabriel has taken the week off and won't be in class.

I'm not that lucky. When I walk into the classroom, he's in the front of the room talking to a girl with an extremely high ponytail and a shirt that says "Porn Star" on it.

Classy. *{And now for a rousing rendition of My Darkest Day's* "Porn Star Dancing."*}*

Their conversation ends. The girl bounces back to her seat, her ponytail swinging back and forth the whole way. Dr. Gabriel starts class. A lengthy monologue about the art of persuasive writing.

Eventually, the persuasive presentations begin. Dr.

Gabriel doesn't ask for any help with comments today. He hasn't even really looked at me.

Not a problem.

Following a presentation about the benefits of changing the drinking age to eighteen, Miss Ponytail Porn Star herself comes to the front to give her speech about saving sex until marriage.

Unreal.

The presentations continue on and on. I listen to the students, try to memorize some of their names and faces, and pick at my nails.

Oh, and think about last night. And him. And tonight.

When class ends, Dr. Gabriel calls me over to talk about topics I'll be teaching. He thinks we should meet for lunch at some point to discuss everything.

Seriously?

In an attempt to avoid any face-to-face meetings, I tell him that I have a rather full schedule over the next week and ask him to email some of the information for me to look over. He seems hesitant, but he does agree to email me.

Excellent.

I leave the classroom and head to my car, pulling out my phone to check for any messages. No text messages, but there is a little number two on my Words with Friends icon.

I click on the icon. He took a turn. He's still losing. I play and further extend my lead. I also have a new game request from Melanie. Of course. She found a way to check if I am surviving while she and Mandy are away. Guess if I'm taking turns it means I'm not in an institution or dead or something…

I take a turn, but she is already beating me. Figures—she is always at least three steps ahead of me in everything.

Okay, time to go home. Before I can even get my key in the ignition, he has played again. He is going to have to wait. Car on. Go home.

WITH FRESHLY WASHED HANDS, I settle on my bed and get to work on my paper. *{R. Kelly's* "Ignition (Remix)" *ends and begins again for the three-hundredth time since I left campus.}* Each time I complete another hand-written page, I allow myself a few minutes to take my turn in our Scrabble-not Scrabble game. He keeps playing only moments after I take my turn. Melanie hasn't played another turn yet at all. Guess she's slacking on checking up on me. *Thank God.*

After a few hours, I have successfully written out all but a conclusion to my paper and, more impressively, beaten him by over one hundred points in our game. He, of course, has already started a new game with me.

Does he ever work?

7:30 p.m. I begin to get ready for the night ahead. I have no idea what to wear so I opt for jeans and a Pierce hoodie.

After my 400-calorie salad dinner, it is time to start my leaving-the-house routine. Thirty-three checks completed three times. Ten minutes until 8:00 p.m.

Nail picking, anti-murderers in my house praying, hallway pacing, him thinking, more nail picking. And it's 8:00 p.m.

The doorbell rings right on time.

Here goes.

In my haste to open the door, I do somehow remember that I should be on the lookout for the murderers so I peek through the little peephole. I'm so glad I do. I can't see much, but I can see his big, relaxed smile and three yellow roses in his hand. Even though I take a few deep breaths, I cannot manage to wipe the gigantic smile off my own face before I open the door.

He meets my eyes and silently hands me the roses. My right hand grazes his when I take the little bouquet, and I feel the smile slip from my face at the sight of his burning eyes. All the fire from the dance floor has been reignited.

"Callie." He breathes out my name and grabs my empty left hand. He pulls it right to his face, rubbing his stubbly cheek against my palm. With another little tug, he has my fingers on his lips. He takes the time to kiss each one, his eyes locked with mine.

By the time he traps my pinkie finger between his lips, I can no longer hold myself back and I fall into him. In less than an instant, his lips find mine, and we drink each other in—arms and hands and bodies scrambling to get closer and closer. More and more entangled.

Just as my lips make their way to his neck, a deafening honk pulls us both out of the moment.

"What the—" I begin, still wrapped in his arms.

"It's okay." He smiles, nodding to the street in front of my house. "Part of tonight's session." Judging by the look in his eyes, he hasn't completely removed himself from our moment.

Can't we just stay he—

Another honk, and my eyes and thoughts are redirected to the street in front of us where a gigantic bus is parked. *Ugh.* The party bus…used to take drunken college students from bar to bar on weekends. *Marvelous.*

As the bus door opens, LMFAO's "Party Rock Anthem" begins to spill out. The greasy driver is staring right at him…at me…us…with a full-blown smirk on his face.

Disgusting.

"Why don't you run your flowers in the house and then we can go." Flowers. In my hand. Right. I forgot about them.

After disentangling myself from him, I place the three roses on the small table in the hallway before meeting him again on the porch. Door locked. Handle twist. Handle twist. Handle twist. *Right in front of him.* He holds out his hand and gives me what I assume is supposed to be a reassuring look. I'm not sure that I can be reassured right now. Not even by him.

Nonetheless, I take his hand and follow him into the huge, loud mode of public transportation. He leads me up two large, relatively clean steps one at a time. No traces of trash, gum, or throw-up—much better than I envisioned. The creepy driver hasn't stopped staring at us, probably since he first pulled up in front of my house. As if we are seriously the most fascinating people he has seen in ages when he spends his weekends driving around drunken freak shows.

Get some perspective, toolbag.

Unfortunately, bigger problems await me when I reach the top of the stairs. College students are everywhere—some in seats, many roaming around in the bus. Why are they allowed to do that?

Some are singing to the radio—now playing FUN's "We are Young." *Perfect. Just perfect*—some are making out, and some are yelling conversations that pretty much consist of sentences about how hammered they are going to get tonight. I guess I'm lucky that most of them aren't already drunk. Thank God we didn't have therapy scheduled for 1:00 in the morning.

"Do you want to sit here?" He has found two empty seats together in the front of the bus. The seats aren't empty though. The blue hotel carpet-looking upholstery has large black splotches in various places. I'm pretty sure that means scraped off gum. There is also a candy bar wrapper shoved in the crevice between the two seats, right by a little tear in the blue fabric.

"Um, no. Let's just stand."

I think he understands that I intend to stand right in the front of the bus and not brave the area in the back with all of the swarming, shouting bodies. His hand begins to reach for the bar above us, but he pulls it back after probably seeing the flinch on my face. He manages to balance himself by jamming one foot beside a seat and the other against a pole in middle of the aisle.

The bus begins moving again. I guess the driver couldn't find it in himself to look at me when it might have been important, like to make sure I'm not just randomly standing in the middle of the bus before peeling away from the front of my house. Fortunately, as I begin to stumble backwards, I am caught by strong and steady arms.

"Relax—I have you," he whispers into my ear before beginning to massage my shoulders. I close my eyes and try to focus on the heat of his breath on my neck and the pressure of his hands.

The bus jolts to briefly pause at the stop sign at the end of my road. His hands fly from my shoulders to around my waist, and he pulls me even closer against him.

"Are you okay?"

My ear brushes his lips as I move my head up and down. His body tenses behind me before he further tightens his grasp around my waist.

{Now a performance from Alison Krauss. "When You Say Nothing at All."*}*

After letting my head drop back against his chest, I close my eyes and allow him to hold me. Or allow myself to be held by him.

I can do this. I am doing this. Even though we're not in the laps of the obnoxious partygoers in the back, we are riding public transportation with them. I'm not even too annoyed by the noise they are making. Their blaring conversations coupled with the songs from the radio distract me from my thoughts, from actually acknowledging that I am here on this bus.

It begins to rain outside, and the patter on the windows joins the mix to create a new kind of white noise. The rain gets stronger and louder, and the partiers get noisier, but I feel fine somehow. In his arms. Safe. Balanced. Dry. *{Let's do that refrain again.}*

I wonder how long we will ride tonight. Hopefully long enough for the rain to stop but not so long that anyone behind me has to pass us on his or her way out.

Good thing your wishes aren't too complicated, Callie.

It doesn't appear that the rain will be stopping for a while. Lightning and some cracks of thunder turn it into an all out storm. But it doesn't matter. I'm content right here, in no rush to leave my spot.

{Ah...one more time.}

The bus lurches to a stop right by one of the dining halls on campus. As the doors creak open, some rain, going sideways now, pounds onto the inside steps. Guess that would have been helpful if they really had been as dirty as I imagined.

Seconds later, two rather bulky guys start to walk up those stairs to get on the bus. I realize that they will have to pass me, and my body stiffens. They are soaking wet and talking loudly. Apparently one of the guys just fell, and the other guy finds it hilarious.

"It will be okay, Callie."

As one of the guys calls the other a "pansy ass" for falling in the rain, I feel myself being pulled, still standing, into the space in front of our would-be front row seats. He is still behind me, almost in the same position as before, but we are now standing sideways in front of the seats. I try to convince myself that I can just throw out my jeans, which are now rubbing against the lower seat cushions, when I see it.

The "pansy ass," the one who just fell, is bleeding. His arm, which he is holding up like a freaking trophy, has a long open gash on it, and he has blood on the front of his Pierce t-shirt.

Dizziness comes upon me as I realize that he is only about two steps away from me. When he takes his next step, I start to taste salad dressing in the back of my throat, and my chest begins to heave. He must notice because in the second before the "pansy ass," the gash, and the blood are right beside me, I am yanked down into a seated position on his lap. We are both sitting in the window seat, and his arms are somehow wrapped more tightly around me than before.

By the time I frantically look up, the two guys have already passed. *But it's too late.* I feel my entire dinner rising in my throat, and I fight to stand up out of his hold.

"Don't move the bus!" he yells as he helps me stand. I am torn between wanting to run for the door and needing to stay as far away from that area as possible (in case some blood dripped on the floor).

That very thought takes the decision out of my hands because I can't hold back any longer. I throw up right there in the aisle of the bus and am overcome with a million separate noises that in no way blend into something comforting. Students are yelling and laughing, the music is still blaring, the bus driver is screaming for me to leave the bus since I'm clearly too drunk to be going out...

And him...repeatedly saying, "I've got you," while squeezing my hand and trying to move me forward. It's too much. I pull my hand from him as tears begin to fall out of my eyes. I feel everything welling up in the back of my throat again.

I try to move forward, but I'm not fast enough. Right beside the driver, right at the top of the stairs, I throw up another time. More yelling, more orders from the driver, and then a hand on my back guiding me around the mess, my mess, down the stairs, and off the bus.

We are both drenched within seconds, but we don't move. The bus peels out of its spot, this time splashing us with dirty rainwater. I move forward, away from his hand on my back, and throw up one more time right there on the side of the street.

Home. I need to be home. In my shower. Now.

"Home," I mouth the word, and he nods before reaching for my hand.

"I can't," I whisper, shaking my head emphatically.

Even though he looks crushed, he nods, moves his hand back to his side, and says he understands. I have no way to deal with his emotions right now so I keep my head down, shielding my eyes from the beating rain, and start walking toward home. He follows suit, walking right beside me in silence.

We make it the whole way to my house just like that—no talking, no touching, no more throwing up. When we get to my doorstep, he quietly asks if I want him to come in, if I want his help. I shake my head, even though I'm sure he already knows my answer. He tells me that he is sorry, and his tormented eyes meet mine.

I can't fix that right now, and it makes me feel even worse. Throwing my hand over my mouth, I nod and run inside my house.

I'M STILL IN THE SHOWER. It's been over an hour, but I can't manage to get out yet.

This isn't working. I really am trying, but I'm not getting any better, and I keep wounding him. I want to get better. I don't want to lose him.

But how? Dozens of little solutions, none of which will actually work, swim through my mind as I stand under the steady stream of hot water.

And then I hear thunder again. The storm seemed to be letting up when we got back to my house, but here it comes again.

Remembering all of my dad's lectures about not bathing during storms, I shut off the water, step out, and wrap myself in a towel, hoping that the storm will end before it's time for my next shower. I then lose myself in my night preparation routine, putting all of my energy and concentration into each task. Rigid, mindless activity for a couple of hours. Just what I need to settle my stomach a bit.

The storm tapers off around midnight. I make my

next shower as quick as I can because I feel certain the thunder and lightning will resume at any moment.

I am right. As I'm putting my hair dryer away, the storm picks up in full force, and the house lights flicker.

Seriously? This had to happen on a night when I'm already alone, completely vulnerable to the murderers?

Grabbing the emergency flashlight out of my nightstand, I continue my routine. The lights flicker some more while I put on lotion and get into my pajamas, and the power goes out completely about three minutes after I turn on the television and settle into bed.

Now what?

Neither the tree branches banging angrily on my windows nor the booms of thunder have much of a chance at lulling me to sleep. Neither do the occasional creaks in my house, noises that I can only assume mean that someone is sneaking up to my room to kidnap me.

Calling Mandy or Melanie would be futile; they are miles and miles away.

Unless…maybe that is my answer. Perhaps I should jump in my car and drive to Pittsburgh now. Hmm…but that would involve…driving through a storm, driving in the dark, and, well, driving in general. Not going to happen.

My body begins to overheat as though straining to hear each and every noise in the house involves strenuous physical exertion.

Throwing off my duvet, I feel less burdened by the covers as well as exposed to the murderers who must be pretty close to my room by now. I consider my options. I could get up and do my routine over, but I would have to do the whole thing with a flashlight in my hand. And if I accidentally drop it, where would that leave me?

I could try to play some of the songs on my iPhone,

but that's never worked before. Music alone has never turned into my white noise so I doubt it will miraculously happen tonight. Besides, playing music would eat the battery of my phone, and then I'd really be in trouble if I did need to call someone.

Little scenarios begin running through my mind. In one, I'm falling out of bed and cracking my head open. In the next, I'm having some sort of seizure or stroke in my bathroom. In another, the murderers are pounding on my bedroom door. In each little scene, music is playing from my iPhone, and when I grab the phone to make a 911 call, the battery dies.

Feeling chilled by my thoughts, I pull the covers back over my body. Okay. Definitely no music. Banging my head back into my pillow, I try to think of a better idea.

If I call Mandy or Melanie or Mom…or even Dad or Jared, I know that any one of them would drive to get me right now. But I can't do that. First of all, it would be unbelievably inconsiderate and selfish, among other adjectives I can't think of right now. More than that, though, it wouldn't be safe. I can't have them driving in the middle of the night in a thunderstorm—I can only imagine what would happen.

Left with no real options, I decide to pray over and over for the storm to end and for the power to come back on. Simultaneously, I seriously consider buying a generator tomorrow.

In the middle of my seventh round of prayers, my phone buzzes on my dresser. Might as well check it as I have nothing else to do. I throw off the covers, lower my legs out of the bed, and grab the phone.

One text message from Unknown Number.

One. Two. Three. Open.

```
Callie—I'm about to ring your
doorbell. Please grab a flash-
light and carefully come to let
me in.
```

What? Now? It's so late. And I'm only wearing shorts and an extremely oversized t-shirt.

That thought makes me jump out of bed to begin a dark search through my dresser drawers. But it's too late. The doorbell is ringing. I can't make him stand out there in the storm…

Clutching my flashlight, I navigate down the stairs, through my house. Before opening the front door, I use the peephole to make sure it's really him.

It is. He's standing on my doorstep just like he was only a few hours ago. No roses this time. No collared shirt either. He does have an umbrella.

I fling open the door and am swept right up in his gaze. A lot anxious. A little sad. And still somewhat heated.

{Lionel Richie's "Hello" st—}

"What would you like me to cook for you tonight?"

I think about my used up calories for the day and my empty refrigerator for a split second before realizing what he is really saying.

"Oh. Anything will do the trick. Hot dogs. Macaroni and cheese. A bowl of cereal."

"Good." He's still standing outside in loose sweatpants and a t-shirt. Rain cascades over his umbrella.

"Come on in." I say it without letting myself think about whether I should or about what it might mean.

Without moving his eyes from mine, he sets his umbrella on the porch and steps inside the house. Right beside me. I point my flashlight up between us so we can both see a little. Still gripping my eyes, he shuts the front door, locks it, and twists the handle three times. He then slips out of his shoes and asks me where he can put them. I point to the towel, my shoe towel, just beside the door, and he breaks our eye contact for a moment to place his sneakers there.

When he turns back around, his eyes take a quick detour, starting at my bare lower legs and sliding up to my exposed left shoulder before again meeting my gaze.

"Callie—I'm having trouble thinking like a doctor when I'm around you. To be honest, I'm having trouble thinking at all." Pause. "Sometimes I just want to ditch this whole therapy thing so I don't have to keep seeing you in so much pain. So I can stop feeling so guilty about being your doctor and wanting…"

He stops talking, but the look on his face finishes the sentence for him.

"And I keep breaking all therapy protocol, not discussing worst case scenarios, trying to do some routines for you, massaging your tension today before letting you try to breathe on your own. Kissing you…"

{Meredith Brooks' "What Would Happen" *tak—}*

"And none of this is your fault, and I shouldn't be burdening you with all of it right now when you have plenty of other things to think about—especially after the day you've had." Another pause. "I'm sorry. I haven't shut up since I walked in. Do you want me to go?"

"No," my lips whisper, my head shaking emphatically back and forth. Silently grabbing his hand, I use my flashlight to guide us back through the house, up the steps, and into my room. He follows me, clutching my hand and walking without saying a word. When we begin going up the stairs, I feel his hand on the lower part of my back. Protecting me. Burning me. I slow down my pace to eliminate almost all of the tiny space between us.

When we reach the top of the steps, I can only hear heavy breathing, but I'm not sure if it's his or mine—or both. We finally make it into my bedroom, and I can't hold back any longer. I turn myself around in his arms and raise my mouth to his. His impatient lips crash into mine while his hands run over my back. Just as I begin to tug him closer to the bed, he pulls back from our kiss.

"Callie—wait."

No. I shake my head, but he probably can't see that so I move one of my hands, one of my fingers, up to his mouth to shush him. He traps my finger between his lips, caressing it with his teeth and tongue.

Yes. Trying to keep a moment's focus, I gently pull back my finger and slide my hand down to hold his. I take him over to my dresser where I click off the flashlight and put it down. Then we both turn toward the bed.

I sit down first and then pull him in to me. As we lie back, my lips find his neck while he begins trailing kisses all over my bare shoulder. Thunder crashes outside, but our bodies keep moving together. Entwining. Exploring. Kissing.

My restless hands find his hard chest underneath his t-shirt. Just as my mouth follows and my lips press against his chest, I feel his entire body tense.

"Callie. Callie. We have to stop, Callie." He breathes out my name as a moan, his own body rejecting his words.

His hand finds my hair, and he presses my head

down sideways to rest on his chest. He runs his fingers through my hair for quite some time before he speaks again.

"Callie, I can't do this. I want to do this. More than I've ever…more than you know. But I can't. We can't."

Lying on his chest, breathing in his magazine page cologne, I wait for him to say more. I don't have to wait very long.

"It wouldn't be fair to you. I know you haven't… that you have fears that…"

He stops speaking, and his hand pauses to rest in my hair.

"I know what happened with, um, what happened before. And I know what you needed him to do before you…I'll do that for you, I mean, if you even want to—"

"Stop." I raise my head up so my chin rests on his chest. If we had any sort of power, I would probably be able to see into his eyes right now.

I continue. "Yes. Yes—I want to do this. But you don't have to—"

"I want to do it for you."

"But I know that it's crazy. That I'm crazy."

I wish I could see his eyes during the silence that follows.

Eventually, his hand begins moving through my hair again, and I hear his mouth open to speak.

"I understand. And I'm starting to love your crazy."

Wow. All of a sudden, I'm unbelievably indebted to the storm for the power outage. Since I can't really see his face, I'm pretty sure he can't see mine right now. *Did he just say—*

"Now, Callie, let's get you to sleep."

He softly moves my head back to its sideways position on his chest as he manages to pull the covers up around me, around us. Once he's tucked us both in, he loses his hands once again in my hair.

"Tonight, we will be preparing a baked macaroni and cheese dish," he begins.

I close my eyes and find myself drifting off rather quickly.

"To begin, we need to preheat the oven to..."

Chapter 20
another weekend

WHEN I AWAKEN, IT IS light outside. I am still in the same position, tucked comfortably in his arms, on his bare chest. Judging from his heavy breathing, I'm pretty sure he is still asleep so I nuzzle my head further into his chest and plant three kisses on his warm skin.

A slight gasp comes from above me. Guess he's awake now. I lift my head to look at him, and he gives me a lazy, boyish smile before starting to talk.

"And that is how you make a delicious dish of baked macaroni and cheese. Simple as that."

After playfully swatting him on the arm, words start spilling out of my mouth.

"You really get me. The food thing with the sleeping." He nods and a somewhat distant look comes to his eyes.

"Mom did it too."

Oh.

"But with her, it was sports. A sports channel had to be on every night all night so she could sleep. But when people asked her about her favorite teams, they were met with a blank stare."

I just nod. Sounds about right.

He is looking at me, but his mind is far away.

"I'm so sorry about your mom. I didn't mean to bring her—"

"No—it's fine." He's coming back. "There are a lot of similarities…" He blinks his eyes, shakes his head, and flashes me a smile. "So, should I make you some real breakfast or what?"

Sure. If you want to make something out of crackers and ketchup packets.

"Well, you might have trouble creating something from the contents of my fridge."

"Right—the not cooking thing. I guess you only buy prepackaged-type foods."

I nod. "Yeah." But he won't find many of those right now either.

In a bold move, I decide to come clean. "My fridge is pretty empty right now in general." I look down at his chest. "I skipped grocery shopping this week."

"Guess I'm not the only one completely sucking at our therapy." He laughs as he says it, and I meet his amused eyes.

"Completely sucking, huh? Is that a technical term, Doctor?"

He manages a pseudo-serious face before firmly saying, "Yes, it is."

Charming. He's freaking charming lying here in my bed. Under me. Making me feel more carefree than I have felt in…forever. Who says he's not good at this therapy stuff?

Just as I begin to reach up to him for a kiss, my cell phone rings. *AARRGGHH.* Giving him a frustrated smile, I get up and grab my phone.

Melanie.

"Hey, Melanie. How is your trip going?"

She talks for a couple of minutes about hanging out with her in-laws and about shopping in Ohio. It sounds like she's having a good time, like she's not actually working every second for once.

While she talks, I notice that my alarm clock is blinking and wonder when the power came back on. I also begin to feel self-conscious about my lack of clothing so I slip into bed and pull the covers up over my legs. He wraps his arms around me and pulls me closer. It feels perfect.

Melanie brings up my trip to Pittsburgh. Of course. She makes me tell her exactly what roads I'll be taking and when I intend to leave. I tell her, mainly because I know she'll just keep calling and asking until I do (if she doesn't make Mandy do it).

She must be at least temporarily satisfied with my answers because she tells me she has to go get Abby dressed. We say our goodbyes and hang up.

"Do you always recite MapQuest directions so early in the morning?" I can hear the smile in his voice.

"If Melanie calls, you never know."

"It sounds like she must be pretty nervous about your trip."

"Yeah. She knows that driving is not my most favorite activity. It will be fine though. For Mom's birthday dinner, I can manage some time in the car."

He runs a finger up and down the exposed part of my arm. It's dizzying. It's even hard to remember how much I despise driving while he does that.

"So the dinner is tomorrow evening?"

"Yep."

His finger moves up and down, up and down, up and down…

"Okay. I have a proposition for you."

"This ought to be good." I can only imagine that this will involve some sort of evil therapy session tomorrow morning or afternoon. Unfortunately, I can also imagine myself going along with whatever it is just so I can see him.

"I want to drive you to Pittsburgh."

What?

"No—did Mandy put you up to this?"

"She didn't. So you don't need to say no. Let me do this. Think of it as an apology for all of the rough stuff you've gone through this week."

Oh, the irony.

He continues. "Or maybe as a thank you for trying. However you want to think of it is fine. Just let me take you. I can drop you off and hang out in Pittsburgh a little until you are ready to go home. Unless you would rather go home with Mandy, of course."

"No, no, no." I shake my head forcefully, bumping into his shoulder as I do. "I will be fine. Really, I'm not even that worried about it."

Guess I'll have to add lying to today's confession list.

"Well, I'm worried about it."

"Ah…so you have no faith in my driving, and you've never really even seen me behind the wheel."

"No, that isn't it. I am concerned about your anxiety levels, your worrying."

"That's not necessary. I'll be fine. New topic."

Nestling my head into his shoulder, I focus on his finger still caressing my arm.

"I'm not ready to change subjects. I told you that I have a proposition—there's something in it for you too. Something that won't be easy to turn down."

"What is it?" I say it with as much irritation as I can muster, considering the fact that I am resting in complete comfort pressed up beside him.

"Well, my guess is that you have something to do this morning. Something that will probably take, I don't know, approximately three hours. Something pretty structured and, I'd imagine, kind of personal." His finger stops moving on my arm. "If you don't let me take you tomorrow, I'll stick around and watch every second of your little morning activity."

Raising my head in surprise, I see his self-satisfied grin.

"Wow, Dr. Blake. Look at you making light of a highly serious, very rational medical condition." I stop to smile. "I'm rather pleased with your progress—two weeks ago, you couldn't see any humor in it."

"Well, I'm trying my best. Especially when it works to my advantage."

As he raises his eyebrows in amusement, his eyes twinkle. They actually twinkle, these eyes that occasionally seem to hold all the sorrow in the world.

He knows that he has me stuck. Obviously, I don't want him to watch my mortifyingly lengthy and precise morning routine. And it's pretty clear that I'm not physically or mentally capable of just skipping it. So it looks like he'll be driving me to Pittsburgh.

"Fine. You can take me. But you can't just drop me off—Mom would kill me for my bad manners. You'll have to sit through dinner." *So there. This won't be all Patty Cake and Go Fish for you either.*

"That sounds nice, if you don't think I'll be imposing. I can't remember the last time I was at a family dinner."

That's right. No relatives for miles and miles. I

can't imagine…

"No—you'll have to stay to eat. They'd be pissed if you didn't."

"Well, I don't want to piss off your family before I even get to meet them." Get to? "So I will keep up my end of the bargain and leave you to your morning festivities."

He squeezes my shoulder, plants a soft kiss on my lips, and takes himself out of my bed.

"I really wish you'd go to the grocery store today, but I know to ask you to do that would be futile. If you want, I can pick up some—"

As I step out of bed, I shake my head to stop him. No, he is not picking up my groceries. Even though it would be nice to avoid going to the store for another week…

We begin walking out of my room.

"All right, well, I'll talk to you later so we can make plans for tomorrow," he says as we go down the stairs.

Nod number 1,263,966.

At my front door, he pulls me in for one more kiss.

"Thanks for letting me stay with you, Callie."

"Thanks for cooking me to sleep."

He smiles and goes. Once I see his car pull away, I close the door, lock it, twist the handle three times, and run to the hallway bathroom to look at my smile in the mirror.

So this is what my face will look like if I'm ever cured of my anxiety. I'm not sure that I'm on a path to a cure though…I think this is something different altogether. With that thought in mind and the smile still on my mouth, I launch my morning preparations.

DESPITE THE FACT THAT I can't stop replaying last night in my mind, I have a rather productive day. My paper on *The Scarlet Letter* is typed and printed. I've played several words in the games on my phone. (I'm still beating him, but Melanie is destroying me.) Another week's worth of sins have been forgiven. (I hope—I'm still not entirely convinced that the slate is wiped after confessing each sin only once.) I've somehow managed to scrounge up enough granola bars, fruit snacks, and cups of yogurt to eat a full day's worth of calories. If I could just knock out some poems for my portfolio, I'd be set.

While I'm trying to focus on inspirational things to say about rainbows, Melanie calls again. She has found a bus that I can take to Pittsburgh tomorrow, and she knows I hate public transportation, but she thinks that maybe this will be better than having to drive, blah, blah, blah. Considering my recent bus trip, I highly doubt I'd rate driving as the greater of the two evils. She doesn't really give me the chance to say that, though, as she's already started to talk prices and departure times.

Even though I don't want to bring it up, I do want her to stop talking (and I don't want her to go ahead and buy me a bus ticket) so I tell her about my new plans for tomorrow. She reacts more maturely than I would have expected. I'm sure that will change once she talks to Mandy.

Using a polite flight attendant or perhaps gala hostess voice, she tells me how kind that is, how nice it is that I've found such a dedicated doctor. I pretend to buy this as real conversation, as her honest thoughts, so the discussion will end already. Might as well let her go so she can call Mandy and Mom and maybe even Jared.

It's probably better this way—if they know in advance, maybe they can get their jokes over with and manage game faces by the time tomorrow night arrives. *Here's hoping.*

We say goodbye, and I go back to my pointless poetry writing attempts.

9:00 P.M. HIS FIRST TEXT COMES after I've already started my night preparations.

Hey—stop playing such big words! You are killing me here.

Smiling, I reply.

Sorry—I find it relaxing to beat you unmercifully. Isn't relaxation the whole point of our game, Doctor?

My phone buzzes again seconds later.

`So you would say I am succeeding in the relaxation portion of your treatment?`

Reply.

`Something like that.`

Carrying my phone with me in my pocket, I continue my routine. My hip starts vibrating as I begin scrubbing the microwave. It only takes me a few moments to rip off my gloves, throw them in the trash, and wash my hands in the kitchen sink. After I towel dry my hands, I pull out my phone.

Another text.

`So...how was your day?`

I threw out a pair of gloves for that?

Reply.

Good. Busy. And yours?

While waiting for his response, I grab a new pair of gloves and finish the microwave. My phone vibrates again as I'm cleaning the front of the dishwasher. I force myself to wait to check his next text until I'm finished with the kitchen and this pair of gloves.

9:33 p.m. Gloves trashed. Hands cleaned. Phone out.

Well, my day started rather nicely. It's been pretty boring since then...

I don't need to run to a mirror to know that I'm blushing.

Reply.

Rather nicely, huh? Is that what you say to all of your patients?

Phone back in pocket. New gloves on. Time for

bathroom cleaning.

My phone buzzes twice while I'm sterilizing my bathroom, but I again force myself to wait until I finish my task to check his messages.

Message one.

`No, Callie, not at all.`

Message two. Sent only seconds after the first.

`I hope you don't think that I would do something like that.`

Fabulous. Now I've not only upset him yet again, but I've also made him wait for my bathroom to be cleaned before giving him a response. *Considerate as always, Calista.*

Count. Reply.

`Of course I don't think that.`

Count. Send.

I stand for quite some time in the middle of my bathroom waiting for a response. One doesn't come.

Eventually, feeling too disgusting to spend any more time not getting clean, I put my phone on the sink counter and start my shower. While scrubbing and shaving and conditioning, I strain to hear any noises from my phone. It's obviously hard to hear with all of the water running over me, but I'm pretty sure I don't miss a buzz. I'm pretty sure there hasn't been one. *He's not going to write back.*

As I shampoo my hair for the second time, I decide that I will send him another message if he hasn't written by the time I've finished drying my hair. Yes, my decision makes me feel like a twelve-year old. *{Cue Justin Bieber with some song that I'm pretty sure is by him but I don't know the name of it.}* I spend the rest of my shower trying to come up with something to say, some magical words that will make him feel better. He can be so freaking serious. How could he think that I would actually accuse him of making middle of the night visits to all of his patients? *Disgusting.*

But he did say he wanted to get tested for me. Guess that means he has made some middle of the night visits to someone. Or someones. How many, I wonder. Probably not a question I should ask in my upcoming text…

By the time I've finished drying my hair, he hasn't sent me a message, and I still have no idea what to write. I guess I could ask about our plans for tomorrow…but what if he's changed his mind?

To buy myself more thinking time and, well, because it's the responsible thing to do, I check my closet one more time for the murderers before applying my body lotion. Then I get dressed for bed. For the first time that I can remember, I put on old pajamas. The same pajamas I wore last night—I couldn't make myself wash them today. Maybe his lingering scent on them will help me get some sleep during my last night without Mandy.

Mandy. She hasn't called or texted since she arrived in Pittsburgh. She's probably busy going—

Stop, Callie. Focus.

After flipping on my television, I grab my phone and get into bed.

Okay…a text…

Still no ideas. I start to type him a good night, and then I hear the TV chef announce tonight's dish.

Baked lobster macaroni and cheese. *Unbelievable. Perfect.*

Erasing the start of my message, I begin again.

It looks like I'll be falling asleep to another cook's take on baked macaroni. This one has lobster in it though. And I hate lobster. Guess your dish wins.

Count. Send.

Please write back. Please write back. Please wr—

Buzz.

Count. Open.

Thanks, I think.

He's still so distant.

I have to fix this—before I go to sleep. Not that I'll be able to sleep anyway…

{Rod Stewart's raspy voice sings most of "So Far Away."*}*

Got it. It's gonna take, as Jared would say, at least one pair of balls.

Count. Reply.

`Maybe you should come over to cook me something better.`

One. Two. Three. One. Two. Three. One. Two. Three.

Onetwothree. Onetwothree. Onetwothree.

Onetwothreeonetwothreeonetwothree.

Send.

Squeezing my eyes shut and trying to block out the swarm of questions and potential outcomes knocking at my brain, I lie completely still in my bed. *{The song begins again.}*

Stupid, stupid, stupid, Callie. He's probably trying to think of a clinical way to say no. Or he's already fallen asleep and will get my message in the morning and think it's ridic—

Buzz.

Ooonnneee. Tttwwwooo. Ttthhhrrreeeeee. Open.

```
Under one condition: You'll have
to be wearing more clothes than
you were yesterday, or I'll nev-
er make it through the night...
```

He's back. And already making me flushed.
Reply.

```
I'll see what I can do.
```

Send.

Time to change clothes, I guess. I change into a slightly longer pair of shorts and a somewhat more fitted t-shirt before folding up my other pajamas and putting them on top of my hamper—just in case I want to wear them tomorrow night. Then I sit down on my bed to wait, not wanting to start something and risk triggering the need to restart my night preparations.

After all ten of my nails are scraped off plus about ten minutes, the doorbell rings.

When I get downstairs (with the help of lights this time), I take only a second at the peephole before opening the front door.

He's smiling.

Thank God.

I smile back and step aside to let him in. He wordlessly takes off his shoes and puts them on the towel before shutting the door and twisting the handle one, two, three times. He then takes my hand and lets me lead him back up to my room.

When we again stand in front of my bed, this time illuminated by the glow of the television, he speaks.

"You aren't really wearing much more than you were last night." He smiles.

"I trust you," I whisper as I stretch my arms around his neck.

"You probably shouldn't." His voice is husky, and the smile has faded from his face. His eyes start sucking me in.

As I move in closer, our lips all but touching, he murmurs, "Callie, you are going to kill me." His lips brush mine as he says the words, making any attempts at resistance entirely worthless.

He covers my lips with his and wraps his arms around my waist. I allow my hands to roam—through his hair, on his chest, down his back…whatever I can get away with. When I reach the bottom of his back, right where his sweats begin, I don't stop, pushing further into him and moving both hands down, down, do—

"Callie—oh my God, you really are killing me."

He pulls back, leaving my hands empty and the rest of me completely breathless.

"Soon," he whispers. And then his eyes search mine anxiously. "And then only if you want to."

"I don't think you have to worry about that," I manage to get out while trying to restore a normal breathing pattern.

"Good." He looks pretty relieved as he kisses my forehead and leads me to my bed.

"I'm planning to take that test early this week," he

continues as he gets under the covers.

In an obscenely bold move (I'm definitely going to check tomorrow morning to see if I've grown testicles), I ask exactly what I want to know.

"Have there, um, been that many others?"

"No." He shakes his head and motions for me to get in beside him.

His eyes glaze over, and he's somewhere else again so I get into the bed, pull up the covers, and wait for more.

{Brandi Carlile starts wailing "The Story."*}*

He takes my hand and then positions himself so he is on his side facing me. His mouth opens and closes a few times before he actually begins to speak.

"There has only been one other person, I mean, other than you when we, if we…"

Oh.

I think he's looking for some sort of reaction from me. I also think he is trying to work his way up to saying more so I squeeze his hand, lie down on my stomach, and nod in the hopes that he'll continue.

It works. *Nice strategy, Callie*. Looks like I'm a degree away from being a psychologist myself–a psychologist with balls, apparently.

Focus, Dr. Royce.

"She was a girl I met in a graduate class. We were, um, engaged."

Wow. I can't say I expected that, but I do my best to keep a game face.

"We dated for a few years before I, ah, proposed. Things didn't get really bad until after I put that ring on her finger."

Where is she now? Who ended it? Do you still love her?

Those are the questions you want to ask, Callie?

Upon further thought, I should probably never study any type of counseling.

He moves to his back and looks up before continuing.

{Brandi's song continues but fades into the background, thank goodness, so I can hear his words.}

"I guess there were signs before we got engaged. She spent a lot of money and always wanted to go out for expensive meals and extravagant activities. But we were dating, and this was my first adult relationship so I really had nothing to judge it against.

"That stuff didn't really bother me anyway. I had money, especially after I finished school and started my job. I guess I was just happy to have someone to spend it on."

He pauses and peeks over at me. To see if he should go on? To see if I have questions?

None that I'd like to voice right now, thank you.

A teeny tiny nod and a brief smile from me, and he goes on.

"She never had much patience for my mom though. That always bothered me. I tried to move my plans around to suit what my mom would or couldn't do. If a restaurant was so crowded that it freaked her out, I would leave with her. If she called and wanted to talk, I would spend long periods of time on the phone with her. And whenever Dad would call to tell me she was in panic mode, I would drop my plans to go over and try to help.

"You know, stuff a son should do for his mom. Just decent human being stuff, really." Pause. "That's how I saw it, but my fiancée didn't agree. I think she was embarrassed by Mom. She seemed much more irritated than concerned when Mom had freak-outs in public. I never really understood why it all irritated her so much. Sure, we might have had to leave a restaurant or two, but it's not like Mom was screaming or making a scene or anything. No one else probably had any idea what was going on so there really was no need for embarrassment.

"But my fiancée, um, Elizabeth, was like that. So concerned about things like whether the shade of her eye makeup was exactly right and whether the buckles on her purse matched her jewelry. It was exhausting."

Maybe he's somehow missed how exhausting I am.

He hasn't. "Not that Mom's issues weren't exhausting. But she couldn't help it."

He is still looking straight up at the ceiling, basically creating a verbal free write. Almost as though he's forgotten I'm here. It's kind of nice though. It seems like his thoughts are less censored this way.

"Anyway, we got engaged. Even though the Mom stuff bothered me, I figured that all relationships had to come with some problems. I proposed, and she started moving ahead with wedding plans right away. Mom even got excited about hearing the plans. I think she really liked it when we'd show her pictures of the dresses or the flowers, or, well, that other wedding stuff.

"I would try to get Elizabeth to take pictures over to Mom, and really, she did go to see her quite a few times. She even took copies of reception menus to her when she was in the hospital. I guess that was probably the last time she saw her."

He stops talking. From my side view, I can easily see the big, labored swallow he takes. He then does this thing where he rubs his upper teeth along his lower lip.

Do I say something? Or move closer? Or—

He shakes his head, appearing to shake off the direction where his mind was heading. When he starts talking again, he sounds all doctory, clinical.

"Mom died shortly after that, a couple of months before the wedding, and I, obviously, was in no frame of mind to be talking tuxes, or program covers, or honeymoon packages.

"That was okay for about a week, and then I guess it was unacceptable. We had some pretty major fights where she yelled at me as I sat and listened. I tried to tell her to just keep making plans, that I would trust her judgment. But that wasn't good enough for her." Pause. Another big gulp. "She called it all off about a month before the wedding, a month after Mom died."

He rolls back over to his side to face me. "All right, now you know a case history of the only person I've ever slept with. I don't anticipate having positive results for any diseases since we were each other's firsts, we always used condoms, and, well, because no symptoms or anything have shown up over the past few years."

He smiles…ish. "Sorry—that's gross to say." Real smile now. "You still want to sleep with me?"

I nod. I don't know what to say. Or how to take this sudden mood change.

Rolling over toward me, he pulls me into the nook of his arm. "Good. Now, I believe I promised you a meal." He begins to "make" London Broil, and I eventually pretend to fall asleep. A little while later, he trails off, and I soon hear heavy sleep breathing beside me.

Luckily, the television is still on to lull me to sleep hours later when I'm exhausted from thinking of possible answers to all of the questions lined up in my head.

HIS STORY STORMS BACK INTO my mind as soon as I open my eyes. {"The Story" *is already playing again too. Or has it been playing all night?}* I try to push it aside as he looks over at me and smiles.

"Hey. You better get up and get your routines moving. We have a road trip to take today."

Mom's dinner. Right. I'm going to have him drive me to my mother's birthday party the day after he's recounted all kinds of events surrounding his own mother's death. *So unbelievably thoughtful, Callie.* I've got it all together just as well as usual.

"You know, I really can drive myself to this. You don't need—"

"Stop. I'm taking you."

He squeezes me further into his side with his arm, the arm that has been around me all night. I really hope it's not asleep.

"Unless, of course, you'd like me to get some popcorn to watch your morning show." I can hear him smiling.

Ugh. "Fine. When should I be ready?"

We discuss our traveling plans, and he soon heads out to leave me to my preparations. He kisses me goodbye, but it's brief. He's still not all here, even though he's trying to pretend otherwise. Perhaps I should tell him that, for him, pretending to be normal should not involve a cheesy smile.

Of course, I don't tell him that. I wave as he drives away, shut the door, and get to work.

Morning routine. Leaving routine. Church. Wrap Mom's presents. Another check-in call from Melanie. Stare at poetry notebook for a couple of hours while picking my nails and never even reaching the point of needing a pen. Leaving routine.

3:30 p.m. He's here. Open door. Grey pants. Royal blue dress shirt unbuttoned at the top. No tie. Casual, comfortable. Big smile. Not fake this time.

He leans in to brush his lips against mine. "Hi," he whispers, only a centimeter from my face. I close the space between us, my lips finding his and my hands grasping the collar of his shirt to pull him closer yet.

{An oldies station accompanies us. The Supremes with "I Hear a Symphony." *They get more than halfway through the song before—}*

"Callie, Callie, Callie," he mumbles against my lips as his hands continue to move up and down my back, my neck, my hair. "We have to go. You know we have to go. Dinner. Your mom's birthday. Remember?"

"Yeah…I remember something like that," I breathe out between kisses on his cheek and neck. As I rub my head against the slight stubble on his cheek, he leans down to my ear, breathing once before speaking. Heated, hot, hot breath on my ear.

"Soon," he promises again in a whisper.

Not soon enough.

Unfortunately, I know he is right so we disentangle ourselves, and he waits as I triple check the lock on the door. He then takes my hand to lead me to his car. His screaming quiet car. Is his radio broken? Does he really not have an iPod?

His car is not quiet for long this time. He fills the silence with constant questions, continuous chatter. He asks for a run down on my family members. I scrounge up what information I can think of, spending more time on Jared and my sisters than on my parents. I probably offer no more than one sentence on Mom.

He seems genuinely interested in my siblings and

tells me how different it is to have grown up as an only child.

{Cue The Beatles (once again) with "Eleanor Rigby." *Guess we really are on an oldies' station today.}*

When we finally arrive at my parents' house, he probably has enough information to write a decent sized research paper on my family. He parks the car, and we head toward the house. He doesn't hesitate to grab my hand, the one not holding Mom's presents.

Guess that sheds some light on the question I couldn't get up the nerve to ask: *How am I supposed to explain you to my parents?* Since we are holding hands, I'm guessing that introducing him as my doctor isn't really good enough. Doctor with benefits? But not really all of them yet because first I'm insisting that he is tested for all possible sexually transmitted diseases. Or, wait, is he the one insisting?

The door opens before we even get up the last porch step. Dad and Mom are both standing in the doorway like they are in some holiday food commercial or something. Melanie has clearly filled them in on my traveling company.

"Glad you could make it," Dad says as he opens the door. Normally they both would have hugged me by now, but I'm still attached to him.

Here goes.

"These are my parents, and Mom, Dad, this is Aiden."

Our hands naturally drop in the jumble of greetings. Dad promptly shakes his hand while Mom gives me a cheesy grin.

"Happy birthday, Mom," I blurt out in an attempt to wipe off her suggestive grin and, well, because I really do hope she is having a nice birthday. As I hug her, I hear that low, soft voice from behind me.

"Yes. Happy birthday, Mrs. Royce." He reaches out to shake my mother's hand as he says it. Smooth. Natural. Charming.

Dad motions for us to go inside so I lead the way to the dining room. Dinner isn't bad. The steaks Dad grilled are good, conversation flows pretty freely, and Mom seems to really like her presents. There are only a couple of differences from any other family dinner—the arm that periodically reaches over under the table to squeeze my hand, and the nudges and looks shared between different sets of my family members when they think no one else is watching.

{Here's Elvis Presley and "Suspicious Minds" *with a special dedication message for my family members: Hello—could you be any more obvious?}* The only person acting completely normal is Abby, who has sung a number of songs, shown us several dance moves, and tried to get out of eating the asparagus on her plate.

When it is eventually time to go, both Melanie and Mandy offer to drive me back. Before I can give either of them a response, they are both gently told no, that he will take me back, that he wants my company on the trip. I, of course, offer no arguments. We say our goodbyes, thank my parents for dinner, and wish Mom a happy birthday once more.

When we finally step back out to the porch, each holding bags of leftovers and extra slices of birthday cake, he smiles, takes my hand again, and leads me down the driveway.

I barely even notice the silence playing in his car because we spend almost the whole ride discussing dinner, particularly my family members and their not so inconspicuous looks at each other. After we imitate looks and nudges, impersonating all the different people from Dad to Jared's girlfriend, he suddenly switches to a more serious tone.

"I guess we should have a better definition for us, for what we are exactly, before I attend another family gathering with you." He says it quietly as he looks ahead at the road in front of us.

Say more. Say more. Say more. What do you want us to be?

Nothing. Guess I have to respond.

"Yeah, you are probably right." I also look ahead as I respond, kind of grateful that he is driving during this awkward discussion.

This is where the silence comes back at full volume; for the next ten minutes or so, until we pull up in front of my house, neither of us says anything. He meets me as I step out of the car and walks me to my front door.

We stop on the porch, and he wraps his arms around me. After a slow, lingering kiss, he pulls back slightly so he can meet my eyes.

"I want you to think about your treatment—where you want to go with it and what we should do." He pauses as he runs a hand over my hair. "I also hope you'll think a little bit about us and what we're doing here, what you want. If you're ready for a relationship with me…"

I start to open my lips, but he puts his finger over them. "Don't answer tonight. Think tonight." He starts to rub his finger slowly across my bottom lip. "I know how difficult it is for me to think clearly around you so I'm going to go in case it's the same for you. Besides, Mandy will probably be back any minute—with plenty of questions, I'm sure." He smiles and presses another light kiss on my mouth. "I'll miss you tonight."

"Me too." *Me too. Me too.*

"Good night, Callie. I'll call you tomorrow."

"Good night, Aiden."

Chapter 21
day six

{THE SCAN BUTTON HAS BEEN pushed, and I'm hearing a new over-the-top love song every three seconds.}

Maybe his scent on my two-day old pajamas triggers the medley. Or maybe it's because his words from last night have been tumbling through my mind for hours. I guess it could also be part of my anticipation about going to see him today—to give him my answer to the question I needed no time to consider. I even have a plan for his first, less interesting, question about my therapy. A plan that might help. A plan that might improve our therapy. But he'll find all of this out when I surprise him before my obligatory appointment with Dr. Spencer.

For now, I need to get moving—time for class in a few hours. On your mark. Get set. Morning Routine.

1:00 P.M. I LEAVE CLASS, RELIEVED to have turned in my paper and already thinking about my *Jane Eyre* assignment. Not for long though. As I get into my car and start to drive toward the therapy office, my stomach starts bouncing around. Nerves? Anticipation? Both, no doubt.

I arrive twenty-five minutes before my appointment. That leaves me with plenty of time. Before I get out of the car, I grab the little pack of tissues I have stored in my glove compartment. I pull out three tissues and shove them into my coat pocket. Just in case I need them. Then I head into the office as another person is leaving. She holds the door open for me. I slide into the waiting room without brushing up against her and without having to use my emergency tissues. Score.

Rather confidently (for me), I go right up to the front desk and ask to see Dr. Blake for a short meeting. It is only at this moment, as Annie starts to fumble around with her computer and an appointment book, that I realize I have no idea what his schedule is today (or any day, for that matter). He might have patients booked all day. It's not like I can just barge into his office. I guess I could leave a note to tell him I was here to see him, but then I really—

"Dr. Blake is out this afternoon. He will return around four o'clock."

Oh. There goes my plan. Clearly, I pretty much suck at surprises. I thank Annie, move a little to the side, and stand to wait for the next twenty-five minutes to be called in for my appointment. Annie doesn't say a word.

Time to think of another plan. Different options run through my head. Calling him. Texting him. Asking him to meet me somewhere to talk. Boring. I could try to surprise him later, but I work until mid-evening, and he'll probably be gone by then. I could go to his house, but I have no clue where he lives, and I'm pretty sure Annie isn't going to hand over an address. Hmm...if I could—

"Miss Royce, Dr. Spencer will see you now." Annie is holding the door open for me.

Impressive. Guess I'm getting some perks now that I'm seeking treatment with two of the doctors in this office—that must be close to a quarter of the practice, after all.

Annie waits for me to pass through the door and then takes the lead again. No long walk this time. We stop at a door in the middle of the first hallway. Annie opens the door and presses her back against it.

"Miss Calista Royce, Doctor Spencer."

"Send her right in." Dr. Spencer's voice. I recognize it from that very first day in this office. Before...well, before everything.

Annie, who must be feeling terribly generous today, waits until I step into the office and then takes the time to grab the handle and pull the door shut behind me. *Thank God I brought emergency tissues.*

"Miss Royce," Dr. Spencer greets me from behind his desk. "Won't you have a seat?" He nods toward a flowery couch to his left. It looks like it was made in the seventies. It's probably been here, in his office, since then too. Hundreds and thousands of patients have sat on it, I'm sure.

"No, thanks." I get right to the point, remaining rigid in the doorway, him looking at me amusedly from his desk chair. "Dr. Lennox wants me to talk to you about a prescription."

"Yes, that's right. Are you interested in starting a medication treatment?"

Here goes my new plan to fix our therapy. I silently pray that a certain someone doesn't refer to my plan as a "medicinal bandage." Then I pray twice more. And finally, I speak. "I am. I'd like to try it in combination with the therapy I've been doing with Dr. Blake—if you think that's okay."

"Definitely. Blending medicine and therapy is a very healthy, effective way to face and control your OCD symptoms."

"Good."

"So you feel you are making progress with your therapy plan then? Dr. Blake hasn't sent me any information since…" He thumbs through the paperwork on his desk. "Since your medical examination."

Wow. Wasn't that a lifetime ago?

He's looking at me, waiting for an answer.

"Um, yes, I think I, we, are making some headway. But I think I need more, and I want to do more to help the therapy succeed. If the medicine just takes some of the edge off, maybe I can make it through tough situations or even just everyday events without losing it right away."

"Well, yes, Miss Royce. The medication is designed to do just that—it should calm you somewhat and make things a little less unbearable." He takes off his glasses and rubs his eyes while he pauses. Like he's given this speech three million times and is bored by it. "But I do have to warn you that the pills won't work miracles. You won't just pop one and be 'cured.' You also won't really begin to feel the benefits until the medicine has some weeks to build up in your system."

"I understand," I mumble. Dr. Blake warned me of this at our first appointment. But it's okay—maybe we can delay the next part of our immersion treatment for a couple of weeks. Maybe we should even start the twelve days over once the medicine is working properly in my system…

"Since I already have your initial diagnosis from

Dr. Lennox, and your consultation and medical examination paperwork from Dr. Blake, I can get you started right away." Dr. Spencer makes some notes in my chart. "I have only a few standard questions for you first."

Dear God. I look down at my purse and pray he doesn't use the same list of questions as Dr. Blake.

"Are you currently taking any other medications?"

"Nope—just a daily vitamin."

"Any known allergies to medications?"

"Not that I know of, no."

"Okay. Great."

Already?

"Today, I am giving you a starter pack of pills. You punch out a pill every day for the next few weeks. The starter pack helps your body ease into the medication—you'll notice that you are on a low dose for the first few days before you begin what will be your larger, standard dose."

I nod. As usual.

Dr. Spencer excuses himself to go to a closet where he retrieves my starter pack. When he comes back, he hands me the medicine. He says that I should start tonight when I eat dinner because I might experience some painful side effects if I don't take the pill with a meal. He also wants to see me in a few weeks to check on my progress and to write out a prescription if things are going well. Lastly, he says he'll type up the information from this appointment and get it to Dr. Blake in a couple of days. I don't bother to tell him that Dr. Blake will already know in a few hours. Instead, I thank him and tell him that I will call to schedule my next appointment.

When he turns to go back to his desk, I grab the emergency tissues from my coat pocket and use them to get out of his office, out of the door to the waiting room, and finally out of the building. I throw the tissues away in my usual trash can, go to my car, and drive home.

I DON'T HAVE MUCH TIME at home, but I try to make the most of it. I start by sending a text to my Unknown Number.

```
Can we meet tonight after I get
off work? Just for a little—I
have a lot of homework, but I
have some stuff to tell you :)
```

Count. Send.

After downloading *Jane Eyre,* I make yet another attempt in my poetry notebook. No luck, as usual. Tonight is going to be a very long night if I'm actually going to get this portfolio done for tomorrow. And I will… because I never turn assignments in late.

I stop not writing poetry to grab an early dinner. Salad with croutons and dressing. Around four hundred calories. Plus one pill from my starter pack. Hopefully no calories there. At least none to speak of.

When I finish eating, I begin my thirty-three checks and then leave for work. My phone buzzes while I'm driving. I wait…not very patiently…to check it until I get to work. As soon as I pull into a parking spot, I yank my phone from my purse. One message from him.

Count. Open.

```
Sure. I'll meet you at the writ-
ing center at 7:00 p.m. I have
some results to show you…
```

Already? Wow. Guess that's where he was when I wanted to surprise him earlier.

Since work starts in three minutes, I don't bother to ask what strings he had to pull for the super fast results. Instead, I hit reply and type.

```
See you then :)
```

Count. Send.

In to work.

MY HEAD STARTS TO POUND around 4:30 p.m. Fortunately, there are only a few people here. Brittany is sitting in her usual chair, but she hasn't sent me any tickets yet. Neither have the other students.

I grab some aspirin from my purse and swallow the pills with a mouthful of saved up saliva. Resting my elbows on my desk, I prop my head up with my hands, trying to keep still, trying to shut down my brain. Every time a new song comes into my head, I try to squelch it, but it doesn't work. Each song stops abruptly with that nasty sound you get when recording on a tape player, and then another song begins immediately.

{First note of a song. Nasty scratching sound. Another song. Scratch. Song number three. Scratch. Scratch. Scratch.}

Ugh.

After a half hour of scratchy music, I still don't have any tickets. My head continues to pound, but I can't concentrate on that anymore because I'm too worried about the hives starting to appear up and down my arms. They look (and feel) just like the ones I get when a cat is nearby. I really don't think there is a cat in the writing center, and I haven't been close enough to anyone's clothing to have come into contact with any lingering cat hair.

My skin is really itchy though. Not just on my arms, but on my legs, my back, and my eyes. Especially my eyes. I can tell that they are starting to swell. *Great*—I don't have any Benadryl with me.

My full out panic begins about ten minutes later when I not only start to feel dizzy, but I also notice my skin turning a shade of blue.

What is going on?

I close my eyes to try to stop the dizziness, but it doesn't help. When I open them again, I can only see a blurry, jumpy mess of computers, chairs, and college students.

I try to blink my vision back to normal, but it only gets worse. After a few more blinks, I can't even distinguish between the different items in the room. If I didn't already know where I was, I would have no idea how to identify any of the objects in front of me.

Okay. Okay. Okay. Gotta get this under control. Very slowly, very cautiously, I start to stand up, pressing my hands onto the top of my desk for support. Before I can even make my way to a full standing position, I feel my legs buckle beneath me, and I begin to fall almost in slow motion.

Voices yelling, a jumble of activity, and the hard, cold floor.

And then nothing.

I DON'T WANT TO OPEN my eyes. I don't want to know what I am lying on, whose soft hand is gripping mine, or when the writing center installed loud siren sound effects. A slew of other questions flail through my mind as well: *Why is part of my face covered with some sort of plastic device? What is the material covering me? Are either of these items clean?*

I hear voices above and around me, but I can't quite catch what they are saying. Only one of the voices sounds vaguely familiar although I can't put a face to it.

The rumbles of unfamiliar pitches and inflections join forces with my overall disorientation, and I'm thrown back into unconsciousness.

NOW I REALLY DON'T WANT to open my eyes. Sterile smell. Beeping noises. Cheap sheets under me. I know I'm in a hospital.

Please don't let me have a gross roommate. Please let these sheets be clean. Please don't stick any needles in me. Please don't expose me to a disease. Please don't expose me to a disease. Please don't expose me to a disease.

My pleas suck up the last of my energy. I feel myself fading away once again.

I CAN FEEL AN IV in my arm. I try to open my mouth, to beg someone to remove it, but I can't get any words out. I can't pry my eyes open either.

"Stop fighting, Miss Royce. Please, stay still." The somewhat familiar voice from the ambulance. "Miss Royce, it's me, Brittany. Try to rest and save your energy."

Brittany. From Computer 7. The voice from the ambulance. The soft hand holding mine on the way here.

"Th-th—" I try to get out some words of gratitude.

"It's okay, Miss Royce. No talking right now. Just rest."

If you want me to rest, get the needle out of my arm. At least cover it up so I don't have to worry about seeing it, if I ever open my eyes again. Get this mask off of my face too.

Please. Please. Plea—

"CALLIE? CAN YOU OPEN YOUR eyes?"

{Cue Boston's "Amanda."*}*

"Callie. Try for me. Try to open your eyes."

Eyes. Won't. Open.

"Callie, Mom and Dad will be here soon. You are going to be okay. The doctors said you got here in time. That one of your students came with you."

Please let me open my eyes. Please let me speak.

Please tell me where he is. Call him. Tell him I won't be able to meet him. Tell him I'm here. Tell him to hurry.

"Callie, it's okay. Stop trying so hard. Rest, just rest."

"I'M HERE, CALLIE. ABBY WANTED to come too, but she was too young to be in the ICU. She sends hugs though."

Hi, Mel. Please get this IV out of my arm.

"Can you open your eyes for me, Callie? The doctors say you are going to get through this. They say you should show some improvement once the medication starts to leave your system. Whenever that will be..."

Medication?

"Why didn't you tell me you were starting medicine? Did Dr. Blake ask you to take it? He will have to really research other medications and allergic reactions if you are going to try another—"

Dr. Blake. Yes. Keep talking about him, Melanie. Where is he? When is he coming?

"—and I guess you still need more rest. Keep resting, Callie. I'll be right here all night."

Chapter 22
day seven

"GOOD MORNING, CAL. ARE YOU going to open those eyes for me today?"

I'm trying, Dad. I'm trying.

"Your mother has been in here with you and your sisters all night. She will be back in with Jared soon."

Mom. Jared. Such a long trip to get here. *I'm sorry. I'm—*

"Cal, stop struggling. You'll be able to talk soon, I know it. Just sleep for now. We are all here with you."

Thank you. Thank you. Thank—

Dad, where is he? Please go get him. Please go get him. Please go get him.

"ALL RIGHT, HONEY. MY SHIFT doesn't end until morning so I'll be in to check on you throughout the night. I'm going to push in a rollaway so your mom can stay with you and maybe get some sleep tonight. Sound okay, honey?”

Yes. Yes, thank you. Can you please get rid of this IV? Or at least cover it?

And please, can you tell me where—

Chapter 23
day eight?

"AND THIS IS CALISTA ROYCE. She's been here the last couple of days. They are going to keep her in the ICU until she fully wakes up." The nurse from last night. "Poor honey has been calling her doctor's name all night."

I have?

"The first time she heard it, her mom thought she was finally waking up so she came to get me. She kept saying 'Aiden.' I even heard it myself. But she was completely out, just talking in her sleep. Apparently, she kept calling for him all night. That's what her mom said when she left to go get coffee a bit ago."

"Who is her doctor?" A new voice. My next nurse?

"Well, Dr. Spencer prescribed her medication. But he is out of town again. She's been calling for her therapist, Dr. Blake. Dr. Aiden Blake. He was in here two nights ago. Well, here at the hospital, not in here."

He was? And he didn't—

"The name sounds familiar. Isn't he that hot, mega-serious one who was in here after his mom killed herself?"

What? She wha—

"That's the one. And he was definitely all serious when he was in here two nights ago. He read her charts, paced around the waiting room, and kept glancing over at this room. Never went in though."

Why? Why no—

"I heard him tell the on-call doctor that he's going to transfer her to another therapist. Something about the whole situation being too much for him, too similar."

"To the stuff with his mother?" The new voice again. "Didn't she take all of her anti-depressants in one shot?"

"Yes, exactly that, honey. God bless her, she did."

"Does he know that this was an accident, an allergic reaction?"

"He knows. He read her chart enough times to know every detail. He even discussed it with the doctor, asking repeatedly if she was going to be okay. It sounds like he's going to call in to monitor her progress, but he wants her new therapist to take over right away."

"So a new therapist might come in today?"

"Could be. Just log it if one does, like usual. Her family members are all in the log already. They've been in and out since she got here so…"

They keep talking, but none of it matters. He's not coming. He's not going to be my doctor. He's not…

Chapter 24
should be day nine

"CALLIE, WHAT'S THE DEAL? WHY don't you wake up already? If you don't wake up soon, I'm going to go to your house and head straight for your bathroom."

No, you won't, Jared. I know you won't.

I'm not even trying to open my eyes today.

Chapter 25
not day ten

"CALISTA HAS BEEN IN THE ICU for four days now. The swelling has gone down, and she doesn't need oxygen anymore. We're just waiting for her to open her eyes."

Another shift change. I don't recognize either of the voices that discuss me as though I'm not here.

Am I even here?

The first voice continues. "She is supposed to be getting a new therapist, but no one has come in yet. It's not like she can talk, though, so I guess there's no hurry."

The other voice. "Unless she is waiting for the comfort of a counselor to ease herself back into consciousness."

"She still calls for her old doctor in her sleep so maybe you are right. Maybe she really does need that new therapist to get here."

Both voices are classic nurse voices. Quiet, gentle, soothing.

It sounds like nurse one is slightly behind me. Straightening up? Putting something into my IV? I can't think about my IV.

Second voice again. “Maybe her old doctor will come in for a visit if the new person can’t make it.”

“I don’t think so. Her old therapist is Dr. Blake. Remember him? All of that stuff with his mother?”

“Yeah, I do. I’m surprised he even took this girl as a patient to begin with. I thought he wasn’t seeing people with his mom’s condition.”

“I know. Maybe he thought this one was different enough.”

“Well, I’m sure he did. Remember how crazy his mom was at the end? I think there were two failed suicide attempts, two stays here in the ICU before she took that bottle of medicine.”

“Oh yeah. I almost forgot about those false alarms. I had just started working here when she came in the first time. I remember having no idea what to say to her.”

“Remember—she kept counting and saying stuff about the music in her head?”

“Yes, that’s right.” Nurse voice number one is close to my bed now. Arranging my pillows? “Apparently, that is why she kept trying to kill herself. I overheard some doctors saying that she had some part of a song, some notes and chords stuck in her head constantly, playing over and over.”

“She killed herself over that?”

“Well, I guess she couldn’t concentrate on anything else because of it. So she couldn’t count properly, or finish her routines…she really lost it.”

“Wow. That’s really strange.”

Their voices are further away now, and I have to struggle to hear. I also have to struggle to stay awake.

Nurse one is talking again. “Alex, the nurse in the psych wing, you know her?”

“Yeah. The blonde?”

"Yep. She told me that Dr. Blake is all anti-medication now. I guess because he is the one who encouraged his mom to see someone who could prescribe meds. He feels responsible or something."

Oh.

God.

The words "medicinal bandage" reverberate through my head. Over and over and over and over and over and—

"Alex also says there are rumors that he doesn't listen to music now, that he has avoided it since she died."

"Sounds like he needs a therapist as much as this one does."

They continue talking about the phantom new therapist and paperwork, but I'm done listening. Back to unconsciousness.

I DON'T KNOW WHAT TIME it is. Or how long I've been asleep.

I do know that I'm still in a hospital bed. I also know he's here.

His magazine cologne fills the air. His hand is squeezing mine, sending familiar shivers up my arm. I think he's talking to me, but his words are no more than a blurry whisper.

{And now George Michael with "Careless Whisper."*}*

Stop, Callie. Focus. Hear him. Hear him. Hear him.

"—and I tried to stay away, but I had to, I had to come, Callie."

His thumb is rubbing against my fingers. Back and forth, back and—

"It's too much though. It's too similar."

You have no idea.

"I can't stay, Callie."

No, Aiden. You have to stay. I need—

"You are going to be fine. I've looked at your charts, and I've been communicating with your doctors. You will be just fine."

No. No, I won't be—

"And you'll be better off this way. I'm such a mess. I can't help you."

Stop, Aiden. You can. You ha—

"I can't help. It's too similar, and I can't think straight, and I—"

He pauses. He is moving. Standing. Leaving?

Eyes open now. Open now. OPEN NOW.

Nothing.

But I can smell his cologne so much better now. And I feel his breath on my cheek.

"I'm so sorry, Callie. I've only known you for about five seconds, but I could really feel it. Feel us. Feel everything…"

His lips are on my forehead. A soft brush of a kiss.

Before I know it, his lips are gone. His hand has let go of mine, and my blanket is pulled up over my arm, over my IV. And then nothing.

My eyes will not open. My mouth won't move. But my ears are working harder than ever.

A few almost inaudible footsteps. The slow, gentle click of the door.

And I know he's gone.

Chapter 26
would have been day eleven

I'M GOING HOME TODAY. WELL, I'm going back to my house anyway. I have strict instructions to rest for an entire week. No classes. No work. No other plans to worry about.

I think I woke up completely at some point on Saturday. The next thirty-some hours were a mess of questions and tests and doctors and medical instruments.

Family. And no one else.

I'm going home today, but I know it won't feel that way.

I'm returning to my empty room. My scheduled routines. My hours of thinking. The comforts of my old life...

{Here is Dionne Warwick with "A House is Not a Home."*}*

Chapter 27
day twelve

My last scheduled day of treatment.
No therapy.
No medication.
No him.
No better at all.
{Sing it, Damien.}

Snippets of Callie's Head Radio

(only the songs mentioned by Callie)

1.) "I'll Stand by You" by the Pretenders (Hynde, Kelly, and Steinberg/1994)
2.) "Fly Me to the Moon" by Frank Sinatra (Howard/1954)
3.) "The Long and Winding Road" by The Beatles (McCartney/1970)
4.) "The Blower's Daughter" by Damien Rice (Rice/2001)
5.) "Boulevard of Broken Dreams" by Green Day (Armstrong/2004)
6.) "Love is Strange" by Mickey & Sylvia (Baker and Vanderpool/1956)
7.) "In Da Club" by 50 Cent (50 Cent, Dr. Dre, and Elizondo/2003)
8.) "Tik Tok" by Ke$ha (Benny Blanco, Dr. Luke, and Ke$ha/2009)
9.) "Against All Odds (Take a Look at Me Now)" by Phil Collins (Collins/1983)
10.) "The Long and Winding Road" by The Beatles (McCartney/1970)
11.) "Complicated" by Avril Lavigne (Lavigne,

Christy, Spock, and Edwards/2002)

12.) "I Have Nothing" by Whitney Houston (Foster and Thompson/1993)

13.) "Sunday Bloody Sunday" by U2 (Bono and The Edge/1983)

14.) "Blowin' in the Wind" by Bob Dylan (Dylan/1962)

15.) "Hollaback Girl" by Gwen Stefani (Stefani, Williams, and Hugo/2004)

16.) "Survivor" by Destiny's Child (B. Knowles, Dent, and M. Knowles/2001)

17.) "I Will Survive" by Gloria Gaynor (Perren and Fekaris/1978)

18.) "Killing Me Softly with His Song" by Roberta Flack (Fox and Gimbel/1973)

19.) "Killing Me Softly" by Fugees (Fox and Gimbel/1996)

20.) "Man of Constant Sorrow" by Soggy Bottom Boys (Burnett/1913)

21.) "Smooth Criminal" by Michael Jackson (Jackson/1988)

22.) "Total Eclipse of the Heart" by Bonnie Tyler (Steinman/1983)

23.) "...Baby One More Time" by Britney Spears (Martin/1998)

24.) "Paparazzi" by Lady Gaga (Fusari and Gaga/2009)

25.) "The Sound of Silence" by Simon & Garfunkel (Simon/1964)

26.) "Feels Like Home" by Chantal Kreviazuk (Newman/1995)

27.) "Hallelujah" by Jeff Buckley (Cohen/1984)

28.) "My Way" by Frank Sinatra (Anka/1969)

29.) "Rhythm of the Night" by Debarge (Warren/1985)

30.) "Paralyzer" by Finger Eleven (Finger Eleven/2007)
31.) "Call Me Maybe" by Carly Rae Jepsen (Jepsen, Ramsay, and Crowe/2011)
32.) "Beautiful Disaster" by Kelly Clarkson (Jordan and Wilder/2003)
33.) "California Gurls" by Katy Perry (Broadus, Gottwald, Martin, McKee, and Perry/2010)
34.) "This is the Moment" by Robert Cuccioli (Wildhorn and Bricusse/1990)
35.) "The Rose" by Bette Midler (McBroom/1979)
36.) "Rainbow Connection" by Kermit the Frog (Williams and Ascher/1979)
37.) "Movin' Right Along" by Kermit the Frog & Fozzie Bear (Williams and Ascher/1979)
38.) "Baby Got Back" by Sir Mix-a-Lot (Sir Mix-a-Lot/1992)
39.) "Somebody That I Used to Know" by Gotye (de Backer/2011)
40.) "Everybody Hurts" by R.E.M (Stipe, Mills, Buck, and Berry/1992)
41.) "The Lazy Song" by Bruno Mars (Mars, Lawrence, Levine, and K'naan/2011)
42.) "Cheeseburger in Paradise" by Jimmy Buffett (Buffett/1978)
43.) "Milkshake" by Kelis (Hugo and Williams/2003)
44.) "Honesty" by Billy Joel (Joel/1978)
45.) "Sway" by Michael Bublé (Ruiz & Gimbel/1954/2004)
46.) "Breathe" by Faith Hill (Bentley and Lamar/1999)
47.) "Someone to Watch over Me" (Gersh-

win/1926)

48.) “Porn Star Dancing” by My Darkest Days (My Darkest Days/2010)
49.) “Ignition (Remix)” by R. Kelly (Kelly/2002)
50.) “When You Say Nothing at All” by Alison Krauss (Overstreet and Schlitz/1998/1995)
51.) “Hello” by Lionel Richie (Richie/1984)
52.) “What Would Happen” by Meredith Brooks (Brooks/1998)
53.) “So Far Away” by Rod Stewart (King/1971)
54.) “The Story” by Brandi Carlile (Hanseroth/2007)
55.) “I Hear a Symphony” by The Supremes (Holland-Dozier-Holland/1965)
56.) “Eleanor Rigby” by The Beatles (Lennon and McCartney/1966)
57.) “Suspicious Minds” by Elvis Presley (James/1969)
58.) “Amanda” by Boston (Scholz/1986)
59.) “Careless Whisper” by George Michael (Michael and Ridgeley/1984)
60.) “A House is Not a Home” by Dionne Warwick (Bacharach and David/1964)

About the Author

Jennifer Jamelli has spent most of her life reading and writing; she holds both a Bachelor of Arts and a Master of Arts in English, and she is an 8th grade English teacher.

She also directs a musical production each school year. Her most recent show was Beauty and the Beast.

Jennifer lives with her husband and her four-year-old son.

She, like the main character in her debut novel, has a rather hopeless case of OCD.

CPSIA information can be obtained at www.ICGtesting.com
Printed in the USA
BVOW02s0529231213

339777BV00001B/4/P